LIN   Lindsay, Jeffry P.

Darkly dreaming
Dexter.

FIC CAT 15th ed.

$22.95

DATE			
e o Lau l oye			

DARKLY
DREAMING
DEXTER

JEFF LINDSAY

DARKLY DREAMING DEXTER

A NOVEL

Doubleday

NEW YORK · LONDON · TORONTO · SYDNEY · AUCKLAND

PUBLISHED BY DOUBLEDAY
a division of Random House, Inc.

DOUBLEDAY and the portrayal of an anchor with a dolphin
are registered trademarks of Random House, Inc.

Book design by Rachel Reiss

Library of Congress Cataloging-in-Publication Data
Lindsay, Jeffry P.
Darkly dreaming Dexter : a novel / by Jeffry Lindsay.—1st ed.
    p. cm.
1. Serial murderers—Fiction. 2. Serial murders—Fiction.
3. Vigilantes—Fiction. I. Title.

PS3562.I51175 D74
813'.54—dc22   2004045460

ISBN 0-385-51123-X

PRINTED IN THE UNITED STATES OF AMERICA
August 2004
First Edition
1 3 5 7 9 10 8 6 4 2

ACKNOWLEDGMENTS

THIS BOOK WOULD NOT HAVE BEEN POSSIBLE WITH-out the generous technical and spiritual help of Einstein and the Deacon. They represent what is best about Miami cops, and they taught me some of what it means to do this very tough job in a tougher place.

I would also like to thank a number of people who made some very helpful suggestions, especially my wife, the Barclays, Julio S., Dr. and Mrs. A. L. Freundlich, Pookie, Bear, and Tinky.

I am deeply indebted to Jason Kaufman for his wisdom and insight in shaping the book.

Thanks also to Doris, the Lady of the Last Laugh.

And very special thanks to Nick Ellison, who is every-thing an agent is supposed to be but almost never is.

DARKLY DREAMING DEXTER

CHAPTER 1

OON. GLORIOUS MOON. FULL, FAT, REDDISH
moon, the night as light as day, the moonlight
flooding down across the land and bringing joy,
joy, joy. Bringing too the full-throated call of the tropical
night, the soft and wild voice of the wind roaring through
the hairs on your arm, the hollow wail of starlight, the
teeth-grinding bellow of the moonlight off the water.

All calling to the Need. Oh, the symphonic shriek of the
thousand hiding voices, the cry of the Need inside, *the
entity*, the silent watcher, the cold quiet thing, the one that
laughs, the Moondancer. The me that was not-me, the thing
that mocked and laughed and came calling with its hunger.
With the Need. And the Need was very strong now, very
careful cold coiled creeping crackly cocked and ready, very
strong, very much ready now—and still it waited and
watched, and it made me wait and watch.

I had been waiting and watching the priest for five
weeks now. The Need had been prickling and teasing and

prodding at me to find one, find the next, find this priest. For three weeks I had known he was it, he was next, we belonged to the Dark Passenger, he and I together. And that three weeks I had spent fighting the pressure, the growing *Need*, rising in me like a great wave that roars up and over the beach and does not recede, only swells more with every tick of the bright night's clock.

But it was careful time, too, time spent making sure. Not making sure of the priest, no, I was long sure of him. Time spent to be certain that it could be done right, made neat, all the corners folded, all squared away. I could not be caught, not now. I had worked too hard, too long, to make this work for me, to protect my happy little life.

And I was having too much fun to stop now.

And so I was always careful. Always tidy. Always prepared ahead of time so it would be *right*. And when it was right, take extra time to be sure. It was the Harry way, God bless him, that farsighted perfect policeman, my foster father. Always be sure, be careful, be exact, he had said, and for a week now I had been sure that everything was just as Harry-right as it could be. And when I left work this night, I knew this was it. This night was the Night. This night felt different. This night it would happen, *had* to happen. Just as it had happened before. Just as it would happen again, and again.

And tonight it would happen to the priest.

His name was Father Donovan. He taught music to the children at St. Anthony's Orphanage in Homestead, Florida. The children loved him. And of course he loved the children, oh very much indeed. He had devoted a whole life to them. Learned Creole and Spanish. Learned their music, too. All for the kids. Everything he did, it was all for the kids.

Everything.

I watched him this night as I had watched for so many nights now. Watched as he paused in the orphanage doorway to talk to a young black girl who had followed him out. She was small, no more than eight years old and small for that. He sat on the steps and talked to her for five minutes. She sat, too, and bounced up and down. They laughed. She leaned against him. He touched her hair. A nun came out and stood in the doorway, looking down at them for a moment before she spoke. Then she smiled and held out a hand. The girl bumped her head against the priest. Father Donovan hugged her, stood, and kissed the girl good night. The nun laughed and said something to Father Donovan. He said something back.

And then he started toward his car. Finally: I coiled myself to strike and—

Not yet. A janitorial service minivan stood fifteen feet from the door. As Father Donovan passed it, the side door slid open. A man leaned out, puffing on a cigarette, and greeted the priest, who leaned against the van and talked to the man.

Luck. Luck again. Always luck on these Nights. I had not seen the man, not guessed he was there. But he would have seen me. If not for Luck.

I took a deep breath. Let it out slow and steady, icy cold.

It was only one small thing. I had not missed any others. I had done it all right, all the same, all the way it had to be done. It would be *right*.

Now.

Father Donovan walked toward his car again. He turned once and called something. The janitor waved from the doorway to the orphanage, then stubbed out his cigarette and disappeared inside the building. Gone.

Luck. Luck again.

Father Donovan fumbled for his keys, opened his car door, got into his car. I heard the key go in. Heard the engine turn over. And then—

NOW.

I sat up in his backseat and slipped the noose around his neck. One quick, slippery, pretty twist and the coil of fifty-pound-test fishing line settled tight. He made a small ratchet of panic and that was it.

"You are mine now," I told him, and he froze as neat and perfect as if he had practiced, almost like he heard the other voice, the laughing watcher inside me.

"Do exactly as I say," I said.

He rasped half a breath and glanced into his rearview mirror. My face was there, waiting for him, wrapped in the white silk mask that showed only my eyes.

"Do you understand?" I said. The silk of the mask flowed across my lips as I spoke.

Father Donovan said nothing. Stared at my eyes. I pulled on the noose.

"Do you understand?" I repeated, a little softer.

This time he nodded. He fluttered a hand at the noose,

not sure what would happen if he tried to loosen it. His face was turning purple.

I loosened the noose for him. "Be good," I said, "and you will live longer."

He took a deep breath. I could hear the air rip at his throat. He coughed and breathed again. But he sat still and did not try to escape.

This was very good.

We drove. Father Donovan followed my directions, no tricks, no hesitations. We drove south through Florida City and took the Card Sound Road. I could tell that road made him nervous, but he did not object. He did not try to speak to me. He kept both hands on the wheel, pale and knotted tight, so the knuckles stood up. That was very good, too.

We drove south for another five minutes with no sound but the song of the tires and the wind and the great moon above making its mighty music in my veins, and the careful watcher laughing quietly in the rush of the night's hard pulse.

"Turn here," I said at last.

The priest's eyes flew to mine in the mirror. The panic was trying to claw out of his eyes, down his face, into his mouth to speak, but—

"Turn!" I said, and he turned. Slumped like he had been expecting this all along, waiting for it forever, and he turned.

The small dirt road was barely visible. You almost had to know it was there. But I knew. I had been there before. The road ran for two and a half miles, twisting three times, through the saw grass, through the trees, alongside a small canal, deep into the swamp and into a clearing.

Fifty years ago somebody had built a house. Most of it was still there. It was large for what it was. Three rooms, half a roof still left, the place completely abandoned now for many years.

Except the old vegetable garden out in the side yard. There were signs that somebody had been digging there fairly recently.

"Stop the car," I said as the headlights picked up the crumbling house.

Father Donovan lurched to obey. Fear had sealed him into his body now, his limbs and thoughts all rigid.

"Turn off the motor," I told him, and he did.

It was suddenly very quiet.

Some small something chittered in a tree. The wind rattled the grass. And then more quiet, silence so deep it almost drowned out the roar of the night music that pounded away in my secret self.

"Get out," I said.

Father Donovan did not move. His eyes were on the vegetable garden.

Seven small mounds of earth were visible there. The heaped soil looked very dark in the moonlight. It must have looked even darker to Father Donovan. And still he did not move.

I yanked hard on the noose, harder than he thought he could live through, harder than he knew could happen to him. His back arched against the seat and the veins stood out on his forehead and he thought he was about to die.

But he was not. Not yet. Not for quite some time, in fact.

I kicked the car door open and pulled him out after me, just to let him feel my strength. He flopped to the sandy roadbed and twisted like an injured snake. The Dark Passenger laughed and loved it and I played the part. I put one boot on Father Donovan's chest and held the noose tight.

"You have to listen and do as I say," I told him. "You *have* to." I bent and gently loosened the noose. "You should know that. It's important," I said.

And he heard me. His eyes, pounding with blood and pain and leaking tears onto his face, his eyes met mine in a rush of understanding and all the things that had to happen were there for him to see now. And he saw. And he knew how important it was for him to be just *right*. He began to know.

"Get up now," I said.

Slowly, very slowly, with his eyes always on mine, Father Donovan got up. We stood just like that for a long time, our eyes together, becoming one person with one need, and then he trembled. He raised one hand halfway to his face and dropped it again.

"In the house," I said, so very softly. In the house where everything was ready.

Father Donovan dropped his eyes. He raised them to me but could not look anymore. He turned toward the house but stopped as he saw again the dark dirt mounds of the garden. And he wanted to look at me, but he could not, not after seeing again those black moonlit heaps of earth.

He started for the house and I held his leash. He went obediently, head down, a good and docile victim. Up the five battered steps, across the narrow porch to the front door, pushed shut. Father Donovan stopped. He did not look up. He did not look at me.

"Through the door," I said in my soft command voice.

Father Donovan trembled.

"Go through the door now," I said again.

But he could not.

I leaned past him and pushed the door open. I shoved the priest in with my foot. He stumbled, righted himself, and stood just inside, eyes squeezed tight shut.

I closed the door. I had left a battery lamp standing on the floor beside the door and I turned it on.

"Look," I whispered.

Father Donovan slowly, carefully, opened one eye.

He froze.

Time stopped for Father Donovan.

"No," he said.

"Yes," I said.

"Oh, no," he said.

"Oh, yes," I said.

He screamed, "NOOOO!"

I yanked on the noose. His scream was cut off and he fell to his knees. He made a wet croaky whimpering sound and covered his face. "Yes," I said. "It's a terrible mess, isn't it?"

He used his whole face to close his eyes. He could not look, not now, not like this. I did not blame him, not really, it *was* a terrible mess. It had bothered me just to know it was there since I had set it up for him. But he had to see it. He had to. Not just for me. Not just for the Dark Passenger. For *him*. He had to see. And he was not looking.

"Open your eyes, Father Donovan," I said.

"Please," he said in a terrible little whimper. It got on my nerves very badly, shouldn't have, icy-clean control, but it got to me, whining in the face of that mess on the floor, and I kicked his legs out from under him. I hauled hard on the noose and grabbed the back of his neck with my right hand, then slammed his face into the filthy warped floorboards. There was a little blood and that made me madder.

"Open them," I said. "Open your eyes. Open them NOW. *Look*." I grabbed his hair and pulled his head back. "Do as you're told," I said. "Look. Or I will cut your eyelids right off your face."

I was very convincing. And so he did it. He did as he was told. He looked.

I had worked hard to make it right, but you have to use what you've got to work with. I could not have done it at all if they had not been there long enough for everything to dry up, but they were so very dirty. I had managed to clean off most of the dirt, but some of the bodies had been in the garden a very long time and you couldn't tell where the dirt began and the body stopped. You never could tell, really, when you stop to think about it. So dirty—

There were seven of them, seven small bodies, seven extra-dirty orphan children laid out on rubber shower sheets, which are neater and don't leak. Seven straight lines pointing straight across the room.

Pointing right at Father Donovan. So he knew.

He was about to join them.

"Hail Mary, full of grace—" he started. I jerked hard on the noose.

"None of that, Father. Not now. Now is for real truth."

"Please," he choked.

"Yes, beg me. That's good. Much better." I yanked again. "Do you think that's it, Father? Seven bodies? Did they beg?" He had nothing to say. "Do you think that's all of them, Father? Just seven? Did I get them all?"

"Oh, God," he rasped out, with a pain that was good to hear.

"And what about the other towns, Father? What about Fayetteville? Would you like to talk about Fayetteville?" He just choked out a sob, no words. "And what about East Orange? Was that three? Or did I miss one there? It's so hard to be sure. Was it four in East Orange, Father?"

Father Donovan tried to scream. There was not enough left of his throat for it to be a very good scream, but it had real feeling behind it, which made up for the poor technique. Then he fell forward onto his face and I let him snivel for a while before I pulled him up and onto his feet. He was not steady, and not in control. His bladder had let loose and there was drool on his chin.

"Please," he said. "I couldn't help myself. I just couldn't help myself. Please, you have to understand—"

"I do understand, Father," I said, and there was something in my voice, the Dark Passenger's voice now, and the sound of it froze him. He lifted his head slowly to face me and what he saw in my eyes made him very still. "I understand perfectly," I told him, moving very close to his face.

The sweat on his cheeks turned to ice. "You see," I said, "I can't help myself, either."

We were very close now, almost touching, and the dirtiness of him was suddenly too much. I jerked up on the noose and kicked his feet out from under him again. Father Donovan sprawled on the floor.

"But *children*?" I said. "I could never do this to children." I put my hard clean boot on the back of his head and slammed his face down. "Not like you, Father. Never kids. I have to find people like you."

"What are you?" Father Donovan whispered.

"The beginning," I said. "And the end. Meet your Unmaker, Father." I had the needle ready and it went into his neck like it was supposed to, slight resistance from the rigid muscles, but none from the priest. I pushed the plunger and the syringe emptied, filling Father Donovan with quick, clean calm. Moments, only moments, and his head began to float, and he rolled his face to me.

Did he truly see me now? Did he see the double rubber gloves, the careful coveralls, the slick silk mask? Did he really see me? Or did that only happen in the other room, the Dark Passenger's room, the Clean Room? Painted white two nights past and swept, scrubbed, sprayed, cleaned as clean as can be. And in the middle of the room, its windows sealed with thick white rubberized sheets, under the lights in the middle of the room, did he finally see me there in the table I had made, the boxes of white garbage bags, the bottles of chemicals, and the small row of saws and knives? Did he see me at last?

Or did he see those seven untidy lumps, and who knows how many more? Did he see himself at last, unable to scream, turning into that kind of mess in the garden?

He would not, of course. His imagination did not allow him to see himself as the same species. And in a way, he was right. He would never turn into the kind of mess he had made of the children. I would never do that, could never allow that. I am not like Father Donovan, not that kind of monster.

I am a very neat monster.

Neatness takes time, of course, but it's worth it. Worth it to make the Dark Passenger happy, keep him quiet for another long while. Worth it just to do it right and tidy. Remove one more heap of mess from the world. A few more neatly wrapped bags of garbage and my one small corner of the world is a neater, happier place. A better place.

I had about eight hours before I had to be gone. I would need them all to do it right.

I secured the priest to the table with duct tape and cut away his clothes. I did the preliminary work quickly; shaving, scrubbing, cutting away the things that stuck out untidily. As always I felt the wonderful long slow build to release begin its pounding throughout my entire body. It would flutter through me while I worked, rising and taking me with it, until the very end, the Need and the priest swimming away together on a fading tide.

And just before I started the serious work Father Donovan opened his eyes and looked at me. There was no fear now; that happens sometimes. He looked straight up at me and his mouth moved.

"What?" I said. I moved my head a little closer. "I can't hear you."

I heard him breathe, a slow and peaceful breath, and then he said it again before his eyes closed.

"You're welcome," I said, and I went to work.

CHAPTER 2

BY FOUR-THIRTY IN THE MORNING THE PRIEST WAS all cleaned up. I felt a lot better. I always did, after. Killing makes me feel good. It works the knots out of darling Dexter's dark schemata. It's a sweet release, a necessary letting go of all the little hydraulic valves inside. I enjoy my work; sorry if that bothers you. Oh, very sorry, really. But there it is. And it's not just any killing, of course. It has to be done the right way, at the right time, with the right partner—very complicated, but very necessary.

And always somewhat draining. So I was tired, but the tension of the last week was gone, the cold voice of the Dark Passenger was quiet, and I could be me again. Quirky, funny, happy-go-lucky, dead-inside Dexter. No longer Dexter with the knife, Dexter the Avenger. Not until next time.

I put all the bodies back in the garden with one new neighbor and tidied the little falling-down house as much as I could. I packed my things into the priest's car and drove south to the small side canal where I had left my boat, a seventeen-foot Whaler with a shallow draft and a big engine. I pushed the priest's car into the canal behind my boat and climbed on board. I watched the car settle and disappear. Then I cranked up my outboard and eased out of the canal, heading north across the bay. The sun was just coming up and bouncing off the brightwork. I put on my very best happy face; just another early-morning fisherman heading home. Red snapper, anyone?

By six-thirty I was home in my Coconut Grove apartment. I took the slide from my pocket, a simple, clean glass strip—with a careful single drop of the priest's blood preserved in the center. Nice and clean, dry now, ready to slip under my microscope when I wanted to remember. I put the slide with the others, thirty-six neat and careful very dry drops of blood.

I took an extra-long shower, letting the hot hot water wash away the last of the tension and ease the knots in my muscles, scrubbing off the small final traces of clinging smell from the priest and the garden of the little house in the swamp.

Children. I should have killed him twice.

Whatever made me the way I am left me hollow, empty inside, unable to feel. It doesn't seem like a big deal. I'm quite sure most people fake an awful lot of everyday human contact. I just fake all of it. I fake it very well, and the feelings are never there. But I like kids. I could never have them, since the idea of sex is no idea at all. Imagine doing those things— How can you? Where's your sense of dignity? But kids—kids are special. Father Donovan deserved to die. The Code of Harry was satisfied, along with the Dark Passenger.

By seven-fifteen I felt clean again. I had coffee, cereal, and headed in for work.

The building where I work is a large modern thing, white with lots of glass, near the airport. My lab is on the second floor, in the back. I have a small office attached to the lab. It is not much of an office, but it's mine, a cubicle off the main blood lab. All mine, nobody else allowed in, nobody to share with, to mess up my area. A desk with a chair, another chair for a visitor, if he's not too big. Computer, shelf, filing cabinet. Telephone. Answering machine.

Answering machine with a blinking light as I came in. A message for me is not a daily thing. For some reason, there are very few people in the world who can think of things to say to a blood spatter pattern analyst during working hours. One of the few people who does have things to say to me is Deborah Morgan, my foster sister. A cop, just like her father.

The message was from her.

I punched the button and heard tinny *Tejano* music, then Deborah's voice. "Dexter, please, as soon as you get in. I'm at a crime scene out on Tamiami Trail, at the Cacique Motel." There was a pause. I heard her put a hand over the mouthpiece of the telephone and say something to somebody. Then there was a blast of Mexican music again and she was back on. "Can you get out here right away? Please, Dex?"

She hung up.

I don't have a family. I mean, as far as I know. Somewhere out there must be people who carry similar genetic material, I'm sure. I pity them. But I've never met them. I haven't tried, and they haven't tried to find me. I was adopted, raised by Harry and Doris Morgan, Deborah's parents. And considering what I am, they did a wonderful job of raising me, don't you think?

Both dead now. And so Deb is the only person in the world who gives a rusty possum fart whether I live or die. For some reason that I can't fathom, she actually prefers me to be alive. I think that's nice, and if I could have feelings at all I would have them for Deb.

So I went. I drove out of the Metro-Dade parking lot and got onto the nearby Turnpike, which took me south to the section of Tamiami Trail that is home to the Cacique Motel and several hundred of its brothers and sisters. In its own way, it is paradise. Particularly if you are a cockroach. Rows of buildings that manage to glitter and molder at the same time. Bright neon over ancient, squalid, sponge-rotted structures. If you don't go at night, you won't go. Because to see these places by daylight is to see the bottom line of our flimsy contract with life.

Every major city has a section like this one. If a piebald dwarf with advanced leprosy wants to have sex with a kangaroo and a teenage choir, he'll find his way here and get a room. When he's done, he might take the whole gang next door for a cup of Cuban coffee and a *medianoche* sandwich. Nobody would care, as long as he tipped.

Deborah had been spending way too much time out here lately. Her opinion, not mine. It seemed like a good place to go if you were a cop and you wanted to increase your statistical chance of catching somebody doing something awful.

Deborah didn't see it that way. Maybe because she was working vice. A good-looking young woman working vice on the Tamiami Trail usually ends up as bait on a sting, standing outside almost naked to catch men who wanted to pay for sex. Deborah hated that. Couldn't get worked up about prostitution, except as a sociological issue. Didn't think bagging johns was real crime fighting. And, known only to me, she hated anything that overemphasized her femininity and her lush figure. She wanted to be a cop; it was not her fault she looked more like a centerfold.

And as I pulled into the parking lot that linked the Cacique and its neighbor, Tito's Café Cubano, I could see that she was currently emphasizing the hell out of her figure. She was dressed in a neon-pink tube top, spandex shorts, black fishnet stockings, and spike heels. Straight from the costume shop for Hollywood Hookers in 3-D.

A few years back somebody in the Vice Bureau got the word that the pimps were laughing at them on the streets. It seems the vice cops, mostly male, were picking the outfits for the women operatives who worked in the sting operations. Their choice of clothing was showing an awful lot about their preferences in kinkiness, but it did not look much like hooker wear. So everybody on the street could tell when the new girl was carrying a badge and gun in her clutch purse.

As a result of this tip, the vice cops began to insist that the girls who went undercover pick their own outfits for the job. After all, girls know more about what looks right, don't they?

Maybe most of them do. Deborah doesn't. She's never

felt comfortable in anything but blues. You should have seen what she wanted to wear to her prom. And now—I had never seen a beautiful woman dressed in such a revealing costume who looked less sexually appealing than Deb did.

But she did stand out. She was working crowd control, her badge pinned to the tube top. She was more visible than the half mile of yellow crime-scene tape that was already strung up, more than the three patrol cars angled in with their lights flashing. The pink tube top flashed a little brighter.

She was off to one side of the parking lot, keeping a growing crowd back from the lab techs who appeared to be going through the Dumpster belonging to the coffee shop. I was glad I hadn't been assigned to that. The stink of it came all the way across the lot and in my car window—a dark stench of Latin coffee grounds mixed with old fruit and rancid pork.

The cop at the entrance to the parking lot was a guy I knew. He waved me in and I found a spot.

"Deb," I said as I strolled over. "Nice outfit. Really shows your figure to full advantage."

"Fuck off," she said, and she blushed. Really something to see in a full-grown cop.

"They found another hooker," she said. "At least, they think it's a hooker. Hard to tell from what's left."

"That's the third in the last five months," I said.

"Fifth," she told me. "There were two more up in Broward." She shook her head. "These assholes keep saying that officially there's no connection."

"It would make for an awful lot of paperwork," I said helpfully.

Deb showed me her teeth. "How about some basic fucking police work?" she snarled. "A moron could see these kills are connected." And she gave a little shudder.

I stared at her, amazed. She was a cop, daughter of a cop. Things didn't bother her. When she'd been a rookie cop and the older guys played tricks on Deborah—showing her the hacked-up bodies that turn up in Miami every day—to get her to blow her lunch, she hadn't blinked. She'd seen it all. Been there, done that, bought the T-shirt.

But this one made her shudder.

Interesting.

"This one is special, is that it?" I asked her.

"This one is on my beat, with the hookers." She pointed a finger at me. "And THAT means I've got a shot to get in on it, get noticed, and pull a transfer into Homicide Bureau."

I gave her my happy smile. "Ambition, Deborah?"

"Goddamned right," she said. "I want out of vice, and I want out of this sex suit. I want into Homicide, Dexter, and this could be my ticket. With one small break—" She paused. And then she said something absolutely amazing. "Please help me, Dex," she said. "I really hate this."

"Please, Deborah? You're saying *please* to me? Do you know how nervous that makes me?"

"Cut the crap, Dex."

"But Deborah, really—"

"Cut it, I said. Will you help me or not?"

When she put it that way, with that strange rare "please"

dangling in the air, what else could I say but, "Of course I will, Deb. You know that."

And she eyed me hard, taking back her please. "I *don't* know it, Dex. I don't know anything with you."

"Of course I'll help, Deb," I repeated, trying to sound hurt. And doing a really good imitation of injured dignity, I headed for the Dumpster with the rest of the lab rats.

Camilla Figg was crawling through the garbage, dusting for fingerprints. She was a stocky woman of thirty-five with short hair who had never seemed to respond to my breezy, charming pleasantries. But as she saw me, she came up onto her knees, blushed, and watched me go by without speaking. She always seemed to stare at me and then blush.

Sitting on an overturned plastic milk carton on the far end of the Dumpster, poking through a handful of waste matter, was Vince Masuoka. He was half Japanese and liked to joke that he got the short half. He called it a joke, anyway.

There was something just slightly off in Vince's bright, Asian smile. Like he had learned to smile from a picture book. Even when he made the required dirty put-down jokes with the cops, nobody got mad at him. Nobody laughed, either, but that didn't stop him. He kept making all the correct ritual gestures, but he always seemed to be faking. That's why I liked him, I think. Another guy pretending to be human, just like me.

"Well, Dexter," Vince said without looking up. "What brings you here?"

"I came to see how real experts operate in a totally professional atmosphere," I said. "Have you seen any?"

"Ha-ha," he said. It was supposed to be a laugh, but it

was even phonier than his smile. "You must think you're in Boston." He found something and held it up to the light, squinting. "Seriously, why are you here?"

"Why wouldn't I be here, Vince?" I said, pretending to sound indignant. "It's a crime scene, isn't it?"

"You do blood spatter," he said, throwing away whatever he'd been staring at and searching for another one.

"I knew that."

He looked at me with his biggest fake smile. "There's no blood here, Dex."

I felt light-headed. "What does that mean?"

"There's no blood in or on or near, Dex. No blood at all. Weirdest thing you ever saw," he said.

No blood at all. I could hear that phrase repeat itself in my head, louder each time. No sticky, hot, messy, awful blood. No splatter. No stain. NO BLOOD AT ALL.

Why hadn't I thought of that?

It felt like a missing piece to something I didn't know was incomplete.

I don't pretend to understand what it is about Dexter and blood. Just thinking of it sets my teeth on edge—and yet I have, after all, made it my career, my study, and part of my real work. Clearly some very deep things are going on, but I find it a little hard to stay interested. I am what I am, and isn't it a lovely night to dissect a child killer?

But this—

"Are you all right, Dexter?" Vince asked.

"I am fantastic," I said. "How does he do it?"

"That depends."

I looked at Vince. He was staring at a handful of coffee

grounds, carefully pushing them around with one rubber-gloved finger. "Depends on what, Vince?"

"On who *he* is and what *it* he's doing," he said. "Ha-ha."

I shook my head. "Sometimes you work too hard at being inscrutable," I said. "How does the killer get rid of the blood?"

"Hard to say right now," he said. "We haven't found any of it. And the body is not in real good shape, so it's going to be hard to find much."

That didn't sound nearly as interesting. I like to leave a neat body. No fuss, no mess, no dripping blood. If the killer was just another dog tearing at a bone, this was all nothing to me.

I breathed a little easier. "Where's the body?" I asked Vince.

He jerked his head at a spot twenty feet away. "Over there," he said. "With LaGuerta."

"Oh, my," I said. "Is LaGuerta handling this?"

He gave me his fake smile again. "Lucky killer."

I looked. A small knot of people stood around a cluster of tidy trash bags. "I don't see it," I said.

"Right there. The trash bags. Each one is a body part. He cut the victim into pieces and then wrapped up each one like it was a Christmas present. Did you ever see anything like that before?"

Of course I had.

That's how I do it.

CHAPTER 3

THERE IS SOMETHING STRANGE AND DISARMING about looking at a homicide scene in the bright daylight of the Miami sun. It makes the most grotesque killings look antiseptic, staged. Like you're in a new and daring section of Disney World. Dahmer Land. Come ride the refrigerator. Please hurl your lunch in the designated containers only.

Not that the sight of mutilated bodies anywhere has ever bothered *me*, oh no, far from it. I do resent the messy ones a little when they are careless with their body fluids—nasty stuff. Other than that, it seems no worse than looking at spare ribs at the grocery store. But rookies and visitors to crime scenes tend to throw up—and for some reason, they throw up much less here than they do up North. The sun just takes the sting out. It cleans things up, makes them neater. Maybe that's why I love Miami. It's such a *neat* town.

And it was already a beautiful, hot Miami day. Anyone

who had worn a suit coat was now looking for a place to hang it. Alas, there was no such place in the grubby little parking lot. There were only five or six cars and the Dumpster. It was shoved over in a corner, next to the café, backed up against a pink stucco wall topped with barbed wire. The back door to the café was there. A sullen young woman moved in and out, doing a brisk business in *café cubano* and *pasteles* with the cops and the technicians on the scene. The handful of assorted cops in suits who hang out at homicide scenes, either to be noticed, to apply pressure, or to make sure they know what's going on, now had one more thing to juggle. Coffee, a pastry, a suit coat.

The crime-lab gang didn't wear suits. Rayon bowling shirts with two pockets was more their speed. I was wearing one myself. It repeated a pattern of voodoo drummers and palm trees against a lime green background. Stylish, but practical.

I headed for the closest rayon shirt in the knot of people around the body. It belonged to Angel Batista-no-relation, as he usually introduced himself. Hi, I'm Angel Batista, no relation. He worked in the medical examiner's office. At the moment he was squatting beside one of the garbage bags and peering inside it.

I joined him. I was anxious to see inside the bag myself. Anything that got a reaction from Deborah was worth a peek.

"Angel," I said, coming up on his side. "What do we have?"

"What you mean *we*, white boy?" he said. "We got no blood with this one. You're out of a job."

"I heard." I crouched down beside him. "Was it done here, or just dumped?"

He shook his head. "Hard to say. They empty the Dumpster twice a week—this has been here for maybe two days."

I looked around the parking lot, then over at the moldy façade of the Cacique. "What about the motel?"

Angel shrugged. "They're still checking, but I don't think they'll find anything. The other times, he just used a handy Dumpster. Huh," he said suddenly.

"What?"

He used a pencil to peel back the plastic bag. "Look at that cut."

The end of a disjointed leg stuck out, looking pale and exceptionally dead in the glare of the sun. This piece ended in the ankle, foot neatly lopped off. A small tattoo of a butterfly remained, one wing cut away with the foot.

I whistled. It was almost surgical. This guy did very nice work—as good as I could do. "Very clean," I said. And it was, even beyond the neatness of the cutting. I had never seen such clean, dry, *neat*-looking dead flesh. Wonderful.

"Me cago en diez on nice and clean," he said. "It's not finished."

I looked past him, staring a little deeper into the bag. Nothing moving in there. "It looks pretty final to me, Angel."

"Lookit," he said. He flipped open one of the other bags. "This leg, he cuts it in four pieces. Almost like with a ruler or something, huh? And so *this* one," and he pointed back to the first ankle that I had admired so deeply, "this one he cuts in two pieces only? How's come, huh?"

"I'm sure I don't know," I said. "Perhaps Detective LaGuerta will figure it out."

Angel looked at me for a moment and we both struggled to keep a straight face. "Perhaps she will," he said, and he turned back to his work. "Why don't you go ask her?"

"Hasta luego, Angel," I said.

"Almost certainly," he answered, head down over the plastic bag.

There was a rumor going around a few years back that Detective Migdia LaGuerta got into the Homicide Bureau by sleeping with somebody. To look at her once you might buy into that. She has all the necessary parts in the right places to be physically attractive in a sullen, aristocratic way. A true artist with her makeup and very well dressed, Bloomingdale's chic. But the rumor can't be true. To begin with, although she seems outwardly very feminine, I've never met a woman who was more masculine inside. She was hard, ambitious in the most self-serving way, and her only weakness seemed to be for model-handsome men a few years younger than she was. So I'm quite sure she didn't get into Homicide using sex. She got into Homicide because she's Cuban, plays politics, and knows how to kiss ass. That combination is far better than sex in Miami.

LaGuerta is very very good at kissing ass, a world-class ass kisser. She kissed ass all the way up to the lofty rank of homicide investigator. Unfortunately, it's a job where her skills at posterior smooching were never called for, and she was a terrible detective.

It happens; incompetence is rewarded more often than not. I have to work with her anyway. So I have used my considerable charm to make her like me. Easier than you might think. Anybody can be charming if they don't mind faking it, saying all the stupid, obvious, nauseating things that a conscience keeps most people from saying. Happily, I don't have a conscience. I say them.

As I approached the little group clustered near the café, LaGuerta was interviewing somebody in rapid-fire Spanish. I speak Spanish; I even understand a little Cuban. But I could only get one word in ten from LaGuerta. The Cuban dialect is the despair of the Spanish-speaking world. The whole purpose of Cuban Spanish seems to be to race against an invisible stopwatch and get out as much as possible in three-second bursts without using any consonants.

The trick to following it is to know what the person is going to say before they say it. That tends to contribute to the clannishness non-Cubans sometimes complain about.

The man LaGuerta was grilling was short and broad, dark, with Indio features, and was clearly intimidated by the dialect, the tone, and the badge. He tried not to look at her as he spoke, which seemed to make her speak even faster.

"No, no hay nadie afuera," he said softly, slowly, looking away. "Todos estan en café." *Nobody was outside, they were all in the café.*

"Donde estabas?" she demanded. *Where were you?*

The man looked at the bags of body parts and quickly looked away. "Cocina." *The kitchen.* "Entonces yo saco la basura." *Then I took out the garbage.*

LaGuerta went on; pushing at him verbally, asking the wrong questions in a tone of voice that bullied and demeaned him until he slowly forgot the horror of finding the body parts in the Dumpster, and turned sullen and uncooperative instead.

A true master's touch. Take the key witness and turn him against you. If you can screw up the case in the first few vital hours, it saves time and paperwork later.

She finished with a few threats and sent the man away. "Indio," she spat, as he lumbered out of earshot.

"It takes all kinds, Detective," I said. "Even campesinos." She looked up and ran her eyes over me, slowly, while I stood and wondered why. Had she forgotten what I looked like? But she finished with a big smile. She really did like me, the idiot.

"Hola, Dexter. What brings you here?"

"I heard you were here and couldn't stay away. Please, Detective, when will you marry me?"

She giggled. The other officers within earshot exchanged a glance and then looked away. "I don't buy a shoe until I try it on," LaGuerta said. "No matter how good the shoe looks." And while I was sure that was true, it didn't actually explain to me why she stared at me with her tongue between her teeth as she said it. "Now go away, you distracting me. I have serious work here."

"I can see that," I said. "Have you caught the killer yet?"

She snorted. "You sound like a reporter. Those assholes will be all over me in another hour."

"What will you tell them?"

She looked at the bags of body parts and frowned. Not because the sight bothered her. She was seeing her career, trying to phrase her statement to the press.

"It is only a matter of time before the killer makes a mistake and we catch him—"

"Meaning," I said, "that so far he hasn't made any mistakes, you don't have any clues, and you have to wait for him to kill again before you can do anything?"

She looked at me hard. "I forget. Why do I like you?"

I just shrugged. I didn't have a clue—but then, apparently she didn't either.

"What we got is nada y nada. That Guatemalan," she made a face at the retreating Indio, "he found the body when he came out with the garbage from the restaurant. He didn't recognize these garbage bags and he opened one up to see if maybe there was something good. And it was the head."

"Peekaboo," I said softly.

"Hah?"

"Nothing."

She looked around, frowning, perhaps hoping a clue would leap out and she could shoot it.

"So that's it. Nobody saw anything, heard anything. Nothing. I have to wait for your fellow nerds to finish up before I know anything."

"Detective," said a voice behind us. Captain Matthews strolled up in a cloud of Aramis aftershave, meaning that the reporters would be here very shortly.

"Hello, Captain," LaGuerta said.

"I've asked Officer Morgan to maintain a peripheral involvement in this case," he said. LaGuerta flinched. "In her capacity as an undercover operative she has resources in the prostitution community that could assist us in expediting the solution." The man talked with a thesaurus. Too many years of writing reports.

"Captain, I'm not sure that's necessary," LaGuerta said.

He winked and put a hand on her shoulder. People management is a skill. "Relax, Detective. She's not going to interfere with your command prerogatives. She'll just check in with you if she has something to report. Witnesses, that sort of thing. Her father was a damn good cop. All right?" His eyes glazed and refocused on something on the other end of the parking lot. I looked. The Channel 7 News van was rolling in. "Excuse me," Matthews said. He straightened his tie, put on a serious expression, and strolled over toward the van.

"Puta," LaGuerta said under her breath.

I didn't know if she meant that as a general observation, or was talking about Deb, but I thought it was a good time to slip away, too, before LaGuerta remembered that Officer Puta was my sister.

As I rejoined Deb, Matthews was shaking hands with Jerry Gonzalez from Channel 7. Jerry was the Miami area's leading champion of if-it-bleeds-it-leads journalism. My kind of guy. He was going to be disappointed this time.

I felt a slight quiver pass over my skin. *No blood at all.*

"Dexter," Deborah said, still trying to sound like a cop, but I could tell she was excited. "I talked to Captain Matthews. He's going to let me in on this."

"I heard," I said. "Be careful."

She blinked at me. "What are you talking about?"

"LaGuerta," I said.

Deborah snorted. "Her," she said.

"Yeah. Her. She doesn't like you, and she doesn't want you on her turf."

"Tough. She got her orders from the captain."

"Uh-huh. And she's already spent five minutes figuring out how to get around them. So watch your back, Debs."

She just shrugged. "What did you find out?" she asked.

I shook my head. "Nothing yet. LaGuerta's already nowhere. But Vince said—" I stopped. Even talking about it seemed too private.

"Vince said what?"

"A small thing, Deb. A detail. Who knows what it means?"

"Nobody will ever know if you don't say it, Dexter."

"There . . . seems to be no blood left with the body. No blood at all."

Deborah was quiet for a minute, thinking. Not a reverent pause, not like me. Just thinking. "Okay," she said at last. "I give up. What does it mean?"

"Too soon to tell," I said.

"But you think it means something."

It meant a strange light-headedness. It meant an itch to find out more about this killer. It meant an appreciative chuckle from the Dark Passenger, who should have been quiet so soon after the priest. But that was all rather tough to explain to Deborah, wasn't it? So I just said, "It might, Deb. Who really knows?"

She looked at me hard for half a moment, then shrugged. "All right," she said. "Anything else?"

"Oh, a great deal," I said. "Very nice blade work. The cuts are close to surgical. Unless they find something in the hotel, which no one expects, the body was killed some-where else and dumped here."

"Where?"

"Very good question. Half of police work is asking the right questions."

"The other half is answering," she told me.

"Well then. Nobody knows where yet, Deb. And I cer-tainly don't have all the forensic data—"

"But you're starting to get a feel for this one," she said.

I looked at her. She looked back. I had developed hunches before. I had a small reputation for it. My hunches were often quite good. And why shouldn't they be? I often know how the killers are thinking. I think the same way. Of course I was not always right. Sometimes I was very wide of the mark. It wouldn't look good if I was always right. And I didn't want the cops to catch *every* serial killer out there. Then what would I do for a hobby? But this one—Which way should I go with this so very interesting escapade?

"Tell me, Dexter," Deborah urged. "Have you got any guesses about this?"

"Possibly," I said. "It's a little early yet."

"Well, Morgan," said LaGuerta from behind us. We both turned. "I see you're dressed for real police work."

Something about LaGuerta's tone was like a slap on the face. Deborah stiffened. "Detective," she said. "Did you find anything?" She said it in a tone that already knew the answer.

A cheap shot. But it missed. LaGuerta waved a hand air-ily. "They are only putas," she said, looking hard at Deb's

cleavage, so very prominent in her hooker suit. "Just hookers. The important thing here is to keep the press from getting hysterical." She shook her head slowly, as if in
disbelief, and looked up. "Considering what you can do
with gravity, that should be easy." And she winked at me
and strolled off, over toward the perimeter, where Captain
Matthews was talking with great dignity to Jerry Gonzalez
from Channel 7.

"Bitch," Deborah said.

"I'm sorry, Debs. Would you prefer me to say, *We'll show
her*? Or should I go with *I told you so*?"

She glared at me. "Goddamn it, Dexter," she said. "I
really want to be the one to find this guy."

And as I thought about that *no blood at all*—

So did I. I really wanted to find him, too.

CHAPTER 4

I TOOK MY BOAT OUT THAT NIGHT AFTER WORK, TO get away from Deb's questions and to sort through what I was feeling. *Feeling.* Me, feeling. What a concept.

I nosed my Whaler slowly out the canal, thinking nothing, a perfect Zen state, moving at idle speed past the large houses, all separated from each other by high hedges and chain-link fences. I threw an automatic big wave and bright smile to all the neighbors out in their yards that grew neatly up to the canal's seawall. Kids playing on the manicured grass. Mom and Dad barbecuing, or lounging, or polishing the barbed wire, hawkeyes on the kids. I waved to everybody. Some of them even waved back. They knew me, had seen me go by before, always cheerful, a big hello for everybody. *He was such a nice man. Very friendly. I can't believe he did those horrible things . . .*

I opened up the throttle when I cleared the canal, heading out the channel and then southeast, toward Cape Florida. The wind in my face and the taste of the salt spray helped clear my head, made me feel clean and a little fresher. I found it a great deal easier to think. Part of it was the calm and peace of the water. And another part was that in the best tradition of Miami watercraft, most of the other boaters seemed to be trying to kill me. I found that very relaxing. I was right at home. This is my country; these are my people.

All day long at work I'd gotten little forensic updates. Around lunchtime the story broke national. The lid was coming off the hooker murders after the "grisly discovery" at the Cacique Motel. Channel 7 had done a masterful job of presenting all the hysterical horror of body parts in a Dumpster without actually saying anything about them. As Detective LaGuerta had shrewdly observed, these were only hookers; but once public pressure started to rise from the media, they might as well be senator's daughters. And so the department began to gear up for a long spell of defensive maneuvering, knowing exactly what kind of heartrending twaddle would be coming from the brave and fearless foot soldiers of the fifth estate.

Deb had stayed at the scene until the captain began to worry about authorizing too much overtime, and then she'd been sent home. She started calling me at two in the afternoon to hear what I'd discovered, which was very little. They'd found no traces of anything at the motel. There were so many tire tracks in the parking lot that none were distinct. No prints or traces in the Dumpster, on the bags, or on the body parts. Everything USDA inspection clean.

The one big clue of the day was the left leg. As Angel had noticed, the right leg had been sectioned into several neat pieces, cut at the hip, knee, and ankle. But the left leg was not. It was a mere two sections, neatly wrapped. Aha, said Detective LaGuerta, lady genius. Somebody had interrupted the killer, surprised him, startled him so he did not finish the cut. He panicked when he was seen. And she directed all her effort at finding that witness.

There was one small problem with LaGuerta's theory of interruption. A tiny little thing, perhaps splitting hairs, but—the entire body had still been meticulously cleaned and wrapped, presumably after it had been cut up. And then it had been transported carefully to the Dumpster, apparently with enough time and focus for the killer to make no mistakes and leave no traces. Either nobody pointed this out to LaGuerta or—wonder of wonders!— could it be that nobody else had noticed? Possible; so much of police work is routine, fitting details into patterns. And if the pattern was brand new, the investigation could seem like three blind men examining an elephant with a microscope.

But since I was neither blind nor hampered by routine, it had seemed far more likely to me that the killer was simply unsatisfied. Plenty of time to work, but—this was the fifth murder in the same pattern. Was it getting boring, simply chopping up the body? Was Our Boy searching for something else, something different? Some new direction, an untried twist?

I could almost feel his frustration. To have come so far, all the way to the end, sectioning the leftovers for gift wrapping. And then the sudden realization: *This isn't it. Something is just not right.* Coitus interruptus.

It wasn't fulfilling him this way anymore. He needed a different approach. He was trying to express something, and hadn't found his vocabulary yet. And in my personal opinion—I mean, if it was *me*—this would make him very frustrated. And very likely to look further for the answer.

Soon.

But let LaGuerta look for a witness. There would be none. This was a cold, careful monster, and absolutely fascinating to me. And what should I do about that fascination? I was not sure, so I had retreated to my boat to think.

A Donzi cut across my bow at seventy miles per hour, only inches away. I waved happily and returned to the present. I was approaching Stiltsville, the mostly abandoned collection of old stilt homes in the water near Cape Florida. I nosed into a big circle, going nowhere, and let my thoughts move back into that same slow arc.

What would I do? I needed to decide now, before I got too helpful for Deborah. I could help her solve this, absolutely, no one better. Nobody else was even moving in the right direction. But did I want to help? Did I want this killer arrested? Or did I want to find him and stop him myself? Beyond this—oh, nagging little thought—did I even want him to stop?

What would I do?

To my right I could just see Elliott Key in the last light of the day. And as always, I remembered my camping trip there with Harry Morgan. My foster father. The Good Cop.

You're different, Dexter.

Yes, Harry, I certainly am.

But you can learn to control that difference and use it con-structively.

All right, Harry. If you think I should. How?

And he told me.

There is no starry sky anywhere like the starry sky in South Florida when you are fourteen and camping out with Dad. Even if he's only your foster dad. And even if the sight of all those stars merely fills you with a kind of satisfaction, emotion being out of the question. You don't feel it. That's part of the reason you're here.

The fire has died down and the stars are exceedingly bright and foster dear old dad has been quiet for some time, taking small sips on the old fashioned hip flask he has pulled from the outside flap of his pack. And he's not very good at this, not like so many other cops, not really a drinker. But it's empty now, and it's time for him to say his piece if he's ever going to say it.

"You're different, Dexter," he says.

I look away from the brightness of the stars. Around the small and sandy clearing the last glow of the fire is making shadows. Some of them trickle across Harry's face. He looks strange to me, like I've never seen him before. Determined, unhappy, a little dazed. "What do you mean, Dad?"

He won't look at me. "The Billups say Buddy has disappeared," he says.

"Noisy little creep. He was barking all night. Mom couldn't sleep."

Mom needed her sleep, of course. Dying of cancer requires plenty of rest, and she wasn't getting it with that awful little dog across the street yapping at every leaf that blew down the sidewalk.

"I found the grave," Harry says. "There were a lot of bones in there, Dexter. Not just Buddy's."

There's very little to say here. I carefully pull at a handful of pine needles and wait for Harry.

"How long have you been doing this?"

I search Harry's face, then look out across the clearing to the beach. Our boat is there, moving gently with the surge of the water. The lights of Miami are off to the right, a soft white glow. I can't figure out where Harry is going, what he wants to hear. But he is my straight-arrow foster dad; the truth is usually a good idea with Harry. He always knows, or he finds out.

"A year and a half," I say.

Harry nods. "Why did you start?"

A very good question, and certainly beyond me at fourteen. "It just—I kind of . . . had to," I tell him. Even then, so young but so smooth.

"Do you hear a voice?" he wants to know. "Something or somebody telling you what to do, and you had to do it?"

"Uh," I say with fourteen-year-old eloquence, "not exactly."

"Tell me," Harry says.

Oh for a moon, a good fat moon, something bigger to look at. I clutch another fistful of pine needles. My face is hot, as if Dad has asked me to talk about sex dreams. Which, in a way— "It, uh . . . I kind of, you know, *feel* something," I say. "Inside. Watching me. Maybe, um. Laughing? But not really a voice, just—" An eloquent teenaged shrug. But it seems to make sense to Harry.

"And this *something*. It makes you kill things."

High overhead a slow fat jet crawls by. "Not, um, doesn't *make* me," I say. "Just—makes it seem like a good idea?"

"Have you ever wanted to kill something else? Something bigger than a dog?"

I try to answer but there is something in my throat. I clear it. "Yes," I say.

"A person?"

"Nobody in particular, Dad. Just—" I shrug again.

"Why didn't you?"

"It's—I thought you wouldn't like it. You and Mom."

"That's all that stopped you?"

"I, uh—I didn't want you, um, mad at me. Uh . . . you know. Disappointed."

I steal a glance at Harry. He is looking at me, not blinking. "Is that why we took this trip, Dad? To talk about this?"

"Yes," Harry says. "We need to get you squared away."

Squared away, oh yes, a completely Harry idea of how life is lived, with hospital corners and polished shoes. And even then I knew; needing to kill something every now and then would pretty much sooner or later get in the way of being squared away.

"How?" I say, and he looks at me long and hard, and then he nods when he sees that I am with him step for step.

"Good boy," he says. "Now." And in spite of saying now,

it is a very long time before he speaks again. I watch the lights on a boat as it goes past, maybe two hundred yards out from our little beach. Over the sound of their motor a radio is blasting Cuban music. "Now," Harry says again, and I look at him. But he is looking away, across the dying fire, off into the future over there somewhere. "It's like this," he says. I listen carefully. This is what Harry says when he is giving you a higher-order truth. When he showed me how to throw a curve ball, and how to throw a left hook. *It's like this*, he would say, and it always was, just like that.

"I'm getting old, Dexter." He waited for me to object, but I didn't, and he nodded. "I think people understand things different when they get older," he says. "It's not a question of getting soft, or seeing things in the gray areas instead of black and white. I really believe I'm just understanding things different. Better." He looks at me, Harry's look, Tough Love with blue eyes.

"Okay," I say.

"Ten years ago I would have wanted you in an institution somewhere," he says, and I blink. That almost hurts, except I've thought of it myself. "Now," he says, "I think I know better. I know what you are, and I know you're a good kid."

"No," I say, and it comes out very soft and weak, but Harry hears.

"Yes," he says firmly. "You're a good kid, Dex, I know that. I *know* it," almost to himself now, for effect maybe, and then his eyes lock onto mine. "Otherwise, you wouldn't care what I thought, or what Mom thought. You'd just do it. You can't help it, I know that. Because—" He stops and just looks at me for a moment. It's very uncomfortable for me. "What do you remember from before?" he asked. "You know. Before we took you in."

That still hurts, but I really don't know why. I was only three. "Nothing."

"Good," he says. "Nobody should remember that." And as long as he lives that will be the most he ever says about it. "But even though you don't remember, Dex, it did things to you. Those things make you what you are. I've talked to some people about this." And strangest of strange, he gives me a very small, almost shy, Harry smile. "I've been expecting this. What happened to you when you were a little kid has shaped you. I've tried to straighten that out, but—" He shrugs. "It was too strong, too much. It got into you too early and it's going to stay there. It's going to make you want to kill. And you can't help that. You can't change that. But," he says, and he looks away again, to see what I can't tell. "But you can channel it. Control it. Choose—" his words come so carefully now, more careful than I've ever heard him talk "—choose what . . . or *who* . . . you kill . . ." And he gave me a smile unlike any I had ever seen before, a smile as bleak and dry as the ashes of our dying fire. "There are plenty of people who deserve it, Dex . . ."

And with those few little words he gave a shape to my whole life, my everything, my who and what I am. The wonderful, all-seeing, all-knowing man. Harry. My dad.

If only I was capable of love, how I would have loved Harry.

So long ago now. Harry long dead. But his lessons had lived on. Not because of any warm and gooey emotional feelings I had. Because Harry was right. I'd proved that over and over. Harry knew, and Harry taught me well.

Be careful, Harry said. And he taught me to be careful as only a cop could teach a killer.

To choose carefully among those who deserved it. To make absolutely sure. Then tidy up. Leave no traces. And always avoid emotional involvement; it can lead to mistakes.

Being careful went beyond the actual killing, of course. Being careful meant building a careful life, too. Compartmentalize. Socialize. Imitate life.

All of which I had done, so very carefully. I was a near perfect hologram. Above suspicion, beyond reproach, and beneath contempt. A neat and polite monster, the boy next door. Even Deborah was at least half fooled, half the time. Of course, she believed what she wanted to believe, too.

Right now she believed I could help her solve these murders, jump-start her career and catapult her out of her Hollywood sex suit and into a tailored business suit. And she was right, of course. I could help her. But I didn't really want to, because I enjoyed watching this other killer work and felt some kind of aesthetic connection, or—

Emotional involvement.

Well. There it was. I was in clear violation of the Code of Harry.

I nosed the boat back toward my canal. It was full dark now, but I steered by a radio tower a few degrees to the left of my home water.

So be it. Harry had always been right, he was right now. *Don't get emotionally involved*, Harry had said. So I wouldn't.

I would help Deb.

CHAPTER 5

THE NEXT MORNING IT WAS RAINING AND THE TRAF-
fic was crazy, like it always is in Miami when it rains.
Some drivers slowed down on the slick roads. That
made others furious, and they leaned on their horns,
screamed out their windows, and accelerated out onto the
shoulder, fishtailing wildly past the slowpokes and waving
their fists.

At the LeJeune on-ramp, a huge dairy truck had roared
onto the shoulder and hit a van full of kids from a Catholic
school. The dairy truck flipped over. And now five young
girls in plaid wool skirts were sitting in a huge puddle of
milk with dazed looks on their faces. Traffic nearly stopped
for an hour. One kid was airlifted to Jackson Hospital. The
others sat in the milk in their uniforms and watched the
grown-ups scream at each other.

I inched along placidly, listening to the radio. Apparently
the police were hot on the trail of the Tamiami Butcher.
There were no specifics available, but Captain Matthews

got a lovely sound bite. He made it seem like he would personally make the arrest as soon as he finished his coffee.

I finally got off onto surface roads and went only a little
faster. I stopped at a doughnut shop not too far from the airport. I bought an apple fritter and a cruller, but the apple
fritter was gone almost before I got back into the car. I have
a very high metabolism. It comes with living the good life.

The rain had stopped by the time I got to work. The sun
shone and steam rose from the pavement as I walked into
the lobby, flashed my credentials, and went upstairs.

Deb was already waiting for me.

She did not look happy this morning. Of course, she does
not look happy very often any more. She's a cop, after all,
and most of them can't manage the trick at all. Too much
time on duty trying not to look human. It leaves their faces
stuck.

"Deb," I said. I put the crisp white pastry bag on my
desk.

"Where were you last night?" she said. Very sour, as I'd
expected. Soon those frown lines would turn permanent,
ruining a wonderful face: deep blue eyes, alive with intelligence, and small upturned nose with just a dash of freckles,
framed by black hair. Beautiful features, at the moment
spattered with about seven pounds of cheap makeup.

I looked at her with fondness. She was clearly coming
from work, dressed today in a lacy bra, bright pink spandex
shorts, and gold high heels. "Never mind me," I said.
"Where were *you*?"

She flushed. She hated to wear anything but clean,
pressed blues. "I tried to call you," she said.

"Sorry," I said.

"Yeah. Sure."

I sat down in my chair and didn't speak. Deb likes to unload on me. That's what family is for. "Why were you so anxious to talk to me?"

"They're shutting me out," she said. She opened my doughnut bag and looked inside.

"What did you expect?" I said. "You know how LaGuerta feels about you."

She pulled the cruller out of the bag and savaged it.

"I expect," she said, mouth full, "to be in on this. Like the captain said."

"You don't have any seniority," I said. "Or any political smarts."

She crumpled the bag and threw it at my head. She missed. "Goddamn it, Dexter," she said. "You know damned well I deserve to be in Homicide. Instead of—" She snapped her bra strap and waved a hand at her skimpy costume. "This bullshit."

I nodded. "Although on you it looks good," I said.

She made an awful face: rage and disgust competing for space. "I hate this," she said. "I can't do this much longer or I swear, I'll go nuts."

"It's a little soon for me to have the whole thing figured out, Deb."

"Shit," she said. Whatever else you could say about police work, it was ruining Deborah's vocabulary. She gave me a cold, hard cop-look, the first I'd ever had from her. It was Harry's look, the same eyes, same feeling of looking right through you to the truth. "Don't bullshit me, Dex," she said. "All you have to do half the time is see the body, and you know who did it. I never asked you how you do that, but if you have any hunches on this one, I want 'em." She kicked out savagely and put a small dent in my metal desk. "Goddamn it, I want out of this stupid outfit."

"And we'd all love to see that, Morgan," came a deep and phony voice from behind her in the doorway. I looked up. Vince Masuoka was smiling in at us.

"You wouldn't know what to do, Vince," Deb told him.

He smiled bigger, that bright, fake, textbook smile. "Why don't we try it and find out?"

"In your dreams, Vince," Debbie said, slumping into a pout that I hadn't seen since she was twelve.

Vince nodded at the crumpled white bag on my desk. "It *was* your turn, goody. What'd you bring me? Where is it?"

"Sorry, Vince," I said. "Debbie ate your cruller."

"I wish," he said, with his sharp, imitation leer. "Then I could eat her jelly roll. You owe me a big doughnut, Dex," he said.

"The only big one you'll ever have," Deborah said.

"It's not the size of the doughnut, it's the skill of the baker," Vince told her.

"Please," I said. "You two are going to sprain a frontal lobe. It's too early to be this clever."

"Ah-ha," Vince said, with his terrible fake laugh. "Ah-ha ha-ha. See you later." He winked. "Don't forget my doughnut." And he wandered away to his microscope down the hall.

"So what have you figured out?" Deb asked me.

Deb believed that every now and then I got hunches. She

had reason to believe. Usually my inspired guesses had to do with the brutal whackos who liked to hack up some poor slob every few weeks just for the hell of it. Several times Deborah had seen me put a quick and clean finger on something that nobody else knew was there. She had never said anything, but my sister is a damned good cop, and so she has suspected me of something for quite a while. She doesn't know what, but she knows there is something wrong there and it bothers the hell out of her every now and then, because she does, after all, love me. The last living thing on the earth that does love me. This is not self-pity but the coldest, clearest self-knowledge. I am unlovable. Following Harry's plan, I have tried to involve myself in other people, in relationships, and even—in my sillier moments—in love. But it doesn't work. Something in me is broken or missing, and sooner or later the other person catches me Acting, or one of Those Nights comes along.

I can't even keep pets. Animals hate me. I bought a dog once; it barked and howled—at *me*—in a nonstop no-mind fury for two days before I had to get rid of it. I tried a turtle. I touched it once and it wouldn't come out of its shell again, and after a few days of that it died. Rather than see me or have me touch it again, it died.

Nothing else loves me, or ever will. Not even—especially—me. I know what I am and that is not a thing to love. I am alone in the world, all alone, but for Deborah. Except, of course, for the Thing inside, who does not come out to play too often. And does not actually play with me but must have somebody else.

So as much as I can, I care about her, dear Deborah. It is probably not love, but I would rather she were happy.

And she sat there, dear Deborah, looking unhappy. My family. Staring at me and not knowing what to say, but coming closer to saying it than ever before.

"Well," I said, "actually—"

"I *knew* it! You *DO* have something!"

"Don't interrupt my trance, Deborah. I'm in touch with the spirit realm."

"Spit it out," she said.

"It's the interrupted cut, Deb. The left leg."

"What about it?"

"LaGuerta thinks the killer was discovered. Got nervous, didn't finish."

Deborah nodded. "She had me asking hookers last night if they saw anything. Somebody must have."

"Oh, not you, too," I said. "*Think*, Deborah. If he was interrupted—too scared to finish—"

"The wrapping," she blurted. "He still spent a lot of time wrapping the body, cleaning up." She looked surprised. "Shit. *After* he was interrupted?"

I clapped my hands and beamed at her. "Bravo, Miss Marple."

"Then it doesn't make sense."

"Au contraire. If there is plenty of time, but the ritual is not completed properly—and remember, Deb, the ritual is nearly everything—what's the implication?"

"Why can't you just tell me, for God's sake?" she snapped.

"What fun would that be?"

She blew out a hard breath. "Goddamn it. All right, Dex. If he wasn't interrupted, but he didn't finish— Shit. The wrapping-up part was more important than the cutting?"

I took pity on her. "No, Deb. Think. This is the fifth one, exactly like all the others. Four left legs cut perfectly. And now number five—" I shrugged, raised an eyebrow at her.

"Aw, shit, Dexter. How should I know? Maybe he only needed four left legs. Maybe . . . I don't know, I swear to God. What?"

I smiled and shook my head. To me it was so clear. "The thrill is gone, Deb. Something just isn't right. It isn't working. Some essential bit of the magic that makes it perfect, isn't there."

"I was supposed to figure that out?"

"Somebody should, don't you think? And so he just sort of dribbles to a stop, looking for inspiration and finding none."

She frowned. "So he's done. He won't do this again?"

I laughed. "Oh my God, no, Deb. Just the opposite. If you were a priest, and you truly believed in God but couldn't find the right way to worship him, what would you do?"

"Keep trying," she said, "until I got it right." She stared hard. "Jesus. That's what you think? He's going to do it again soon?"

"It's just a hunch," I said modestly. "I could be wrong." But I was sure I was not wrong.

"We should be setting up a way to catch him when he does," she said. "Not looking for a nonexistent witness."

She stood and headed out the door. "I'll call later. Bye!" And she was gone.

I poked at the white paper bag. There was nothing left inside. Just like me: a clean, crisp outside and nothing at all on the inside.

I folded the bag and placed it in the trash can beside my desk. There was work to do this morning, real official police lab work. I had a long report to type up, accompanying pictures to sort, evidence to file. It was routine stuff, a double homicide that would probably never go to trial, but I like to make sure that whatever I touch is well organized.

Besides, this one had been interesting. The blood spatter had been very difficult to read; between the arterial spurting, the multiple victims—obviously moving around—and the cast-off pattern from what had to be a chain saw, it had been almost impossible to find an impact site. In order to cover the whole room, I'd had to use two bottles of Luminol, which reveals even the faintest of blood spots and is shockingly expensive at $12 a bottle.

I'd actually had to lay out strings to help me figure the primary spatter angles, a technique ancient enough to seem like alchemy. The splat patterns were startling, vivid; there were bright, wild, feral splatters across the walls, furniture, television, towels, bedspreads, curtains—an amazing wild horror of flying blood. Even in Miami you would think someone would have heard something. Two people being hacked up alive with a chain saw, in an elegant and expensive hotel room, and the neighbors simply turned up their TVs.

You may say that dear diligent Dexter gets carried away in his job, but I like to be thorough, and I like to know where all the blood is hiding. The professional reasons for this are obvious, but not quite as important to me as the personal ones. Perhaps someday a psychiatrist retained by the state penal system will help me discover exactly why.

In any case, the body chunks were very cold by the time we got to the scene, and we would probably never find the guy in the size 7½ handmade Italian loafer. Right-handed and overweight, with a terrific backhand.

But I had persevered and done a very neat piece of work. I don't do my job to catch the bad guys. Why would I want to do that? No, I do my job to make order out of chaos. To force the nasty blood stains to behave properly, and then go away. Others may use my work to catch criminals; that's fine by me, but it doesn't matter.

If I am ever careless enough to be caught, they will say I am a sociopathic monster, a sick and twisted demon who is not even human, and they will probably send me to die in Old Sparky with a smug self-righteous glow. If they ever catch Size 7½, they will say he is a bad man who went wrong because of social forces he was too unfortunate to resist, and he will go to jail for ten years before they turn him loose with enough money for a suit and a new chain saw.

Every day at work I understand Harry a little better.

CHAPTER 6

FRIDAY NIGHT. DATE NIGHT IN MIAMI. AND BE-
lieve it or not, Date Night for Dexter. Oddly enough,
I had found somebody. What, what? Deeply dead
Dexter dating debutante doxies? Sex among the Undead?
Has my need to imitate life gone all the way to faking
orgasms?

Breathe easy. Sex never entered into it. After years of
dreadful fumbling and embarrassment trying to look normal, I had finally hooked up with the perfect date.

Rita was almost as badly damaged as I am. Married too
young, she had fought to make it work for ten years and two
kids. Her charming life mate had a few small problems.
First alcohol, then heroin, believe it or not, and finally crack.
He beat her, the brute. Broke furniture, screamed, and threw
things and made threats. Then raped her. Infected her with
some dreadful crack-house diseases. All this on a regular
basis, and Rita endured, worked, fought him through rehab

twice. Then he went after the kids one night and Rita finally put her foot down.

Her face had healed by now, of course. And broken arms and ribs are routine for Miami physicians. Rita was quite presentable, just what the monster ordered.

The divorce was final, the brute was locked up, and then? Ah, the mysteries of the human mind. Somehow, somewhy, dear Rita had decided to date again. She was quite sure it was the Right Thing to do—but as a result of her frequent battery at the hands of the Man She Loved, she was completely uninterested in sex. Just, maybe, some masculine company for a while.

She had searched for just the right guy: sensitive, gentle, and willing to wait. Quite a long search, of course. She was looking for some imaginary man who cared more about having someone to talk to and see movies with than someone to have sex with, because she was Just Not Ready for That.

Did I say imaginary? Well, yes. Human men are not like that. Most women know this by the time they've had two kids and their first divorce. Poor Rita had married too young and too badly to learn this valuable lesson. And as a by-product of recovering from her awful marriage, instead of realizing that all men are beasts, she had come up with this lovely romantic picture of a perfect gentleman who would wait indefinitely for her to open slowly, like a little flower.

Well. Really. Perhaps such a man existed in Victorian England—when there was a knocking shop on every corner where he could blow off steam between flowery protestations of frictionless love. But not, to my knowledge, in twenty-first-century Miami.

And yet—I could imitate all those things perfectly. And I actually wanted to. I had no interest in a sexual relationship. I wanted a disguise; Rita was exactly what I was looking for.

She was, as I say, very presentable. Petite and pert and spunky, a slim athletic figure, short blond hair, and blue eyes. She was a fitness fanatic, spending all her off-hours running and biking and so on. In fact, sweating was one of our favorite activities. We had cycled through the Everglades, done 5K runs, and even pumped iron together.

And best of all were her two children. Astor was eight and Cody was five and they were much too quiet. They would be, of course. Children whose parents frequently attempt to kill each other with the furniture tend to be slightly withdrawn. Any child brought up in a horror zone is. But they can be brought out of it eventually—look at me. I had endured nameless and unknown horrors as a child, and yet here I was: a useful citizen, a pillar of the community.

Perhaps that was part of my strange liking for Astor and Cody. Because I did like them, and that made no sense to me. I know what I am and I understand many things about myself. But one of the few character traits that genuinely mystifies me is my attitude toward children.

I like them.

They are important to me. They matter.

I don't understand it, really. I genuinely wouldn't care if every human in the universe were suddenly to expire, with the possible exception of myself and maybe Deborah. Other people are less important to me than lawn furniture. I do not, as the shrinks put it so eloquently, have any sense of the reality of others. And I am not burdened with this realization.

But kids—kids are different.

I had been "dating" Rita for nearly a year and a half, and in that time I had slowly and deliberately won over Astor and Cody. I was okay. I wouldn't hurt them. I remembered their birthdays, report-card days, holidays. I could come into their house and would do no harm. I could be trusted.

Ironic, really. But true.

Me, the only man they could really trust. Rita thought it was part of my long slow courtship of her. Show her that the kids liked me and who knows? But in fact, they mattered to me more than she did. Maybe it was already too late, but I didn't want to see them grow up to be like me.

This Friday night Astor answered the door. She was wearing a large T-shirt that said RUG RATS and hung below her knees. Her red hair was pulled back in two pigtails and she had no expression at all on her small still face.

"Hello Dexter," she said in her too-quiet way. For her, two words were a long conversation.

"Good evening, beautiful young lady," I said in my best Lord Mountbatten voice. "May I observe that you are looking very lovely this evening?"

"Okay," she said, holding the door open. "He's here," she said over her shoulder to the darkness around the couch.

I stepped past her. Cody was standing behind her, just inside, like he was backing her up, just in case. "Cody," I said. I handed him a roll of Necco Wafers. He took them without taking his eyes off me and simply let his hand drop to his side without looking at the candy. He wouldn't open them until I was gone, and then he would split them with his sister.

"Dexter?" Rita called from the next room.

"In here," I said. "Can't you teach these children to behave?"

"No," said Cody softly.

A joke. I stared at him. What next? Would he sing someday? Tap dance in the streets? Address the Democratic National Convention?

Rita rustled in, fastening a hoop earring. She was rather provocative, considering. She wore a practically weightless light blue silk dress that fell to mid-thigh, and of course her very best New Balance cross-training shoes. I'd never before met, or even heard of, a woman who actually wore comfortable shoes on dates. The enchanting creature.

"Hey, handsome," Rita said. "Let me talk to the sitter and we're out of here." She went into the kitchen, where I heard her going over instructions with the teenage neighbor who did her babysitting. Bedtimes. Homework. TV dos and don'ts. Cell phone number. Emergency number. What to do in case of accidental poisoning or decapitation.

Cody and Astor still stared at me.

"Are you going to a movie?" Astor asked me.

I nodded. "If we can find one that doesn't make us throw up."

"Yuk," she said. She made a very small sour face and I felt a tiny glow of accomplishment.

"Do you throw up at the movies?" Cody asked.

"Cody," Astor said.

"Do you?" he insisted.

"No," I said. "But I usually want to."

"Let's go," said Rita, sailing in and bending to give each kid a peck on the cheek. "Listen to Alice. Bedtime at nine."

"Will you come back?" Cody asked.

"Cody! Of course I'll be back," Rita said.

"I meant Dexter," Cody said.

"You'll be asleep," I said. "But I'll wave at you, okay?"

"I won't be asleep," he said grimly.

"Then I'll stop in and play cards with you," I said.

"Really?"

"Absolutely. High-stakes poker. Winner gets to keep the horses."

"Dexter!" Rita said, smiling anyway. "You'll be asleep, Cody. Now good night, kids. Be good." And she took my arm and lead me out the door. "Honestly," she murmured. "You've got those two eating out of your hand."

The movie was nothing special. I didn't really want to throw up, but I'd forgotten most of it by the time we stopped at a small place in South Beach for a late-night drink. Rita's idea. In spite of living in Miami for most of her life, she still thought South Beach was glamorous. Perhaps it was all the Rollerblades. Or maybe she thought that any-place so full of people with bad manners *had* to be glamorous.

In any case, we waited twenty minutes for a small table and then sat and waited another twenty for service. I didn't mind. I enjoyed watching good-looking idiots looking at each other. A great spectator sport.

We strolled along Ocean Boulevard afterward, making pointless conversation—an art at which I excel. It was a lovely night. One corner was chewed off the full moon of a few nights ago, when I had entertained Father Donovan.

And as we drove back to Rita's South Miami house after our standard evening out, we passed an intersection in one of Coconut Grove's less wholesome areas. A winking red light caught my eye and I glanced down the side street. Crime scene: the yellow tape was already up, and several cruisers were nosed into a hurried splay.

It's him again, I thought, and even before I knew what I meant by that I was swinging the car down the street to the crime scene.

"Where are we going?" Rita asked, quite reasonably.

"Ah," I said. "I'd like to check here and see if they need me."

"Don't you have a beeper?"

I gave her my best Friday-night smile. "They don't always *know* they need me," I said.

I might have stopped anyway, to show off Rita. The whole point of wearing a disguise was to be seen wearing her. But in truth, the small irresistible voice yammering in my ear would have made me stop no matter what. *It's him again*. And I had to see what he was up to. I left Rita in the car and hurried over.

He was up to no good again, the rascal. There was the same stack of neatly wrapped body parts. Angel-no-relation bent over it in almost the same position he'd been in when I left him at the last scene.

"*Hijo de puta*," he said when I approached him.

"Not me, I trust," I said.

"The rest of us are complaining that we have to work on Friday night," Angel said. "You show up with a date. And there is *still* nothing for you here."

"Same guy, same pattern?"

"Same," he said. He flipped the plastic away with his pen. "Bone dry, again," he said. "No blood at all."

The words made me feel slightly light-headed. I leaned in for a look. Once again the body parts were amazingly clean and dry. They had a near blue tinge to them and seemed preserved in their small perfect moment of time. Wonderful.

"A small difference in the cuts this time," Angel said. "In four places." He pointed. "Very rough here, almost emotional. Then here, not so much. Here and here, in between. Huh?"

"Very nice," I said.

"And then lookit this," he said. He nudged aside the bloodless chunk on top with a pencil. Underneath another piece gleamed white. The flesh had been flayed off very carefully, lengthwise, to reveal a clean bone.

"Why he would do like that?" Angel asked softly.

I breathed. "He's experimenting," I said. "Trying to find the right way." And I stared at the neat, dry section until I became aware that Angel had been looking at me for a very long moment.

"Like a kid playing with his food," is how I described it to Rita when I returned to the car.

"My God," Rita said. "That's horrible."

"I think the correct word is *heinous*," I said.

"How can you joke about it, Dexter?"

I gave her a reassuring smile. "You kind of get used to it in my line of work," I said. "We all make jokes to hide our pain."

"Well, good lord, I hope they catch this maniac soon."

I thought of the neatly stacked body parts, the variety of the cuts, the wonderful total lack of blood. "Not too soon," I said.

"What did you say?" she asked.

"I said, I don't think it will be too soon. The killer is extremely clever, and the detective in charge of the case is more interested in playing politics than in solving murders."

She looked at me to see if I was kidding. Then she sat quietly for a while as we drove south on U.S. 1. She didn't speak until South Miami. "I can never get used to seeing . . . I don't know. The underside? The way things really are? The way you see it," she finally said.

She took me by surprise. I had been using the silence to think about the nicely stacked body parts we had just left. My mind had been hungrily circling the clean dry chopped-up limbs like an eagle looking for a chunk of meat to rip out. Rita's observation was so unexpected I couldn't even stutter for a minute. "What do you mean?" I managed to say at last.

She frowned. "I—I'm not sure. Just— We all assume that . . . *things* . . . really are a certain way. The way they're supposed to be? And then they never are, they're always more . . . I don't know. Darker? More human. Like this. I'm thinking, of course the detective wants to catch the killer, isn't that what detectives do? And it never occurred to me before that there could be anything at all political about murder."

"Practically everything," I said. I turned onto her street and slowed down in front of her neat and unremarkable house.

"But you," she said. She didn't seem to notice where we were or what I had said. "That's where you start. Most people would never really think it through that far."

"I'm not all that deep, Rita," I said. I nudged the car into park.

"It's like, everything really is two ways, the way we all pretend it is and the way it really is. And you already know that and it's like a game for you."

I had no idea what she was trying to say. In truth, I had given up trying to figure it out and, as she spoke, I'd let my mind wander back to the newest murder; the cleanness of the flesh, the improvisational quality of the cuts, the complete dry spotless immaculate lack of blood—

"Dexter—" Rita said. She put a hand on my arm.

I kissed her.

I don't know which one of us was more surprised. It really wasn't something I had thought about doing ahead of time. And it certainly wasn't her perfume. But I mashed my lips against hers and held them there for a long moment.

She pushed away.

"No," she said. "I— No, Dexter."

"All right," I said, still shocked at what I had done.

"I don't think I want to—I'm not *ready* for— Damn it, Dexter," she said. She unclipped her seat belt, opened the car door, and ran into her house.

Oh, dear, I thought. *What on earth have I done now?*

And I knew I should be wondering about that, and perhaps feeling disappointed that I had just destroyed my disguise after a year and a half of hard maintenance.

But all I could think about was that neat stack of body parts.

No blood.

None at all.

CHAPTER 7

THIS BODY IS STRETCHED OUT JUST THE WAY I LIKE it. *The arms and legs are secure and the mouth is stopped with duct tape so there will be no noise and no spill into my work area. And my hand feels so steady with the knife that I am quite sure this will be a good one, very satisfying—*

Except it's not a knife, it's some kind of—

Except it's not my hand. Even though my hand is moving with this hand, it's not mine that holds the blade. And the room really is sort of small, it's so narrow, which makes sense because it's— what?

And now here I am floating above this perfect tight work space and its tantalizing body and for the first time I feel the cold blowing around me and even through me somehow. And if I could only feel my teeth I am quite sure they would chatter. And my hand in perfect unison with that other hand goes up and arches back for a perfect cut—

And of course I wake up in my apartment. Standing somehow by the front door, completely naked. Sleepwalking I could understand, but sleep stripping? Really. I stumble back to my little trundle bed. The covers are in a heap on the floor. The air conditioner has kicked the temperature down close to sixty. It had seemed like a good idea at the time, last night, feeling a little estranged from it all after what had happened with Rita. Preposterous, if it had really happened. Dexter, the love bandit, stealing kisses. And so I had taken a long hot shower when I got home and shoved the thermostat all the way down as I climbed into bed. I don't pretend to understand why, but in my darker moments I find cold cleansing. Not refreshing so much as necessary.

And cold it was. Far too cold now, for coffee and the start of the day amid the last tattered pieces of the dream.

As a rule I don't remember my dreams, and don't attach any importance to them if I do. So it was ridiculous that this one was staying with me.

—*floating above this perfect tight work space—my hand in perfect unison with that other hand goes up and arches back for a perfect cut—*

I've read the books. Perhaps because I'll never be one, humans are interesting to me. So I know all the symbolism: Floating is a form of flying, meaning sex. And the knife—

Ja, Herr Doktor. The knife ist eine mother, ja?

Snap out of it, Dexter.

Just a stupid, meaningless dream.

The telephone rang and I almost jumped out of my skin.

"How about breakfast at Wolfie's?" said Deborah. "My treat."

"It's Saturday morning," I said. "We'll never get in."

"I'll get there first and get a table," she said. "Meet you there."

Wolfie's Deli on Miami Beach was a Miami tradition. And because the Morgans are a Miami family, we had been eating there all our lives on those special deli occasions. Why Deborah thought today might be one of those occasions was beyond me, but I was sure she would enlighten me in time. So I took a shower, dressed in my casual Saturday best, and drove out to the Beach. Traffic was light over the new improved MacArthur Causeway, and soon I was politely elbowing my way through the teeming throngs at Wolfie's.

True to her word, Deborah had corralled a corner table. She was chatting with an ancient waitress, a woman even I recognized. "Rose, my love," I said, bending to kiss her wrinkled cheek. She turned her permanent scowl on me. "My wild Irish Rose."

"Dexter," she rasped, with her thick middle-European accent. "Knock off with the kiss, like some faigelah."

"Faigelah. Is that Irish for fiancé?" I asked her, and slid into my chair.

"Feh," she said, trudging off to the kitchen and shaking her head at me.

"I think she likes me," I told Deborah.

"Somebody should," said Deb. "How was your date last night?"

"A lot of fun," I said. "You should try it sometime."

"Feh," said Deborah.

"You can't spend all your nights standing on Tamiami Trail in your underwear, Deb. You need a life."

"I need a transfer," she snarled at me. "To Homicide Bureau. Then we'll see about a life."

"I understand," I said. "It would certainly sound better for the kids to say Mommie's in homicide."

"Dexter, for Christ's sake," she said.

"It's a natural thought, Deborah. Nephews and nieces. More little Morgans. Why not?"

She blew out a long breath. "I thought Mom was dead," she said.

"I'm channeling her," I said. "Through the cherry Danish."

"Well, change the channel. What do you know about cell crystallization?"

I blinked. "Wow," I said. "You just blew away all the competition in the Subject Changing Tournament."

"I'm serious," she said.

"Then I really am floored, Deb. What do you mean, cell crystallization?"

"From cold," she said. "Cells that have crystallized from cold."

Light flooded my brain. "Of course," I said, "beautiful," and somewhere deep inside small bells began to ring. *Cold . . . Clean, pure cold and the cool knife almost sizzling as it slices into the warm flesh. Antiseptic clean coldness, the blood slowed and helpless, so absolutely right and totally necessary; cold.* "Why didn't I—" I started to say. I shut up when I saw Deborah's face.

"What," Deb demanded. "What of course?"

I shook my head. "First tell me why you want to know."

She looked at me for a long hard moment and blew out

another breath. "I think you know," she said at last. "There's been another murder."

"I know," I said. "I passed it last night."

"I heard you didn't actually pass it."

I shrugged. Metro Dade is such a small family.

"So what did that 'of course' mean?"

"Nothing," I said, mildly irritated at last. "The flesh of the body just looked a little different. If it was subjected to cold—" I held out my hands. "That's all, okay? How cold?"

"Like meat-packing cold," she said. "Why would he do that?"

Because it's beautiful, I thought. "It would slow the flow of blood," I said.

She studied me. "Is that important?"

I took a long and perhaps slightly shaky breath. Not only could I never explain it, she would lock me up if I tried. "It's vital," I said. For some reason I felt embarrassed.

"Why vital?"

"It, ah—I don't know. I think he has a thing about blood, Deb. Just a feeling I got from—I don't know, no evidence, you know."

She was giving me that look again. I tried to think of something to say, but I couldn't. Glib, silver-tongued Dexter, with a dry mouth and nothing to say.

"Shit," she said at last. "That's it? Cold slows the blood, and that's vital? Come on. What the hell good is that, Dexter?"

"I don't do 'good' before coffee, Deborah," I said with a heroic effort at recovery. "Just accurate."

"Shit," she said again. Rose brought our coffee. Deborah

sipped. "Last night I got an invite to the seventy-two-hour briefing," she said.

I clapped my hands. "Wonderful. You've arrived. What do you need me for?" Metro Dade has a policy of pulling the homicide team together approximately seventy-two hours after a murder. The investigating officer and her team talk it over with the Medical Examiner and, sometimes, someone from the prosecutor's office. It keeps everyone on the same heading. If Deborah had been invited, she was on the case.

She scowled. "I'm not good at politics, Dexter. I can feel LaGuerta pushing me out, but I can't do anything about it."

"Is she still looking for her mystery witness?"

Deborah nodded.

"Really. Even after the new kill last night?"

"She says that proves it. Because the new cuts were all complete."

"But they were all *different*," I protested.

She shrugged.

"And you suggested—?"

Deb looked away. "I told her I thought it was a waste of time to look for a witness when it was obvious that the killer wasn't interrupted, just unsatisfied."

"Ouch," I said. "You really *don't* know anything about politics."

"Well, goddamn it, Dex," she said. Two old ladies at the next table glared at her. She didn't notice. "What you said made sense. It *is* obvious, and she's ignoring me. And even worse."

"What could be worse than being ignored?" I said.

She blushed. "I caught a couple of the uniforms snicker-
ing at me afterward. There's a joke going around, and I'm
it." She bit her lip and looked away. "Einstein," she said.

"I'm afraid I don't get it."

"If my tits were brains, I'd be Einstein," she said bitterly.
I cleared my throat instead of laughing. "That's what she's
spreading about me," Deb went on. "That kind of crappy
little tag sticks to you, and then they don't promote you
because they think nobody will respect you with a nickname like that. God*damn* it, Dex," she said again, "she's
ruining my career."

I felt a little surge of protective warmth. "She's an idiot."

"Should I tell her that, Dex? Would that be political?"

Our food arrived. Rose slammed the plates down in
front of us as though she had been condemned by a corrupt
judge to serve breakfast to baby killers. I gave her a gigantic smile and she trudged away, muttering to herself.

I took a bite and turned my thoughts to Deborah's problem. I had to try to think of it that way, Deborah's problem.
Not "those fascinating murders." Not "that amazingly
attractive MO," or "the thing so similar to what I would
love to do someday." I had to stay uninvolved, but this was
pulling at me so very hard. Even last night's dream, with its
cold air. Pure coincidence, of course, but unsettling anyway.

This killer had touched the heart of what my killing was
about. In the way he worked, of course, and not in his selec-
tion of victims. He had to be stopped, certainly, no question. Those poor hookers.

Still . . . The need for cold . . . So very interesting to
explore sometime. Find a nice dark, narrow place . . .

Narrow? Where had that come from?

My dream, naturally. But that was just saying that my unconscious wanted me to think about it, wasn't it? And narrow felt right somehow. Cold and narrow—

"Refrigerated truck," I said.

I opened my eyes. Deborah struggled mightily with a mouthful of eggs before she could speak. "What?"

"Oh, just a guess. Not a real insight, I'm afraid. But wouldn't it make sense?"

"Wouldn't what make sense?" she asked.

I looked down at my plate and frowned, trying to picture how this would work. "He wants a cold environment. To slow the blood flow, and because it's, uh—cleaner."

"If you say so."

"I do say so. And it has to be a narrow space—"

"Why? Where the hell did that come from, narrow?"

I chose not to hear that question. "So a refrigerated truck would fit those conditions, and it's mobile, which makes it much easier to dump the garbage afterward."

Deborah took a bite of bagel and thought for a moment while she chewed. "So," she said at last, and swallowed. "The killer might have access to one of these trucks? Or own one?"

"Mmm, maybe. Except the kill last night was the first that showed signs of cold."

Deborah frowned. "So he went out and bought a truck?"

"Probably not. This is still experimental. It was probably an impulse to try cold."

She nodded. "And we would never get lucky enough that he drives one for a living or something, right?"

I gave her my happy shark smile. "Ah, Deb. How quick you are this morning. No, I'm afraid our friend is much too smart to connect himself that way."

Deborah sipped her coffee, put the cup down, and leaned back. "So we're looking for a stolen refrigerator truck," she said at last.

"I'm afraid so," I said. "But how many of those can there be in the last forty-eight hours?"

"In Miami?" She snorted. "Somebody steals one, word gets out that it's worth stealing, and suddenly every god-damn two-bit original gangsta, marielito, crackhead, and junior wise guy has to steal one, just to keep up."

"Let's hope word isn't out yet," I said.

Deborah swallowed the last of her bagel. "I'll check," she said. And then she reached across the table and squeezed my hand. "I really appreciate this," she said. She gave me a couple of seconds of a shy, hesitant smile. "But I worry about how you come up with this stuff, Dex. I just . . ." She looked down at the table and squeezed my hand again.

I squeezed back. "Leave the worrying to me," I said. "You just find that truck."

CHAPTER 8

I N THEORY, METRO'S SEVENTY-TWO-HOUR MEETING gives everyone enough time to get somewhere with a case, but is soon enough that the leads are still warm. And so Monday morning, in a conference room on the second floor, the crack crime-fighting team led by the indomitable Detective LaGuerta assembled once again for the seventy-two-hour. I assembled with them. I got some looks, and a few good-hearted remarks from the cops who knew me. Just simple, cheerful wit, like, "Hey, blood boy, where's your squeegee?" Salt of the earth, these people, and soon my Deborah would be one of them. I felt proud and humble to be in the same room.

Unfortunately, these feelings were not shared by all present. "The fuck you doing here?" grunted Sergeant Doakes. He was a very large black man with an injured air of permanent hostility. He had a cold ferocity to him that would certainly come in handy for somebody with my hobby. It was a shame we couldn't be friends. But for some reason he hated all lab techs, and for some additional reason that had always meant especially Dexter. He also held the Metro Dade record for the bench press. So he rated my political smile.

"I just dropped in to listen, Sergeant," I told him.

"Got no fucking call to be here," he said. "The fuck outta here."

"He can stay, Sergeant," LaGuerta said.

Doakes scowled at her. "The fuck for?"

"I don't want to make anybody unhappy," I said, edging for the door without any real conviction.

"It's perfectly all right," LaGuerta said with an actual smile for me. She turned to Doakes. "He can stay," she repeated.

"Gimme the fucking creeps," Doakes grumbled. I began to appreciate the man's finer qualities. Of course I gave him the fucking creeps. The only real question was why he was the only one in a room filled with cops who had the insight to get the fucking creeps from my presence.

"Let's get started," LaGuerta said, cracking her whip gently, leaving no room for doubt that she was in charge. Doakes slouched back in his chair with a last scowl at me.

The first part of the meeting was a matter of routine; reports, political maneuvers, all the little things that make us human. Those of us who are human, anyway. LaGuerta briefed the information officers on what they could and could not release to the press. Things they could release included a new glossy photo of LaGuerta she'd made up for the occasion. It was serious and yet glamorous; intense but refined. You could almost see her making lieutenant in that picture. If only Deborah had that kind of PR smarts.

It took most of an hour before we got around to the actual murders. But finally LaGuerta asked for reports on the progress in finding her mystery witness. Nobody had anything to report. I tried hard to look surprised.

LaGuerta gave the group a frown of command. "Come on, people," she said. "Somebody needs to find something here." But nobody did, and there was a pause while the group studied their fingernails, the floor, the acoustic tiles in the ceiling.

Deborah cleared her throat. "I, uh," she said and cleared her throat again. "I had a, um, an idea. A different idea. About trying something in a slightly different direction." She said it like it was in quotation marks, and indeed it was. All my careful coaching couldn't make her sound natural when she said it, but she had at least stuck to my carefully worded politically correct phrasing.

LaGuerta raised an artificially perfect eyebrow. "An idea? Really?" She made a face to show how surprised and delighted she was. "Please, by all means, share it with us, Officer Ein—I mean, Officer Morgan."

Doakes snickered. A delightful man.

Deborah flushed, but slogged on. "The, um, cell crystallization. On the last victim. I'd like to check and see if any refrigerated trucks have been reported stolen in the last week or so."

Silence. Utter, dumb silence. The silence of the cows. They didn't get it, the brickheads, and Deborah was not

making them see it. She let the silence grow, a silence
LaGuerta milked with a pretty frown, a puzzled glance
around the room to see if anybody else was following this,
then a polite look at Deborah.

"Refrigerated . . . trucks?" LaGuerta said.

Deborah looked completely flustered, the poor child.
This was not a girl who enjoyed public speaking. "That's
right," she said.

LaGuerta let it hang, enjoying it. "Mm-hmm," she said.

Deborah's face darkened; not a good sign. I cleared my
throat, and when that didn't do any good I coughed, loud
enough to remind her to stay cool. She looked at me. So did
LaGuerta. "Sorry," I said. "I think I'm getting a cold."

Could anyone really ask for a better brother?

"The, um, *cold*," Deborah blurted, lunging at my lifeline.
"A refrigerated vehicle could probably cause that kind of
tissue damage. And it's mobile, so he'd be harder to catch.
And getting rid of the body would be a lot easier. So, uh, if
one was stolen, I mean a truck . . . a refrigerated . . . that
might give us a lead."

Well, that was most of it, and she did get it out there. One
or two thoughtful frowns blossomed around the room. I
could almost hear gears turning.

But LaGuerta just nodded. "That's a very . . . *interesting*
thought, Officer," she said. She put just the smallest emphasis on the word *officer*, to remind us all that this was a
democracy where anybody could speak up, but really . . .
"But I still believe that our best bet is to find the witness. We
know he's out there." She smiled, a politically shy smile.
"Or *she*," she said, to show that she could be sharp. "But

somebody saw something. We know that from the *evidence*. So let's concentrate on that, and leave grasping at straws for the guys in Broward, okay?" She paused, waiting for a little chuckle to run around the room. "But Officer Morgan, I would appreciate your continued help talking to the hookers. They know you down there."

My God, she was good. She had deflected anyone from possibly thinking about Deb's idea, put Deb in her place, and brought the team back together behind her with the joke about our rivalry with Broward County. All in a few simple words. I felt like applauding.

Except, of course, that I was on poor Deborah's team, and she had just been flattened. Her mouth opened for a moment, then closed, and I watched her jaw muscles knot as she carefully pushed her face back into Cop Neutral. In its own way, a fine performance, but truly, not even in the same league as LaGuerta's.

The rest of the meeting was uneventful. There was really nothing to talk about beyond what had been said. So very shortly after LaGuerta's masterful putdown, the meeting broke up and we were in the hall again.

"Damn her," Deborah muttered under her breath. "Damn, damn, *damn* her!"

"Absolutely," I agreed.

She glared at me. "Thanks, bro. Some help you were."

I raised my eyebrows at her. "But we agreed I would stay out of it. So you would get the credit."

She snarled. "Some credit. She made me look like an idiot."

"With absolute respect, sister dear, you met her halfway."

Deborah looked at me, looked away, threw up her hands with disgust. "What was I supposed to say? I'm not even on the team. I'm just there because the captain said they had to let me in."

"And he didn't say they had to listen to you," I said.

"And they don't. And they won't," Deborah said bitterly. "Instead of getting me into homicide, this is going to kill my career. I'll die a meter maid, Dexter."

"There is a way out, Deb," I said, and the look she turned on me now was only about one-third hope.

"What," she said.

I smiled at her, my most comforting, challenging, I'm-not-really-a-shark smile. "Find the truck," I said.

It was three days before I heard from my dear foster sister again, a longish period for her to go without talking to me. She came into my office just after lunch on Thursday, looking sour. "I found it," she said, and I didn't know what she meant.

"Found what, Deb?" I asked. "The Fountain of Grumpiness?"

"The truck," she said. "The refrigerated truck."

"But that's great news," I said. "Why do you look like you're searching for somebody to slap?"

"Because I am," she said, and flung four or five stapled pages onto my desk. "Look at this."

I picked it up and glanced at the top page. "Oh," I said. "How many altogether?"

"Twenty-three," she said. "In the last month, twenty-three refrigerator trucks have been reported stolen. The guys over on traffic say most of 'em turn up in canals, torched for the insurance money. Nobody pushes too hard to find them. So nobody's been pushing on these, and nobody's going to."

"Welcome to Miami," I said.

Deborah sighed and took the list back from me, slouching into my extra chair like she'd just lost all her bones. "There's no way I can check them all, not by myself. It would take months. Goddamn it, Dex," she said. "Now what do we do?"

I shook my head. "I'm sorry, Deb," I said. "But now we have to wait."

"That's it? Just wait?"

"That's it," I said.

And it was. For two more weeks, that was it. We waited. And then . . .

CHAPTER 9

I WOKE UP COVERED WITH SWEAT, NOT SURE WHERE I was, and absolutely certain that another murder was about to happen. Somewhere not so far away *he* was searching for his next victim, sliding through the city like a shark around the reef. I was so certain I could almost hear the purr of the duct tape. He was out there, feeding his Dark Passenger, and it was talking to mine. And in my sleep I had been riding with him, a phantom remora in his great slow circles.

I sat up in my own little bed and peeled away the twisted sheets. The bedside clock said it was 3:14. Four hours since I'd gone to bed, and I felt like I'd been slogging through the jungle the entire time with a piano on my back. I was sweaty, stiff, and stupid, unable to form any thoughts at all beyond the certainty that it was happening out there without me.

Sleep was gone for the night, no question. I turned on the light. My hands were clammy and trembling. I wiped them on the sheet, but that didn't help. The sheets were just as wet. I stumbled into the bathroom to wash my hands. I held them under the running water. The tap let out a stream that was warm, room temperature, and for a moment I was washing my hands in blood and the water turned red; just for a second, in the half-light of the bathroom, the sink ran bloodred.

I closed my eyes.

The world shifted.

I had meant to get rid of this trick of light and my half-sleeping brain. Close the eyes, open them, the illusion would be over and it would be simple clean water in my sink. Instead, it was like closing my eyes had opened a second set of eyes into another world.

I was back in my dream, floating like a knife blade above the lights of Biscayne Boulevard, flying cold and sharp and homing in on my target and—

I opened my eyes again. The water was just water.

But what was I?

I shook my head violently. Steady, old boy; no Dexter off the deep end, please. I took a long breath and peeked at myself. In the mirror I looked the way I was supposed to look. Carefully composed features. Calm and mocking blue eyes, a perfect imitation of human life. Except that my hair stuck up like Stan Laurel's, there was no sign of whatever it was that had just zipped through my half-sleeping brain and rattled me out of my slumber.

I carefully closed my eyes again.

Darkness.

Plain, simple, darkness. No flying, no blood, no city

lights. Just good old Dexter with his eyes closed in front of the mirror.

I opened them again. Hello, dear boy, so good to have you back. But where on earth have you been?

That, of course, was the question. I have spent most of my life untroubled by dreams and, for that matter, hallucinations. No visions of the Apocalypse for me; no troubling Jungian icons burbling up from my subconscious, no mysterious recurring images drifting through the history of my unconsciousness. Nothing ever goes bump in Dexter's night. When I go to sleep, all of me sleeps.

So what had just happened? Why were these pictures appearing to me?

I splashed water on my face and pushed my hair down. That did not, of course, answer the question, but it made me feel a little better. How bad could things be if my hair was neat?

In truth, I did not know. Things could be plenty bad. I might be losing all, or many, of my marbles. What if I had been slipping into insanity a piece at a time for years, and this new killer had simply triggered the final headlong fall into complete craziness? How could I hope to measure the relative sanity of somebody like me?

The images had looked and felt so real. But they couldn't be; I had been right here in my bed. Yet I had almost been able to smell the tang of salt water, exhaust, and cheap perfume floating over Biscayne Boulevard. Completely real—and wasn't that one of the signs of insanity, that the delusions were indistinguishable from reality? I had no answers, and no way to find any. Talking to a shrink was out of the question, of course; I would frighten the poor thing to death, and he might feel honor bound to have me locked away somewhere. Certainly I could not argue with the wisdom of that idea. But if I was losing my hold on sanity as I had built it, it was all my problem, and the first part of the problem was that there was no way to know for sure.

Although, come to think of it, there was one way.

Ten minutes later I was driving past Dinner Key. I drove slowly, since I didn't actually know what I was looking for. This part of the city slept, as much as it ever did. A few people still swirled across the Miami landscape: tourists who'd had too much Cuban coffee and couldn't sleep. People from Iowa looking for a gas station. Foreigners looking for South Beach. And the predators, of course—thugs, robbers, crackheads; vampires, ghouls, and assorted monsters like me. But in this area, at this time, very few of them altogether. This was Miami deserted, as deserted as it got, a place made lonely by the ghost of the daytime crowd. It was a city that had whittled itself down to a mere hunting ground, without the gaudy disguises of sunlight and bright T-shirts.

And so I hunted. The other night eyes tracked me and dismissed me as I passed without slowing. I drove north, over the old drawbridge, through downtown Miami, still not sure what I was looking for and still not seeing it—and yet, for some uncomfortable reason, absolutely sure that I would find it, that I was going in the right direction, that *it* was waiting for me ahead.

Just beyond the Omni the nightlife picked up. More activity, more things to see. Whooping on the sidewalks, tinny music coming and going through the car windows. The night girls came out, flocks of them on the street corners, giggling with each other, or staring stupidly at the passing cars. And the cars slowed to stare back, gawking at the costumes and what they left uncovered. Two blocks ahead of me a new Corniche stopped and a pack of the girls flew out of the shadows, off the sidewalk, and into the street, surrounding the car immediately. Traffic stumbled to a half stop, horns blattered. Most of the drivers sat for a minute, content to watch, but an impatient truck pulled around the knot of cars and into the oncoming lane.

A refrigerator truck.

This was nothing, I said to myself. Nighttime yogurt delivery; pork link sausages for breakfast, freshness guaranteed. A load of grouper headed north or to the airport. Refrigerated trucks moved through Miami around the clock, even now, even in the night hours— This it was and nothing more.

But I put my foot down on the gas pedal anyway. I moved up, in and out of traffic. I got within three cars of the Corniche and its besieged driver. Traffic stopped. I looked ahead at the truck. It was running straight up Biscayne, moving into a series of traffic lights. I would lose him if I got too far behind. And I suddenly wanted very badly not to lose him.

I waited for a gap in traffic and quickly nosed out into the oncoming lane. I was around the Corniche and then speeding up, closing on the truck. Trying not to move too fast, not to be conspicuous, but slowly closing the space between us. He was three traffic lights ahead, then two.

Then his light turned red and before I could gloat and catch up, mine did, too. I stopped. I realized with some surprise that I was chewing on my lip. I was tense; me, Dexter the Ice Cube. I was feeling human anxiety, desperation, actual emotional distress. I wanted to catch up to this truck and see for myself, oh how I wanted to put my hand on the truck, open the door to the cabin, look inside—

And then what? Arrest him single-handed? Take him by the hand to dear Detective LaGuerta? See what I caught? Can I keep him? It was just as likely that he would keep me. He was in full hunting mode, and I was merely tagging along behind like an unwanted little brother. And why was I tagging along? Did I just want to prove to myself that it was him, *the* him, that he was out here prowling and I was not crazy? And if I was not crazy—how had I known? What was going on in my brain? Perhaps crazy would be a happier solution after all.

An old man shuffled in front of my car, crossing the street with incredibly slow and painful steps. For a moment I watched him, marveling at what life must be like when you moved that slow, and then I glanced ahead at the refrigerator truck.

His light had turned green. Mine had not.

The truck accelerated quickly, moving north at the upper end of the speed limit, taillights growing smaller as I watched, waiting for my light to change.

Which it refused to do. And so grinding my teeth— steady, Dex!—I ran the light, narrowly missing the old man. He didn't look up or break step.

The speed limit on this stretch of Biscayne Boulevard

was thirty-five. In Miami that means if you go under fifty they will run you off the road. I pushed up to sixty-five, moving through the sparse traffic, desperate now to close the distance. The lights of the truck winked out as he went around a curve—or had he turned? I moved up to seventy-five and roared past the turn for the 79th Street Causeway, around the bend by the Publix Market, and into the straightaway, searching frantically for the truck.

And saw it. There—ahead of me—

Moving *toward* me.

The bastard had doubled back. Did he feel me on his tail? Smell my exhaust drifting up on him? No matter—it was him, the same truck, no question, and as I raced past him he turned out onto the causeway.

I squealed into a mall parking lot and slowed, turning the car and accelerating back out onto Biscayne Boulevard, southbound now. Less than a block and I turned onto the causeway, too. Far, far in front, nearly to the first bridge, I saw the small red lights, winking, mocking me. My foot crashed down on the gas pedal and I charged ahead.

He was on the up-slope of the bridge now, picking up speed, keeping the distance steady between us. Which meant he must know, must realize somebody was following. I pushed my car a little harder; I got closer, little by little, a few lengths closer.

And then he was gone, over the hump at the top of the bridge and down the far side, heading much too fast into North Bay Village. It was a heavily patrolled area. If he went too fast he would be seen and pulled over. And then—

I was up the bridge and onto the hump now and below me—

Nothing.

Empty road.

I slowed, looking in all directions from the vantage point at the top of the bridge. A car moved toward me—not the truck, just a Mercury Marquis with one smashed fender. I started down the far side of the bridge.

At the bottom of the bridge North Bay Village split off the causeway into two residential areas. Behind a gas station on the left a row of condos and apartments made a slow circle. To the right were houses; small but expensive. Nothing moved on either side. There were no lights showing, no sign of anything, neither traffic nor life.

Slowly I moved through the village. Empty. He was gone. On an island with only one through street, he had lost me. But how?

I circled back, pulled off onto the shoulder of the road and closed my eyes. I don't know why; perhaps I hoped I might *see* something again. But I didn't. Just darkness, and little bright lights dancing on the inside of my eyelids. I was tired. I felt stupid. Yes, me; ditzy Dexter, trying to be Boy Wonder, using my great psychic powers to track down the evil genius. Pursuing him in my supercharged crime-fighting vehicle. And in all likelihood he was simply a stoked-up delivery boy playing macho head games with the only other driver on the road that night. A Miami thing that happened every day to every driver in our fair city. Chase me, you can't catch me. Then the uplifted finger, the waved gun, ho-hum and back to work.

Just a refrigerated truck, nothing more, now speeding away across Miami Beach with the heavy metal station ripping from the radio speaker. And not my killer, not some mysterious bond pulling me out of bed and across the city in the dead of night. Because that was just too silly for words, and far too silly for level-headed empty-hearted Dexter.

I let my head drop onto the steering wheel. How wonderful to have such an authentic *human* experience. Now I knew what it was like to feel like a total idiot. I could hear the bell on the drawbridge in the near distance, clanging its warning that the bridge was about to go up. Ding ding ding. The alarm bell on my expired intellect. I yawned. Time to go home, go back to bed.

Behind me an engine started. I glanced back.

From behind the gas station at the foot of the bridge he came out fast in a tight circle. He passed me fishtailing and still accelerating and through the blur of motion in the driver's window a shape spun at me, wild and hard. I ducked. Something thumped into the side of my car, leaving behind it the sound of an expensive dent. I waited for a moment, just to be safe. Then I raised my head and looked. The truck was speeding away, crashing the wooden barrier at the drawbridge and powering through, leaping across the bridge as it started to raise up, and making it easily to the other side as the bridge keeper leaned out and yelled. Then the truck was gone, down the far side of the bridge and back into Miami, far away on the other side of the widening gap as the bridge went up. Gone, hopelessly gone, gone as if he had never been. And I would never know if it had been my killer or just another normal Miami jerk.

I got out of my car to look at the dent. It was a big one. I looked around to see what he had thrown.

It had rolled ten or fifteen feet away and wobbled out into the middle of the street. Even from this distance there was no mistaking it, but just to make sure I was absolutely without any doubt, the headlights from an oncoming car lit it up. The car swerved and smashed into a hedge and over the sound of its now-constant horn I could hear the driver screaming. I walked over to the thing to be sure.

Yes indeed. That's what it was.

A woman's head.

I bent to look. It was a very clean cut, very nice work. There was almost no blood around the lip of the wound.

"Thank God," I said, and I realized I was smiling—and why not?

Wasn't it nice? I wasn't crazy after all.

CHAPTER 10

AT A LITTLE AFTER 8 AM LaGuerta came over to where I was sitting on the trunk of my car. She leaned her tailored haunch onto the car and slid over until our thighs were touching. I waited for her to say something, but she didn't seem to have any words for the occasion. Neither did I. So I sat there for several minutes looking back at the bridge, feeling the heat of her leg against mine and wondering where my shy friend had gone with his truck. But I was yanked out of my quiet daydream by a pressure on my thigh.

I looked down at my pants leg. LaGuerta was kneading my thigh as if it were a lump of dough. I looked up at her face. She looked back.

"They found the body," she said. "You know. The rest of it that goes with the head."

I stood up. "Where?"

She looked at me the way a cop looks at somebody who

finds corpseless heads in the street. But she answered. "Office Depot Center," she said.

"Where the Panthers play?" I asked, and a little icy-fingered jolt ran through me. "On the ice?"

LaGuerta nodded, still watching me. "The hockey team," she said. "Is that the Panthers?"

"I think that's what they're called," I said. I couldn't help myself.

She pursed her lips. "They found it stuffed into the goalie's net."

"Visitor's or home?" I asked.

She blinked. "Does that make a difference?"

I shook my head. "Just a joke, Detective."

"Because I don't know how to tell the difference. I should get somebody there who knows about hockey," she said, her eyes finally drifting away from me and across the crowd, searching for somebody carrying a puck. "I'm glad you can make a joke about it," she added. "What's a—" she frowned, trying to remember, "—a sam-bolie?"

"A what?"

She shrugged. "Some kind of machine. They use it on the ice?"

"A Zamboni?"

"Whatever. The guy who drives it, he takes it out on the ice to get ready for practice this morning. A couple of the players, they like to get there early? And they like the ice fresh, so this guy, the—" she hesitated slightly "—the sam-bolie driver? He comes in early on practice days. And so he drives this thing out onto the ice? And he sees these pack-

ages stacked up. Down there in the goalie's net? So he gets
down and he takes a look." She shrugged again. "Doakes is
over there now. He says they can't get the guy to calm
down enough to say any more than that."

"I know a little about hockey," I said.

She looked at me again with somewhat heavy eyes. "So
much I don't know about you, Dexter. You play hockey?"

"No, I never played," I said modestly. "I went to a few
games." She didn't say anything and I had to bite my lip to
keep from blathering on. In truth, Rita had season tickets
for the Florida Panthers, and I had found to my very great
surprise that I liked hockey. It was not merely the frantic,
cheerfully homicidal mayhem I enjoyed. There was something about sitting in the huge, cool hall that I found relaxing, and I would happily have gone there even to watch
golf. In truth, I would have said anything to make LaGuerta
take me to the rink. I wanted to go to the arena very badly.
I wanted to see this body stacked in the net on the ice more
than anything else I could think of, wanted to undo the neat
wrapping and see the clean dry flesh. I wanted to see it so
much that I felt like a cartoon of a dog on point, wanted to
be there with it so much that I felt self-righteous and pos-
sessive about the body.

"All right," LaGuerta finally said, when I was about to
vibrate out of my skin. And she showed a small, strange
smile that was part official and part—what? Something else
altogether, something human, unfortunately, putting it
beyond my understanding. "Give us a chance to talk."

"I'd like that very much," I said, absolutely oozing
charm. LaGuerta didn't respond. Maybe she didn't hear

me, not that it mattered. She was totally beyond any sense of sarcasm where her self-image was concerned. It was possible to hit her with the most horrible flattery in the world and she would accept it as her due. I didn't really enjoy flattering her. There's no fun where there's no challenge. But I didn't know what else to say. What did she imagine we would talk about? She had already grilled me mercilessly when she first arrived on the scene.

We had stood beside my poor dented car and watched the sun come up. She had looked out across the causeway and asked me seven times if I had seen the driver of the truck, each time with a slightly different inflection, frowning in between questions. She'd asked me five times if I was sure it had been a refrigerated truck—I'm sure that was subtlety on her part. She wanted to ask about that one a lot more, but held back to avoid being obvious. She even forgot herself once and asked in Spanish. I told her I was *seguro*, and she had looked at me and touched my arm, but she did not ask again.

And three times she had looked up the incline of the bridge, shaken her head, and spat "Puta!" under her breath. Clearly, that was a reference to Officer Puta, my dear sister Deborah. In the face of an actual refrigerator truck as predicted by Deborah, a certain amount of spin control was going to be necessary, and I could tell by the way LaGuerta nibbled at her lower lip that she was hard at work on the problem. I was quite sure she would come up with something uncomfortable for Deb—it was what she did best— but for the time being I was hoping for a modest rise in my sister's stock. Not with LaGuerta, of course, but one could hope that others might notice that her brilliant bit of attempted detective work had panned out.

Oddly enough, LaGuerta did not ask me what I had been doing driving around at that hour. Of course, I'm not a detective, but it did seem like a rather obvious question. Perhaps it would be unkind to say that the oversight was typical of her, but there it is. She just didn't ask.

And yet there was more for us to talk about, apparently. So I followed her to her car, a big two-year-old light blue Chevrolet that she drove on duty. After hours she had a little BMW that nobody was supposed to know about.

"Get in," she said. And I climbed into the neat blue front seat.

LaGuerta drove fast, in and out of traffic, and in a very few minutes we were over the causeway to the Miami side again, across Biscayne and a half mile or so to I-95. She drove onto the freeway and wove north through traffic at speeds that seemed a little much even for Miami. But we got to 595 and turned west. She looked at me sideways, out of the corner of her eye, three times before she finally spoke. "That's a nice shirt," she said.

I glanced down at my nice shirt. I had thrown it on to chase out of my apartment and saw it now for the first time, a polyester bowling shirt with bright red dragons on it. I had worn it all day at work and it was a trifle ripe, but yes, more or less clean looking. Somewhat nice, of course, but still—

Was LaGuerta making small talk so I would relax enough to make some damaging admission? Did she suspect that I knew more than I was saying and think she could get me to drop my guard and say it?

"You always wear such nice clothes, Dexter," she said. She looked over at me with a huge, goofy smile, unaware that she was about to ram her car into a tanker truck. She looked back in time and turned the wheel with one finger and we slid around the tanker and west on I-595.

I thought about the nice clothes that I always wore. Well of course I did. I took pride in being the best-dressed monster in Dade County. Yes, certainly, he chopped up that nice Mr. Duarte, but he was so well dressed! Proper clothing for all occasions—by the way, what did one wear to attend an early-morning decapitation? A day-old bowling shirt and slacks, naturally. I was *à la mode*. But aside from this morning's hasty costume, I really was careful. It was one of Harry's lessons: stay neat, dress nicely, avoid attention.

But why should a politically minded homicide detective either notice or care? It was not as if—

Or was it? A nasty little idea began to grow. Something in the strange smile that flicked across her face and then away gave me the answer. It was ridiculous, but what else could it be? LaGuerta was not looking for a way to put me off my guard and ask more penetrating questions about what I had seen. And she did not truly give a winged fart about my hockey expertise.

LaGuerta was being social.

She *liked* me.

Here I was still trying to recover from the horrible shock of my bizarre, lurching, slobbering attack on Rita—and

now this? LaGuerta *liked* me? Had terrorists dumped something in the Miami water supply? Was I exuding some kind
of strange pheromone? Had every woman in Miami suddenly realized how hopeless real men are, and I had
become attractive by default? What, in all very seriousness,
the hell was going on?

Of course I could be wrong. I lunged at the thought like
a barracuda at a shiny silver spoon. After all, what colossal
egotism to think that a polished, sophisticated, career-track
woman like LaGuerta might show any kind of interest in
me. Wasn't it more likely that, that—

That what? As unfortunate as it was, it did make a kind
of sense. We were in the same line of work and therefore,
conventional cop wisdom said, more likely to understand
and forgive each other. Our relationship could survive her
cop hours and stressful lifestyle. And although I take no
credit for it, I am presentable enough; I clean up good, as
we natives like to say. And I had put myself out to be
charming to her for several years now. It had been purely
political schmoozing, but she did not have to know that. I
was *good* at being charming, one of my very few vanities. I
had studied hard and practiced long, and when I applied
myself no one could tell I was faking it. I was really very
good at sprinkling seeds of charm. Perhaps it was natural
that the seeds would eventually sprout.

But sprout into this? What now? Was she going to pro-
pose a quiet dinner some evening? Or a few hours of
sweaty bliss at the Cacique Motel?

Happily, we arrived at the arena just before panic took
me over completely. LaGuerta circled the building once,

looking for the correct entrance. It wasn't too hard to find. A cluster of police cars stood scattered outside one row of double doors. She nosed her big car in among them. I jumped out of the car quickly, before she could put her hand on my knee. She got out and looked at me for a moment. Her mouth twitched.

"I'll take a look," I said. I did not quite run into the arena. I was fleeing LaGuerta, yes—but I was also very anxious to get inside; to see what my playful friend had done, to be near his work, to inhale the wonder, to learn.

The inside echoed with the organized bedlam typical of any murder scene—and yet it seemed to me that there was a special electricity in the air, a slightly hushed feeling of excitement and tension that you wouldn't find at any ordinary murder, a sense that this one was different somehow, that new and wonderful things might happen because we were out here on the cutting edge. But maybe that was just me. A clot of people stood around the nearby net. Several of them wore Broward uniforms; they had their arms folded and watched as Captain Matthews argued about jurisdiction with a man in a tailored suit. As I got closer I saw Angel-no-relation in an unusual position, standing above a balding man who was on one knee poking at a stack of carefully wrapped packages.

I stopped at the railing to look through the glass. There it was, only ten feet away. It looked so perfect in the cold purity of the newly Zambonied hockey rink. Any jeweler will tell you that finding the right setting is vitally important, and this— It was stunning. Absolutely perfect. I felt just a little dizzy, uncertain of whether the railing would hold my weight, as if I might simply pass straight down through the hard wood like a mist.

Even from the railing I could tell. He had taken the time, he had done it right, in spite of what must have seemed like a very close call on the causeway only minutes before. Or had he known somehow that I meant him no harm?

And since I brought it up anyway, did I, in fact, mean him no harm? Did I truly mean to track him to his lair and come up on point all aquiver for advancing Deborah's career? Of course that was what I thought I was doing—but would I be strong enough to carry through with it if things kept getting so interesting? Here we were at the hockey rink where I had whiled away many pleasant and contemplative hours; wasn't this even more proof that this artist—excuse me, I mean "killer" of course—was moving on a track parallel to mine? Just look at the lovely work he had done here.

And the head—that was the key. Surely it was too important as a piece of what he was doing simply to leave it behind. Had he thrown it to frighten me, send me into paroxysms of terror, horror, and dread? Or had he known somehow that I felt the same way he did? Could he, too, feel the connection between us, and he just wanted to be playful? Was he teasing me? He had to have some important reason for leaving me such a trophy. I was experiencing powerful, dizzying sensations—how could he be feeling nothing?

LaGuerta came up beside me. "You're in such a hurry," she said, a slight edge of complaint in her voice. "Are you afraid she'll get away?" She nodded at the stacked body parts.

I knew that somewhere inside me was a clever answer, something that would make her smile, charm her a little more, smooth over my awkward run from her clutches. But standing there at the rail, looking down at the body on the ice, in the goalie's net—in the presence of greatness, one might say—no wit came out. I did manage not to yell at her to shut up, but it was a very near thing.

"I had to see," I said truthfully, and then recovered enough to add, "It's the home team's net."

She slapped my arm playfully. "You're awful," she said. Luckily Sergeant Doakes came over to us and the detective didn't have time for a kittenish giggle, which would have been more than I could take. As always, Doakes seemed more interested in finding a way to get a good grip on my ribs and pull me open than anything else, and he gave me such a warm and penetrating look of welcome that I faded quickly away and left him to LaGuerta. He stared after me, watching me with an expression that said I had to be guilty of something and he would very much like to examine my entrails to find out what. I'm sure he would have been happier someplace where the police were permitted to break the occasional tibia or femur. I circled away from him, moving slowly around the rink to the nearest place where I could get in. I had just found it when something came at me on my blind side and hit me, rather hard, in the ribs.

I straightened up to face my assailant with a certain bruise and a strained smile. "Hello, dear sister," I said. "So nice to see a friendly face."

"Bastard!" she hissed at me.

"Quite probably," I said. "But why bring it up now?"

"Because, you miserable son of a bitch, you had a lead and you didn't call me!"

"A lead?" I almost stuttered. "What makes you think—"

"Cut the crap, Dexter," Deborah snarled. "You weren't driving around at four AM looking for hookers. You knew where he was, goddamn it."

Light dawned. I had been so wrapped up in my own problems, starting with the dream—and the fact that it had obviously been something more than that—and continuing on through my nightmarish encounter with LaGuerta, that it did not occur to me that I had wronged Deborah. I had not shared. Of course she would be angry. "Not a lead, Deb," I said, trying to soothe her feelings a bit. "Nothing solid like that. Just—a feeling. A thought, that's all. It was really nothing—"

She shoved again. "Except that it was *something,*" she snarled. "You found him."

"Actually, I'm not sure," I said. "I think he found me."

"Quit being clever," she said, and I spread my hands to show how impossible that would be. "You promised, god-damn you."

I did not remember making any kind of promise that might cover calling her in the middle of the night and telling her my dreams, but this didn't seem like a very politic thing to say, so I didn't. "I'm sorry, Deb," I said instead. "I really didn't think it would pan out. It was just a . . . a hunch, really." I was certainly not going to attempt any explanation of the parapsychology involved, even with Deb. Or perhaps especially not with her. But another thought hit me. I lowered my voice. "Maybe you could help me a little. What am

I supposed to tell them if *they* ever decide to ask what I was doing driving around down there at four AM?"

"Has LaGuerta interviewed you yet?"

"Exhaustively," I said, fighting down a shudder.

Deb made a disgusted face. "And she didn't ask." It was not a question.

"I'm sure the detective has a great deal on her mind," I said. I did not add that apparently some of it was me. "But sooner or later, somebody will ask." I looked over to where she was Directing the Operation. "Probably Sergeant Doakes," I said with real dread.

She nodded. "He's a decent cop. If he could just lose some attitude."

"Attitude may be all he is," I said. "But he doesn't like me for some reason. He'll ask anything if he thinks it will make me squirm."

"So tell him the truth," Deborah said deadpan. "But first, tell it to me." And she poked me again in the same spot.

"Please, Deb," I said. "You know how easily I bruise."

"I don't know," she said. "But I feel like finding out."

"It won't happen again," I promised. "It was just one of those 3 AM inspirations, Deborah. What would you have said if I had called you about it, and then it turned out to be nothing?"

"But it didn't. It turned out to be something," she said with another push.

"I really didn't think it would. And I would have felt stupid dragging you in on it."

"Imagine how I would have felt if he had killed you," she said.

It took me by surprise. I couldn't even begin to imagine how she would have felt. Regret? Disappointment? Anger? That sort of thing is way beyond me, I'm afraid. So I just repeated, "I'm sorry, Deb." And then, because I am the kind of cheerful Pollyanna who always finds the bright side, I added, "But at least the refrigerated truck was there."

She blinked at me. "The truck was where?" she said.

"Oh, Deb," I said. "They didn't tell you?"

She hit me even harder in the same place. "Goddamn it, Dexter," she hissed. "What about the truck?"

"It was there, Deb," I said, somewhat embarrassed by her nakedly emotional reaction—and also, of course, by the fact that a good-looking woman was beating the crap out of me. "He was driving a refrigerated truck. When he threw the head."

She grabbed my arms and stared at me. "The fuck you say," she finally said.

"The fuck I do."

"Jesus—!" she said, staring off into space and no doubt seeing her promotion floating there somewhere above my head. And she was probably going to go on but at that moment Angel-no-relation lifted his voice over the echoing din of the arena. "Detective?" he called, looking over at LaGuerta. It was a strange, unconscious sound, the half-strangled cry of a man who never makes loud noises in public, and something about it brought instant quiet to the room. The tone was part shock and part triumph—I found something important but oh-my-God. All eyes turned to Angel and he nodded down at the crouching bald man who was slowly, carefully, removing something from the top package.

The man finally pulled the thing out, fumbled, and dropped it, and it skittered across the ice. He reached for it and slipped, sliding after the brightly gleaming thing from the package until they both came to rest against the boards. Hand shaking, Angel grabbed for it, got it and held it up for all of us to see. The sudden quiet in the building was awe inspiring, breathtaking, beautiful, like the overwhelming crash of applause at the unveiling of any work of genius.

It was the rearview mirror from the truck.

CHAPTER 11

THE GREAT BLANKET OF STUNNED SILENCE LASTED for only a moment. Then the buzz of talk in the arena took on a new note as people strained to see, to explain, to speculate.

A mirror. What the hell did it mean?

Good question. In spite of feeling so very moved by the thing, I didn't have any immediate theories about what it meant. Sometimes great art is like that. It affects you and you can't say why. Was it deep symbolism? A cryptic message? A wrenching plea for help and understanding? Impossible to say, and to me, not the most important thing at first. I just wanted to breathe it in. Let others worry about how it had gotten there. After all, maybe it had just fallen off and he had decided to throw it away in the nearest handy garbage bag.

Not possible, of course not. And now I couldn't help thinking about it. The mirror was there for some very important reason. These were not garbage bags to him. As he had now proved so elegantly with this hockey-rink set-ting, presentation was an important part of what he was doing. He would not be casual in any detail. And because of that, I began to think about what the mirror might mean. I had to believe that, as improvised as it might be, putting it in with the body parts was exceedingly deliberate. And I had the further feeling, burbling up from somewhere behind my lungs, that this was a very careful, very private message.

To me?

If not me, then whom? The rest of the act was speaking to the world at large: See what I am. See what we all are. See what I am doing about it. A truck's mirror wasn't part of the statement. Segmenting the body, draining the blood—this was necessary and elegant. But the mirror—and especially if it turned out to be from the truck that I had chased—that was different. Elegant, yes; but what did it say about the way things really are? Nothing. It was added on for some other purpose, and that purpose had to be a new and different kind of statement. I could feel the electricity of the thought surging through me. If it was from that truck, it could only be meant for me.

But what did it mean?

"What the hell is that about?" Deb said beside me. "A mirror. Why?"

"I don't know," I said, still feeling its power throb through me. "But I will bet you dinner at Joe's Stone Crabs that it came from the refrigerator truck."

"No bet," she said. "But at least it settles one important question."

I looked at her, startled. Could she really have made some intuitive jump that I had missed? "What question, sis?"

She nodded at the cluster of management-level cops still squabbling at the edges of the rink. "Jurisdiction. This one is ours. Come on."

On the surface, Detective LaGuerta was not impressed with this new piece of evidence. Perhaps she was hiding a deep and abiding concern for the symbolism of the mirror and all it implied under a carefully crafted façade of indifference. Either that or she really was dumb as a box of rocks. She was still standing with Doakes. To his credit, he looked troubled, but maybe his face had simply gotten tired from its perpetual mean glare and he was trying something new.

"Morgan," LaGuerta said to Deb, "I didn't recognize you with clothes on."

"I guess it's possible to miss a lot of obvious things, Detective," Deb said before I could stop her.

"It is," LaGuerta said. "That's why some of us never make detective." It was a complete and effortless victory, and LaGuerta didn't even wait to see the shot go home. She turned away from Deb and spoke to Doakes. "Find out who has keys to the arena. Who could get in here whenever they wanted."

"Uh-huh," said Doakes. "Check all the locks, see if somebody busted in?"

"No," LaGuerta told him with a pretty little frown. "We got our ice connection now." She glanced at Deborah. "That refrigerated truck is just to confuse us." Back to Doakes.

"The tissue damage had to come from the ice, from here. So the killer is connected to the ice in this place." She looked one last time at Deborah. "Not the truck."

"Uh-huh," said Doakes. He didn't sound convinced, but he wasn't in charge.

LaGuerta looked over at me. "I think you can go home, Dexter," she said. "I know where you live when I need you." At least she didn't wink.

Deborah walked me to the big double doors of the arena. "If this keeps up, I'll be a crossing guard in a year," she grumbled at me.

"Nonsense, Deb," I said. "Two months, max."

"Thanks."

"Well really. You can't challenge her *openly* like that. Didn't you see how Sergeant Doakes did it? Have some subtlety, for God's sake."

"Subtlety." She stopped dead in her tracks and grabbed me. "Listen, Dexter," she said. "This isn't some kind of game here."

"But it is, Deb. A political game. And you're not playing it properly."

"I'm not playing anything," she snarled. "There are human lives at stake. There's a butcher running loose, and he's going to stay loose as long as that half-wit LaGuerta is running things."

I fought down a surge of hope. "That may be so—"

"It *is* so," Deb insisted.

"—but Deborah, you can't change that by getting yourself exiled to Coconut Grove traffic duty."

"No," she said. "But I can change it by finding the killer."

Well there it was. Some people just have no idea how the world works. She was otherwise a very smart person, truly she was. She had simply inherited all of Harry's earthy directness, his straightforward way of dealing with things, without latching on to any of his accompanying wisdom. With Harry, bluntness had been a way to cut through the fecal matter. With Deborah, it was a way of pretending there wasn't any.

I got a ride back to my car with one of the patrol units outside the arena. I drove home, imagining I had kept the head, wrapped it carefully in tissue paper, and placed it in the backseat to take home with me. Terrible and silly, I know. For the first time I understood those sad men, usually Shriners, who fondle women's shoes or carry around dirty underwear. An awful feeling that made me want a shower almost as much as I wanted to stroke the head.

But I didn't have it. Nothing for it but to go home. I drove slowly, a few miles per hour under the speed limit. In Miami that's like wearing a KICK ME sign on your back. No one actually kicked me, of course. They would have had to slow down for that. But I was honked at seven times, flipped off eight, and five cars simply roared around me, either onto the sidewalk or through oncoming traffic.

But today even the energetic high spirits of the other drivers couldn't cheer me. I was dead tired and bemused and I needed to think, away from the echoing din of the arena and the bonehead blather of LaGuerta. Driving slowly gave me time to wonder, to work through the meaning of all that had happened. And I found that one silly phrase kept ringing in my head, bouncing off the rocks and

crannies of my exhausted brain. It took on a life of its own.
The more I heard it in my thoughts, the more sense it made.
And beyond sense, it became a kind of seductive mantra. It
became the key to thinking about the killer, the head rolling
into the street, the rearview mirror tucked away amid the
wonderfully dry body parts.

If it had been me—

As in, "If it had been me, what would I be saying with
the mirror?" and "If it had been me, what would I have
done with the truck?"

Of course it had not been me, and that kind of envy is
very bad for the soul, but since I was not aware of having
one it didn't matter. If it *had* been me, the truck would be
run into a ditch somewhere not too far from the arena. And
then I would get far away from there fast—in a stashed car?
A stolen one? It would depend. If it had been me, would I
have planned on leaving the body at the arena all along, or
had that come up as a response to the chase on the causeway?

Except that made no sense. He could not have counted
on anyone chasing him out to North Bay Village—could
he? But then why did he have the head ready to throw?
And then why take the rest to the arena? It seemed like an
odd choice. Yes, there was a great deal of ice there, and the
coldness was all to the good. But the vast clattery space was
really not appropriate for my kind of intimate moment—if
it had been me. There was a terrible, wide-open desolation
that was not at all conducive to real creativity. Fun to visit,
but not a real artist's studio. A dumping ground, and not a
work space. It just didn't have the proper feeling to it.

If it had been me, that is.

So the arena was a bold stroke into unexplored territory. It would give the police fits, and it would most definitely lead them in the wrong direction. If they ever figured out that there was a direction to be led in, which seemed increasingly unlikely.

And to top it off with the mirror—if I was right about the reasons for selecting the arena, then the addition of the mirror would of course support that. It would be a comment on what had just happened, connected to leaving the head. It would be a statement that would bring together all the other threads, wrap them up as neatly as the stacked body parts, an elegant underlining to a major work. Now what would the statement be, if it was me?

I see you.

Well. Of course that was it, in spite of being somewhat obvious. I see you. I know you're behind me, and I am watching you. But I am far ahead of you, too, controlling your course and setting your speed and watching you follow me. I see you. I know who you are and where you are, and all you know about me is that I am watching. I see you.

That felt right. Why didn't it make me feel better?

Further, how much of this should I tell poor dear Deborah? This was becoming so intensely personal that it was a struggle to remember that there was a public side to it, a side that was important to my sister and her career. I could not begin to tell her—or anyone—that I thought the killer was trying to tell me something, if I had the wit to hear and reply. But the rest—was there something I needed to tell her, and did I actually want to?

It was too much. I needed sleep before I could sort all this out.

I did not quite whimper as I crawled into my bed, but it was a very near thing. I allowed sleep to roll over me quickly, just letting go into the darkness. And I got nearly two and a half full hours of sleep before the telephone rang.

"It's me," said the voice on the other end.

"Of course it is," I said. "Deborah, wasn't it?" And of course it was.

"I found the refrigerated truck."

"Well, congratulations, Deb. That's very good news."

There was a rather long silence on the other end.

"Deb?" I said finally. "That is good news, isn't it?"

"No," she said.

"Oh." I felt the need for sleep thumping my head like carpet beaters on a prayer rug, but I tried to concentrate. "Um, Deb—what did you . . . what happened?"

"I made the match," she said. "Made absolutely certain. Pictures and part numbers and everything. So I told LaGuerta like a good scout."

"And she didn't believe you?" I asked incredulously.

"She probably did."

I tried to blink, but my eyes wanted to stick shut so I gave it up. "I'm sorry, Deb, one of us isn't making much sense. Is it me?"

"I tried to explain it to her," Deborah said in a very small, very tired voice that gave me a terrible feeling of sinking under the waves without a bailing bucket. "I gave her the whole thing. I was even polite."

"That's very good," I said. "What did she say?"

"Nothing," Deb said.

"Nothing at all?"

"Nothing at all," Deb repeated. "Except she just says thanks, in a kind of way like you'd say it to the valet parking attendant. And she gives me this funny little smile and turns away."

"Well, but Deb," I said, "you can't really expect her to—"

"And then I found out why she smiled like that," Deb said. "Like I'm some kind of unwashed half-wit and she's finally figured out where to lock me up."

"Oh, no," I said. "You mean you're off the case?"

"We're all off the case, Dexter," Deb said, her voice as tired as I felt. "LaGuerta's made an arrest."

There was far too much silence on the line all of a sudden and I couldn't think at all, but at least I was wide awake. "What?" I said.

"LaGuerta has arrested somebody. Some guy who works at the arena. She has him in custody and she's sure he's the killer."

"That's not possible," I said, although I knew it was possible, the brain-dead bitch. LaGuerta, not Deb.

"I know that, Dexter. But don't try to tell LaGuerta. She's sure she got the right guy."

"How sure?" I asked. My head was spinning and I felt a little bit like throwing up. I couldn't really say why.

Deb snorted. "She has a press conference in one hour," she said. "For her, that's positive."

The pounding in my head got too loud to hear what Deb might have said next. LaGuerta had made an arrest? Who? Who could she possibly have tagged for it? Could she truly ignore all the clues, the smell and feel and taste of these kills, and arrest somebody? Because nobody who could do what this killer had done—was doing!—could possibly allow a pimple like LaGuerta to catch him. Never. I would bet my life on it.

"No, Deborah," I said. "No. Not possible. She's got the wrong guy."

Deborah laughed, a tired, dirty-up-to-here cop's laugh. "Yeah," she said. "I know it. You know it. But she doesn't know it. And you want to know something funny? Neither does he."

That made no sense at all. "What are you saying, Deb? Who doesn't know?"

She repeated that awful little laugh. "The guy she arrested. I guess he must be almost as confused as LaGuerta, Dex. Because he confessed."

"What?"

"He confessed, Dexter. The bastard confessed."

CHAPTER 12

His name was Daryll Earl McHale and he was what we liked to call a two-time loser. Twelve of his last twenty years had been spent as a guest of the State of Florida. Dear Sergeant Doakes had managed to dig his name out of the arena's personnel files. In a computer cross-check for employees with a record of violence or felony convictions, McHale's name had popped up twice.

Daryll Earl was a drunk and a wife beater. Apparently he occasionally knocked over filling stations, too, just for the entertainment value. He could be relied on to hold down a minimum wage job for a month or two. But then some fine Friday night he'd throw back a few six-packs and start to believe he was the Wrath of God. So he'd drive around until he found a gas station that just pissed him off. He'd charge in waving a weapon, take the money, and drive away. Then he'd use his massive $80 or $90 haul to buy a few more six-packs until he felt so good he just had to beat up on somebody. Daryll Earl was not a large man: five six and scrawny. So to play it safe, the somebody he beat on usually turned out to be his wife.

Things being what they were, he'd actually gotten away with it a couple of times. But one night he went a little too far with his wife and put her into traction for a month. She pressed charges, and since Daryll Earl already had a record, he'd done some serious time.

He still drank, but he'd apparently been frightened enough at Raiford to straighten out just a bit. He'd gotten a job as a janitor at the arena and actually held on to it. As far as we could tell, he hadn't beaten up his wife for ages.

And more, Our Boy had even had a few moments of fame when the Panthers made their run at the Stanley Cup. Part of his job had been to run out and clean up when the fans threw objects on the ice. That Stanley Cup year, this had been a major job, since every time the Panthers scored the fans threw three or four thousand plastic rats onto the rink. Daryll Earl had to schlep out and pick them all up, boring work, no doubt. And so encouraged by a few snorts of very cheap vodka one night, he'd picked up one of the plastic rats and done a little "Rat Dance." The crowd ate it up and yelled for more. They began to call for it when Daryll Earl skidded out onto the ice. Daryll Earl did the dance for the rest of the season.

Plastic rats were forbidden nowadays. Even if they had been required by federal statute, nobody would have been throwing them. The Panthers hadn't scored a goal since the days when Miami had an honest mayor, sometime in the last century. But McHale still showed up at the games hoping for one last on-camera two-step.

At the press conference LaGuerta played that part beautifully. She made it sound like the memory of his small fame had driven Daryll Earl over the edge into murder. And of course with his drunkenness and his record of violence toward women, he was the perfect suspect for this series of stupid and brutal murders. But Miami's hookers could rest easy; the killing was over. Driven by the overwhelming pressure of an intense and merciless investigation, Daryll Earl had confessed. Case closed. Back to work, girls.

The press ate it up. You couldn't really blame them, I suppose. LaGuerta did a masterful job of presenting just enough fact colored with high-gloss wishful thinking that nearly anyone would have been convinced. And of course you don't actually have to take an IQ test to become a reporter. Even so, I always hope for just the smallest glimmer. And I'm always disappointed. Perhaps I saw too many black-and-white movies as a child. I still thought the cynical, world-weary drunk from the large metropolitan daily was supposed to ask an awkward question and force the investigators to carefully reexamine the evidence.

But sadly, life does not always imitate art. And at LaGuerta's press conference, the part of Spencer Tracy was played by a series of male and female models with perfect hair and tropical-weight suits. Their penetrating questions amounted to, "How did it feel to find the head?" and "Can we have some pictures?"

One lone reporter, Nick Something from the local NBC TV affiliate, asked LaGuerta if she was sure McHale was the killer. But when she said that the overwhelming preponderance of evidence indicated that this was the case and anyway the confession was conclusive, he let it go. Either he was satisfied or the words were too big.

And so there it was. Case closed, justice done. The mighty machinery of Metro Miami's awesome crime-fighting apparatus had once again triumphed over the dark forces besieging Our Fair City. It was a lovely show. LaGuerta handed out some very sinister-looking mug shots of Daryll Earl stapled to those new glossy shots of herself investigating a $250-an-hour high-fashion photographer on South Beach.

It made a wonderfully ironic package; the appearance of danger and the lethal reality, so very different. Because however coarse and brutal Daryll Earl looked, the real threat to society was LaGuerta. She had called off the hounds, closed down the hue and cry, sent people back to bed in a burning building.

Was I the only one who could see that Daryll Earl McHale could not possibly be the killer? That there was a style and wit here that a brickhead like McHale couldn't even understand?

I had never been more alone than I was in my admiration for the real killer's work. The very body parts seemed to sing to me, a rhapsody of bloodless wonder that lightened my heart and filled my veins with an intoxicating sense of awe. But it was certainly not going to interfere with my zeal in capturing the real killer, a cold and wanton executioner of the innocent who absolutely must be brought to justice. Right, Dexter? Right? Hello?

I sat in my apartment, rubbing my sleep-crusted eyes and thinking about the show I had just watched. It had been as near perfect as a press conference could be without free food and nudity. LaGuerta had clearly pulled every string she had ever gotten a hand on in order to make it the biggest, splashiest press conference possible, and it had been. And for perhaps the first time in her Gucci-licking career, LaGuerta really and truly believed she had the right man. She had to believe it. It was kind of sad, really. She thought she had done everything right this time. She wasn't just making political moves; in her mind she was cashing in on a clean and well-lit piece of work. She'd solved the crime, done it her way, caught the bad guy, stopped the killing. Well-earned applause all around for a job well done. And what a lovely surprise she would get when the next body turned up.

Because I knew with no room for doubt that the killer was still out there. He was probably watching the press conference on Channel 7, the channel of choice for people with an eye for carnage. At the moment he would be laughing too hard to hold a blade, but that would pass. And when it did his sense of humor would no doubt prompt him to comment on the situation.

For some reason the thought did not overwhelm me with fear and loathing and a grim determination to stop this madman before it was too late. Instead I felt a little surge of anticipation. I knew it was very wrong, and perhaps that made it feel even better. Oh, I wanted this killer stopped, brought to justice, yes, certainly—but did it have to be soon?

There was also a small trade-off to make. If I was going to do my little part to stop the real killer, then I should at least make something positive happen at the same time. And as I thought it, my telephone rang.

"Yes, I saw it," I said into the receiver.

"Jesus," said Deborah on the other end. "I think I'm going to be sick."

"Well, I won't mop your fevered brow, sis. There's work to be done."

"Jesus," she repeated. Then, "What work?"

"Tell me," I asked her. "Are you in ill odor, sis?"

"I'm tired, Dexter. And I'm more pissed off than I've ever been in my life. What's that in English?"

"I'm asking if you are in what Dad would have called the doghouse. Is your name mud in the department? Has your professional reputation been muddied, damaged, sullied, colored, rendered questionable?"

"Between LaGuerta's backstabbing and the Einstein thing? My professional reputation is shit," she said with more sourness than I would have thought possible in someone so young.

"Good. It's important that you don't have anything to lose."

She snorted. "Glad I could help. 'Cause I'm there, Dexter. If I sink any lower in the department, I'll be making coffee for community relations. Where is this going, Dex?"

I closed my eyes and leaned all the way back in my chair.

"You are going to go on record—with the captain and the department itself—as believing that Daryll Earl is the wrong man and that another murder is going to take place. You will present a couple of compelling reasons culled from your investigation, and you will be the laughingstock of Miami Metro for a little while."

"I already am," she said. "No big deal. But is there some reason for this?"

I shook my head. It was sometimes hard for me to believe she could be so naïve. "Sister dearest," I said, "you don't truly believe Daryll Earl is guilty, do you?"

She didn't answer. I could hear her breathing and it occurred to me that she must be tired, too, every bit as tired as I was, but without the jolt of energy I got from being certain I was right. "Deb?"

"The guy confessed, Dexter," she said at last, and I heard the utter fatigue in her voice. "I don't—I've been wrong before, even when— I mean, but he *confessed*. Doesn't that, that . . . Shit. Maybe we should just let it go, Dex."

"Oh ye of little faith," I said. "She's got the wrong guy, Deborah. And you are now going to rewrite the politics."

"Sure I am."

"Daryll Earl McHale is not it," I said. "There's absolutely no doubt about it."

"Even if you're right, so what?" she said.

Now it was my turn to blink and wonder. "Excuse me?"

"Well, look, if I'm this killer, why don't I realize I'm off the hook now? With this other guy arrested, the heat's off, you know. Why don't I just stop? Or even take off for some-place else and start over?"

"Impossible," I said. "You don't understand how this guy thinks."

"Yeah, I know," she said. "How come you do?"

I chose to ignore that. "He's going to stay right here and he's going to kill again. He has to show us all what he thinks of us."

"Which is what?"

"It's not good," I admitted. "We've done something stupid by arresting an obvious twinky like Daryll Earl. That's funny."

"Ha, ha," Deb said with no amusement.

"But we've also insulted him. We've given this lowbrow brain-dead redneck all the credit for his work, which is like telling Jackson Pollock your six-year-old could have painted that."

"Jackson Pollock? The *painter*? Dexter, this guy's a butcher."

"In his own way, Deborah, he is an artist. And he thinks of himself that way."

"For Christ's sake. That's the stupidest—"

"Trust me, Deb."

"Sure, I trust you. Why shouldn't I trust you? So we have an angrily amused artist who's not going anywhere, right?"

"Right," I said. "He has to do it again, and it has to be under our noses, and it probably has to be a little bigger."

"You mean he's going to kill a fat hooker this time?"

"Bigger in scale, Deborah. Larger in concept. Splashier."

"Oh. Splashier. Sure. Like with a mulcher."

"The stakes have gone up, Debs. We've pushed him and insulted him a little and the next kill will reflect that."

"Uh-huh," she said. "And how would that work?"

"I don't really know," I admitted.

"But you're sure."

"That's right," I said.

"Swell," she said. "Now I know what to watch for."

CHAPTER 13

I KNEW WHEN I WALKED IN MY FRONT DOOR AFTER work on Monday that something was wrong. Someone had been in my apartment.

The door was not broken, the windows were not jimmied, and I couldn't see any signs of vandalism, but I knew. Call it sixth sense or whatever you like. Someone had been here. Maybe I was smelling pheromones the intruder had left in my air molecules. Or perhaps my La-Z-Boy recliner's aura had been disturbed. It didn't matter how I knew: I knew. Somebody had been in my apartment while I had been at work.

That might seem like no big deal. This was Miami, after all. People come home every day to find their TVs gone, their jewelry and electronics all taken away; their space violated, their possessions rifled, and their dog pregnant. But this was different. Even as I did a quick search through the apartment, I knew I would find nothing missing.

And I was right. Nothing was missing.

But something had been added.

It took me a few minutes to find it. I suppose some work-induced reflex made me check the obvious things first. When an intruder has paid a visit, in the natural course of events your things are gone: toys, valuables, private relics, the last few chocolate chip cookies. So I checked.

But all my things were unmolested. The computer, the sound system, the TV and VCR—all right where I had left them. Even my small collection of precious glass slides was tucked away on the bookcase, each with its single drop of dried blood in place. Everything was exactly as I had left it.

I checked the private areas next, just to be sure: bedroom, bathroom, medicine cabinet. There were all fine, too, all apparently undisturbed, and yet there was a feeling suspended in the air over every object that it had been examined, touched, and replaced—with such perfect care that even the dust motes were in their proper positions.

I went back into the living room, sank into my chair, and looked around, suddenly unsure. I had been absolutely positive that someone had been here, but why? And who did I imagine was so interested in little old me that they would come in and leave my modest home exactly as it had been? Because nothing was missing, nothing disturbed. The pile of newspapers in the recycle box might be leaning slightly to the left—but was that my imagination? Couldn't it have been a breeze from the air conditioner? Nothing was really different, nothing changed or missing; nothing.

And why would anyone break into my apartment at all? There was nothing special about it—I'd made sure of that. It was part of building my Harry Profile. Blend in. Act normal, even boring. Don't do anything or own anything that might cause comment. So had I done. I had no real valuables other than a stereo and a computer. There were other, far more attractive targets in the immediate neighborhood.

And in any case, why would somebody break in and then take nothing, do nothing, leave no sign? I leaned back and closed my eyes; almost certainly I was imagining the whole thing. This was surely just jangled nerves. A symptom of sleep deprivation and worrying too much about Deborah's critically injured career. Just one more small sign that Poor Old Dexter was drifting off into Deep Water. Making that last painless transition from sociopath to psychopath. It is not necessarily crazy in Miami to assume that you are surrounded by anonymous enemies—but to act like it is socially unacceptable. They would have to put me away at last.

And yet the feeling was so strong. I tried to shake it off: just a whim, a twitch of the nerves, a passing indigestion. I stood up, stretched, took a deep breath, and tried to think pretty thoughts. None came. I shook my head and went into the kitchen for a drink of water and there it was.

There it was.

I stood in front of the refrigerator and looked, I don't know how long, just staring stupidly.

Attached to the refrigerator, hair pinned to the door with one of my small tropical-fruit magnets, was a Barbie doll's head. I did not remember leaving it there. I did not remember ever owning one. It seemed like the kind of thing I would remember.

I reached to touch the little plastic head. It swung gently, thumping against the freezer door with a small *thack* sound. It turned in a tiny quarter circle until Barbie looked up at me with alert, Collie-dog interest. I looked back.

Without really knowing what I was doing or why, I opened the freezer door. Inside, lying carefully on top of the ice basket, was Barbie's body. The legs and arms had been pulled off, and the body had been pulled apart at the waist. The pieces were stacked neatly, wrapped, and tied with a pink ribbon. And stuck into one tiny Barbie hand was a small accessory, a Barbie vanity mirror.

After a long moment I closed the freezer door. I wanted to lie down and press my cheek against the cool linoleum. Instead I reached out with my little finger and flipped Barbie's head. It went *thack thack* against the door. I flipped it again. *Thack thack*. Whee. I had a new hobby.

I left the doll where it was and went back to my chair, sinking deep into the cushions and closing my eyes. I knew I should be feeling upset, angry, afraid, violated, filled with paranoid hostility and righteous rage. I didn't. Instead I felt—what? More than a little light-headed. Anxious, perhaps—or was it exhilaration?

There was of course no possible doubt about who had been in my apartment. Unless I could swallow the idea that some stranger, for unknown reasons, had randomly chosen my apartment as the ideal spot to display his decapitated Barbie doll.

No. I had been visited by my favorite artist. How he had found me was not important. It would have been easy enough to jot down my license number on the causeway that night. He'd had plenty of time to watch me from his hiding place behind the filling station. And then anyone with computer literacy could find my address. And having found it, it would be easy enough to slip in, take a careful look around, and leave a message.

And here was the message: the head hung separately, the body parts stacked on my ice tray, and that damned mirror again. Combined with the total lack of interest in everything else in the apartment, it all added up to only one thing.

But what?

What was he saying?

He could have left anything or nothing. He could have jammed a bloody butcher knife through a cow's heart and into my linoleum. I was grateful he hadn't—what a mess—but why Barbie? Aside from the obvious fact that the doll reflected the body of his last kill, why tell me about it? And was this more sinister than some other, gooier message—or less? Was it, "I'm watching and I'll get you"?

Or was he saying, "Hi! Wanna play?"

And I did. Of course I did.

But what about the mirror? To include it this time gave it meaning far beyond the truck and the chase on the causeway. Now it had to mean much more. All I could come up with was, "Look at yourself." And what sense did that make? Why should I look at myself? I am not vain enough to enjoy that—at least, I am not vain about my physical appearance. And why would I even want to look at myself, when what I really wanted was to see the killer? So there had to be some other meaning to the mirror that I was not getting.

But even here I could not be sure. It was possible that there was no real meaning at all. I did not want to believe that of so elegant an artist, but it was possible. And the message could very well be a private, deranged, and sinister one. There was absolutely no way to know. And so, there was also no way to know what I should do about it. If indeed I should do anything.

I made the human choice. Funny when you think about it; me, making a human choice. Harry would have been proud. Humanly, I decided to do nothing. Wait and see. I would not report what had happened. After all, what was there to report? Nothing was missing. There was nothing at all to say officially except: "Ah, Captain Matthews, I thought you should know that someone apparently broke into my apartment and left a Barbie doll in my freezer."

That had a very good ring to it. I was sure that would go over well with the department. Perhaps Sergeant Doakes would investigate personally and finally be allowed to indulge some hidden talents for unfettered interrogation. And perhaps they would simply fling me on the Mentally Unable to Perform list, along with poor Deb, since officially the case was closing and even when open had nothing to do with Barbie dolls.

No, there was really nothing to tell, not in any way that I could explain. So at the risk of another savage elbowing, I would not even tell Deborah. For reasons I could not begin to explain, even to myself, this was personal. And by keeping it personal, there was a greater chance that I could get closer to my visitor. In order to bring him to justice, of course. Naturally.

With the decision made I felt much lighter. Almost giddy, in fact. I had no idea what might come of it, but I was ready to go with whatever came. The feeling stayed with me through the night, and even through the next day at work, as I prepared a lab report, comforted Deb, and stole a doughnut from Vince Masuoka. It stayed with me during my drive home through the happily homicidal evening traffic. I was in a state of Zen readiness, prepared for any surprise.

Or so I thought.

I had just returned to my apartment, leaned back in my chair, and relaxed, when the phone rang. I let it ring. I wanted to breathe for a few minutes, and I could think of nothing that couldn't wait. Besides, I had paid almost $50 for an answering machine. Let it earn its keep.

Two rings. I closed my eyes. Breathed in. Relax, old boy. Three rings. Breathe out. The answering machine clicked and my wonderfully urbane message began to play.

"Hello, I'm not in right now, but I'll get back to you right away if you'll please leave a message, after the beep. Thank you."

What fabulous vocal tone. What acid wit! A truly great message altogether. It sounded nearly human. I was very proud. I breathed in again, listening to the melodic BEEEEP! that followed.

"Hi, it's me."

A female voice. Not Deborah. I felt one eyelid twitch in irritation. Why do so many people start their messages with "It's me"? Of course it is you. We all know that. But who the hell ARE you? In my case the choices were rather limited. I knew it wasn't Deborah. It didn't sound like LaGuerta, although anything was possible. So that left—

Rita?

"Um, I'm sorry, I—" A long breath sighing out. "Listen, Dexter, I'm sorry. I thought you would call me and then when you didn't I just—" Another long breath out. "Anyway. I need to talk. Because I realized . . . I mean—oh hell. Could you, um, call me? If—you know."

I didn't know. Not at all. I wasn't even sure who it was. Could that really be Rita?

Another long sigh. "I'm sorry if—" And a very long pause. Two full breaths. In deeply, out. In deeply, then blown out abruptly. "Please call me, Dexter. Just—" A long pause. Another sigh. Then she hung up.

Many times in my life I have felt like I was missing something, some essential piece of the puzzle that everybody else carried around with them without thinking about it. I don't usually mind, since most of those times it turns out to be an astonishingly stupid piece of humania like understanding the infield fly rule or not going all the way on the first date.

But at other times I feel like I am missing out on a great reservoir of warm wisdom, the lore of some sense I don't possess that humans feel so deeply they don't need to talk about it and can't even put it into words.

This was one of those times.

I knew I was supposed to understand that Rita was actually saying something very specific, that her pauses and stutters added up to a great and marvelous thing that a human male would intuitively grasp. But I had not a single clue as to what it might be, nor how to figure it out. Should I count the breaths? Time the pauses and convert the numbers to Bible verses to arrive at the secret code? What was she trying to tell me? And why, for that matter, was she trying to tell me anything at all?

As I understood things, when I had kissed Rita on that strange and stupid impulse, I had crossed a line we had both agreed to keep uncrossed. With that thing done there was no undoing it, no going back. In its own way the kiss had been an act of murder. At any rate, it was comforting to think so. I had killed our careful relationship by driving my tongue through its heart and pushing it off a cliff. Boom, a dead thing. I hadn't even thought about Rita since. She was gone, shoved out of my life by an incomprehensible whim.

And now she was calling me and recording her breathing for my amusement.

Why? Did she want to chastise me? Call me names, rub my nose in my folly, force me to understand the immensity of my offense?

The whole thing began to irritate me beyond measure. I paced around my apartment. Why should I have to think about Rita at all? I had more important concerns at the moment. Rita was merely my beard, a silly kid's costume I wore on weekends to hide the fact that I was the kind of person who did the things that this other interesting fellow was now doing and I wasn't.

Was this jealousy? Of course I wasn't doing those things. I had just recently finished for the time being. I certainly wouldn't do it again anytime soon. Too risky. I hadn't prepared anything.

And yet—

I walked back into the kitchen and flicked the Barbie head. *Thack. Thack thack.* I seemed to be feeling something here. Playfulness? Deep and abiding concern? Professional jealousy? I couldn't say, and Barbie wasn't talking.

It was just too much. The obviously fake confession, the violation of my inner sanctum, and now Rita? A man can take only so much. Even a phony man like me. I began to feel unsettled, dizzy, confused, hyperactive and lethargic at the same time. I walked to the window and looked out. It was dark now and far away over the water a light rose up in the sky and at the sight of it a small and evil voice rose up to meet it from somewhere deep inside.

Moon.

A whisper in my ear. Not even a sound; just the slight sense of someone speaking your name, almost heard, somewhere nearby. Very near, perhaps getting closer. No words at all, just a dry rustle of not-voice, a tone off-tone, a thought on a breath. My face felt hot and I could suddenly hear myself breathing. The voice came again, a soft sound dropped on the outer edge of my ear. I turned, even though I knew no one was there and it was not my ear but my dear friend inside, kicked into consciousness by who knows what and the moon.

Such a fat happy chatterbox moon. Oh how much it had to say. And as much as I tried to tell it that the time was wrong, that this was much too soon, there were other things to do now, important things—the moon had words for all of it and more. And so even though I stood there for a quarter of an hour and argued, there was never really any question.

I grew desperate, fighting it with all the tricks I had, and when that failed I did something that shocked me to my very core. I called Rita.

"Oh, Dexter," she said. "I just—I was afraid. Thank you for calling. I just—"

"I know," I said, although of course I did not know.

"Could we—I don't know what you— Can I see you later and just—I would really like to talk to you."

"Of course," I told her, and as we agreed to meet later at her place, I wondered what she might possibly have in mind. Violence? Tears of recrimination? Full-throated name-calling? I was on foreign turf here—I could be walking into anything.

And after I hung up, the whole thing distracted me wonderfully for almost half an hour before the soft interior voice came sliding back into my brain with its quiet insistence that tonight really ought to be special.

I felt myself pulled back to the window and there it was again, the huge happy face in the sky, the chuckling moon. I pulled the curtain and turned away, circled my apartment from room to room, touching things, telling myself I was checking once more for whatever might be missing, knowing nothing was missing, and knowing why, too. And each time around the apartment I circled closer and closer to the small desk in the living room where I kept my computer, knowing what I wanted to do and not wanting to do it, until finally, after three-quarters of an hour, the pull was too strong. I was too dizzy to stand and thought I would just slump into the chair since it was close at hand, and since I was there anyway I turned on the computer, and once it was on . . .

But it's not done, I thought, *I'm not ready.*

And of course, that didn't matter. Whether I was ready or not made no difference at all. *It* was ready.

CHAPTER 14

I WAS ALMOST CERTAIN HE WAS THE ONE, BUT ONLY almost, and I had never been only *almost* certain before. I felt weak, intoxicated, half sick with a combination of excitement and uncertainty and complete wrongness—but of course, the Dark Passenger was driving from the backseat now and how I felt was not terribly important anymore because *he* felt strong and cold and eager and ready. And I could feel him swelling inside me, surging up out of the Dexter-dark corners of my lizard brain, a rising and swelling that could only end one way and that being the case it rather had to be with this one.

I had found him several months ago, but after a little bit of observation I'd decided that the priest was a sure thing and this one could wait a little longer until I was positive.

How wrong I had been. I now found he couldn't wait at all.

He lived on a small street in Coconut Grove. A few blocks to one side of his crummy little house the neighborhood was low-income black housing, barbecue joints, and crumbling churches. Half a mile in the other direction the millionaires lived in overgrown modern houses and built coral walls to keep out people like him. But Jamie Jaworski was right in between, in a house he shared with a million palmetto bugs and the ugliest dog I had ever seen.

It was still a house he shouldn't have been able to afford. Jaworski was a part-time janitor at Ponce de Leon Junior High, and as far as I could tell that was his only source of income. He worked three days a week, which might be just enough to live on but not much more. Of course, I was not interested in his finances. I was very interested in the fact that there had been a small but significant increase in runaway children from Ponce since Jaworski had begun to work there. All of them twelve- to thirteen-year-old light-haired girls.

Light-haired. That was important. For some reason it was the kind of detail that police often seem to overlook but always jumped out at someone like me. Perhaps it didn't seem politically correct; dark-haired girls, and dark-skinned girls, should have an equal opportunity to be kidnapped, sexually abused, and then cut up in front of a camera, don't you think?

Jaworski, too, often seemed to be the missing kid's last witness. The police had talked to him, held him overnight, questioned him, and had not been able to make anything stick to him. Of course, they have to meet certain petty legal requirements. Torture, for example, was frowned on lately, for the most part. And without some very forceful persuasion, Jamie Jaworski was never going to open up about his hobby. I know I wouldn't.

But I knew he was doing it. He was helping those girls disappear into very quick and final movie careers. I was almost positive. I had not found any body parts and hadn't seen him do it, but everything fit. And on the Internet I did manage to locate some particularly inventive pictures of three of the missing girls. They did not look very happy in those pictures, although some of the things they were doing were supposed to bring joy, I have been told.

I could not positively connect Jaworski with the pictures. But the mailbox address was South Miami, a few minutes from the school. And he was living above his means. And in any case I was being reminded with increasing force from the dark backseat that I was out of time, that this was not a case where certainty was terribly important.

But the ugly dog worried me. Dogs were always a problem. They don't like me and they quite often disapprove of what I do to their masters, especially since I don't share the good pieces. I had to find a way around the dog to Jaworski. Perhaps he would come out. If not, I had to find a way in.

I drove past Jaworski's house three times but nothing occurred to me. I needed some luck and I needed it before the Dark Passenger made me do something hasty. And just as my dear friend began to whisper imprudent suggestions, I got my small piece of luck. Jaworski came out of his house and climbed into his battered red Toyota pickup as I drove past. I slowed down as much as I could, and in a moment he backed out and yanked his little truck toward Douglas Road. I turned around and followed.

I had no idea how I was going to do this. I was not prepared. I had no safe room, no clean coveralls, nothing but a roll of duct tape and a filet knife under my seat. I had to be unseen, unnoticed, and perfect, and I had no idea how. I hated to improvise, but I was not being offered a choice.

Once again I was lucky. Traffic was very light as Jaworski drove south to Old Cutler Road, and after a mile or so he turned left toward the water. Another huge new development was going up to improve life for all of us by turning trees and animals into cement and old people from New Jersey. Jaworski drove slowly through the construction, past half a golf course with the flags in place but no grass on it, until he came almost to the water. The skeleton of a large, half-finished block of condos blotted out the moon. I dropped far back, turned out my headlights, and then inched close enough to see what my boy was up to.

Jaworski had pulled in beside the block of condos-to-be and parked. He got out and stood between his little truck and a huge pile of sand. For a moment he just looked around and I pulled onto the shoulder and turned off the engine. Jaworski stared at the condos and then down the road toward the water. He seemed satisfied and went into the building. I was quite certain that he was looking for a guard. I was, too. I hoped he had done his homework. Most often in these huge uberdevelopments one guard rides around from site to site in a golf cart. It saves money, and anyway, this is Miami. A certain amount of the overhead on any project is for material that is expected to disappear quietly. It looked to me like Jaworski planned to help the builder meet his quota.

I got out of my car and slipped my filet knife and duct tape into a cheap tote bag I'd brought along. I had already stuffed some rubberized gardening gloves and a few pictures inside it, nothing much. Just trifles I'd downloaded from the Internet. I shrugged the bag onto my shoulder and moved quietly through the night until I came to his grungy little truck. The bed was as empty as the cab. Heaps of Burger King cups and wrappers, empty Camel packs on the floor. Nothing that wasn't small and dirty, like Jaworski himself.

I looked up. Above the rim of the half-condo I could just see the glow of the moon. A night wind blew across my face, bringing with it all the enchanting odors of our tropical paradise: diesel oil, decaying vegetation, and cement. I inhaled it deeply and turned my thoughts back to Jaworski.

He was somewhere inside the shell of the building. I didn't know how long I had, and a certain small voice was urging me to hurry. I left the truck and went into the building. As I stepped through the door I heard him. Or rather, I heard a strange whirring, rattling sound that had to be him, or—

I paused. The sound came from off to one side and I whisper-footed over to it. A pipe ran up the wall, an electrical conduit. I placed a hand on the pipe and felt it vibrate, as if something inside was moving.

A small light went on in my brain. Jaworski was pulling out the wire. Copper was very expensive, and there was a thriving black market for copper in any form. It was one more small way to supplement a meager janitorial salary, helping to cover the long, poverty-strewn stretches between young runaways. He could make several hundred dollars for one load of copper.

Now that I knew what he was up to, a vague outline of an idea began to take root in my brain. From the sound, he was above me somewhere. I could easily track him, shadow him until the time was right, and then pounce. But I was practically naked here, completely exposed and unready. I was used to doing these things a certain way. To step outside my own careful boundaries made me extremely uncomfortable.

A small shudder crawled up my spine. Why was I doing this?

The quick answer, of course, was that I wasn't doing it at all. My dear friend in the dark backseat was doing it. I was just along because I had the driver's license. But we had reached an understanding, he and I. We had achieved a careful, balanced existence, a way to live together, through our Harry solution. And now he was rampaging outside Harry's careful, beautiful chalk lines. Why? Anger? Was the invasion of my home really such an outrage that it woke him to strike out in revenge?

He didn't *feel* angry to me—as always he seemed cool, quietly amused, eager for his prey. And I didn't feel angry either. I felt—half drunk, high as a kite, teetering on the knife edge of euphoria, wobbling through a series of inner ripples that felt curiously like I have always thought emotions must feel. And the giddiness of it had driven me to this dangerous, unclean, unplanned place, to do something on the spur of the moment that always before I had planned carefully. And even knowing all this, I badly wanted to do it. *Had* to do it.

Very well then. But I didn't have to do it undressed. I looked around. A large pile of Sheetrock squatted at the far end of the room, bound with shrink-wrap. A moment's work and I had cut myself an apron and a strange transparent mask from the shrink-wrap; nose, mouth, and eyes sliced away so I could breathe, talk, and see. I pulled it tight, feeling it mash my features into something unrecognizable. I twisted the ends behind my head and tied a clumsy knot in the plastic. Perfect anonymity. It might seem silly, but I was used to hunting with a mask. And aside from a neurotic compulsion to make everything *right*, it was simply one less thing to think about. It made me relax a little, so it was a good idea. I took the gloves from the tote bag and slipped them on. I was ready now.

I found Jaworski on the third floor. A pile of electrical wire pooled at his feet. I stood in the shadows of the stairwell and watched as he pulled out wire. I ducked back into the stairwell and opened my tote bag. Using my duct tape, I hung up the pictures I had brought along. Sweet little photos of the runaway girls, in a variety of endearing and very explicit poses. I taped them to the concrete walls where Jaworski would see them as he stepped through the door onto the stairs.

I looked back in at Jaworski. He pulled out another twenty yards of wire. It stuck on something and would pull no more. Jaworski yanked twice, then pulled a pair of heavy cutters from his back pocket and snipped the wire. He picked up the wire lying at his feet and wound it into a tight coil on his forearm. Then he walked toward the stairs—toward me.

I shrank back into the stairwell and waited.

Jaworski wasn't trying to be quiet. He was not expecting any interruption—and he certainly wasn't expecting me. I listened to his footsteps and the small rattle of the wire coil dragging behind him. Closer—

He came through the door and a step past without seeing me. And then he saw the pictures.

"Whooof," he said, as though he had been hit hard in the stomach. He stared, slack-jawed, unable to move, and then I was behind him with my knife at his throat.

"Don't move and don't make a sound," we said.

"Hey, lookit—" he said.

I turned my wrist slightly and pushed the knife point into his skin under the chin. He hissed as a distressing, awful little spurt of blood squirted out. So unnecessary. Why can't people ever listen?

"I said, don't make a sound," we told him, and now he was quiet.

And then the only sound was the ratcheting of the duct tape, Jaworski's breathing, and the quiet chuckle from the Dark Passenger. I taped over his mouth, twisted a length of the janitor's precious copper wire around his wrists, and dragged him over to another stack of shrink-wrapped Sheetrock. In just a few moments I had him trussed up and secured to the makeshift table.

"Let's talk," we said in the Dark Passenger's gentle, cold voice.

He didn't know if he was allowed to speak, and the duct tape would have made it difficult in any case, so he stayed silent.

"Let's talk about runaways," we said, ripping the duct tape from his mouth.

"Yaaaooww— Whu—whataya mean?" he said. But he was not very convincing.

"I think you know what I mean," we told him.

"Nuh-no," he said.

"Yuh-yes," we said.

Probably one word too clever. My timing was off, the whole evening was off. But he got brave. He looked up at me in my shiny face. "What are you, a cop or something?" he asked.

"No," we said, and sliced off his left ear. It was closest. The knife was sharp and for a moment he couldn't believe it was happening to him, permanent and forever no left ear. So I dropped the ear on his chest to let him believe. His eyes got huge and he filled his lungs to scream, but I stuffed a wad of plastic wrap in his mouth just before he did.

"None of that," we said. "Worse things can happen." And they would, oh definitely, but he didn't need to know that yet.

"The runaways?" we asked gently, coldly, and waited for just a moment, watching his eyes, to make sure he wouldn't scream, then removed the gag.

"Jesus," he said hoarsely. "My ear—"

"You have another, just as good," we said. "Tell us about the girls in those pictures."

"Us? What do you mean, us? Jesus, that hurts," he whimpered.

Some people just don't get it. I put the plastic stuff back in his mouth and went to work.

I almost got carried away; easy to do, under the circumstances. My heart was racing like mad and I had to fight hard to keep my hand from shaking. But I went to work, exploring, looking for something that was always just beyond my fingertips. Exciting—and terribly frustrating. The pressure was rising inside me, climbing up into my ears and screaming for release—but no release came. Just the growing pressure, and the sense that something wonderful was just beyond my senses, waiting for me to find it and dive in. But I did not find it, and none of my old standards gave me any joy at all. What to do? In my confusion I opened up a vein and a horrible puddle of blood formed on the plastic wrap alongside the janitor. I stopped for a moment, looking for an answer, finding nothing. I looked away, out the shell of the window. I stared, forgetting to breathe.

The moon was visible over the water. For some reason I could not explain that seemed so right, so *necessary*, that for a moment I just looked out across the water, watching it shimmer, so very perfect. I swayed and bumped against my makeshift table and came back to myself. But the moon . . . or was it the water?

So close . . . I was so close to something I could almost smell—but what? A shiver ran through me—and that was right, too, so right it set off a whole chain of shivers until my teeth chattered. But why? What did it mean? Something was there, something *important*, an overwhelming purity and clarity riding the moon and the water just beyond the tip of my filet knife, and I couldn't catch it.

I looked back at the janitor. He made me so angry, the way he was lying there, covered with improvised marks and unnecessary blood. But it was hard to stay angry, with the beautiful Florida moon pounding at me, the tropical breeze blowing, the wonderful night sounds of flexing duct tape and panic breathing. I almost had to laugh. Some people choose to die for some very unusual things, but this horrid little bug, dying for copper wire. And the look on his face: so hurt and confused and desperate. It would have been funny if I hadn't felt so frustrated.

And he really did deserve a better effort from me; after all, it wasn't his fault I was off my usual form. He wasn't even vile enough to be at the top of my TO DO list. He was just a repulsive little slug who killed children for money and kicks, and only four or five of them as far as I knew. I almost felt sorry for him. He truly wasn't ready for the major leagues.

Ah, well. Back to work. I stepped back to Jaworski's side. He was not thrashing as much now, but he was still far too lively for my usual methods. Of course I did not have all my highly professional toys tonight and the going must have been a little rough for Jaworski. But like a real trouper, he had not complained. I felt a surge of affection and slowed down my slapdash approach, spending some quality time on his hands. He responded with real enthusiasm and I drifted away, lost in happy research.

Eventually it was his muffled screams and wild thrash-

ing that called me back to myself. And I remembered I had
not even made sure of his guilt. I waited for him to calm
down, then removed the plastic from his mouth.

"The runaways?" we asked.

"Oh Jesus. Oh God. Oh Jesus," he said weakly.

"I don't think so," we said. "I think we may have left
them behind."

"Please," he said. "Oh, please . . ."

"Tell me about the runaways," we said.

"Okay," he breathed.

"You took those girls."

"Yes. . . ."

"How many?"

He just breathed for a moment. His eyes were closed and
I thought I might have lost him a little early. He finally
opened his eyes and looked at me. "Five," he said at last.
"Five little beauties. I'm not sorry."

"Of course you're not," we said. I placed a hand on his
arm. It was a beautiful moment. "And now, I'm not sorry
either."

I stuffed the plastic into his mouth and went back to
work. But I had really only just started to recapture my
rhythm when I heard the guard arrive downstairs.

CHAPTER 15

IT WAS THE STATIC OF HIS RADIO THAT GAVE HIM away. I was deeply involved in something I'd never tried before when I heard it. I was working on the torso with the knife point and could feel the first real tinglings of response down my spine and through my legs and I didn't want to stop. But a radio— This was worse news than a mere guard arriving. If he called for backup or to have the road blocked, it was just possible that I might find a few of the things I had been doing a little difficult to explain.

I looked down at Jaworski. He was nearly done now, and yet I was not happy with how things had gone. Far too much mess, and I had not really found what I was looking for. There had been a few moments where I felt on the brink of some wonderful thing, some amazing revelation to do with—what? the water flowing by outside the window?— but it had not happened, whatever it had been. Now I was left with an unfinished, unclean, untidy, unsatisfying child rapist, and a security guard on his way to join us.

I hate to rush the conclusion. It's such an important moment, and a real relief for both of us, the Dark Passenger and I. But what choice did I have? For a long moment—far too long, really, and I'm quite ashamed—I thought about killing the guard and going on. It would be easy, and I could continue to explore with a fresh start—

But no. Of course not. It wouldn't do. The guard was innocent, as innocent as anyone can be and still live in Miami. He'd probably done nothing worse than shoot at other drivers on the Palmetto Expressway a few times. Practically snow-white. No, I had to make a hasty retreat, and that was all there was to it. And if I had to leave the janitor not quite finished and me not quite satisfied—well, better luck next time.

I stared down at the grubby little insect and felt myself fill with loathing. The thing was drooling snot and blood all together, the ugly wet slop burbling across his face. A trickle of awful red came from his mouth. In a quick fit of pique, I slashed across Jaworski's throat. I immediately regretted my rashness. A fountain of horrible blood came out and the sight made it all seem even more regrettable, a messy mistake. Feeling unclean and unsatisfied, I sprinted for the stairwell. A cold and petulant grumbling from my Dark Passenger followed me.

I turned out onto the second floor and slid sideways over to a glassless window. Below me I could see the guard's golf cart parked, pointing in the direction of Old Cutler—meaning, I hoped, that he had come from the other direction and had not seen my car. Standing beside the cart, a fat olive-skinned young man with black hair and a wispy black mustache was looking up at the building—luckily, looking at the other end at the moment.

What had he heard? Was he merely on his regular route? I had to hope so. If he had actually heard something— If he stood outside and called for help, I was probably going to be caught. And as clever and glib-tongued as I was, I did not think I was good enough to talk my way out of this.

The young guard touched a thumb to his mustache and stroked it as if to encourage fuller growth. He frowned, swept his gaze along the front of the building. I ducked back. When I peeked out again a moment later I could just see the top of his head. He was coming in.

I waited until I heard his feet in the stairwell. Then I was out the window, halfway between the first and second floors, hanging by my fingertips from the coarse cement of the windowsill, then dropping. I hit badly, one ankle twisting on a rock, one knuckle skinned. But in my very best rapid limp I hurried into the shadows and scurried for my car.

My heart was pounding when I finally slid into the driver's seat. I looked back and saw no sign of the guard. I started the engine and, with the lights still off, I drove as quickly and quietly as I could out onto Old Cutler Road, heading toward South Miami and taking the long way home along Dixie Highway. My pulse still pounded in my ears. What a stupid risk to take. I had never before done anything so impulsive, never before done anything at all without careful planning. That was the Harry Way: be careful, be safe, be prepared. The Dark Scouts.

And instead, this. I could have been caught. I could have

been seen. Stupid, stupid—if I had not heard the young security guard in time I might have had to kill him. Kill an innocent man with violence; I was quite sure Harry would disapprove. And it was so messy and unpleasant, too.

Of course I was still not safe—the guard might easily have written down my license number if he had passed my car in his little golf cart. I had taken brainless, terrible risks, gone against all my careful procedures, gambled my entire carefully built life—and for what? A thrill kill? Shame on me. And deep in the shaded corner of my mind the echo came, *Oh yes, shame*, and the familiar chuckle.

I took a deep breath and looked at my hand on the steering wheel. But it *had* been thrilling, hadn't it? It had been wildly exciting, full of life and new sensations and profound frustration. It had been something entirely new and interesting. And the odd sensation that it was all going somewhere, an important place that was new and yet familiar—I would really have to explore that a little better next time.

Not that there was going to be a next time, of course. I would certainly never again do anything so foolish and impulsive. Never. But to have done it once—kind of fun.

Never mind. I would go home and take an exceptionally long shower, and by the time I was done—

Time. It came into my mind unwanted and unasked. I had agreed to meet with Rita at—right about now, according to my dashboard clock. And for what dark purpose? I couldn't know what went on in the human female mind. Why did I even have to think about "for what" at a time like this, when all my nerve endings were standing up and yodeling with frustration? I did not care what Rita wanted to yell at me about. It would not really bother me, whatever sharp observations she had to make on my character defects, but it was irritating to be forced to spend time listening when I had other, far more important things to think about. Most particularly, I wanted to wonder what I should have done that I had not done with dear departed Jaworski. Up to the cruelly interrupted and unfinished climax so many new things had happened that needed my very best mental efforts; I needed to reflect, to consider, and to understand where it had all been leading me. And how did it relate to that other artist out there, shadowing me and challenging me with his work?

With all this to think about, why did I need Rita right now?

But of course I would go. And of course, it would actually serve some humble purpose if I should need an alibi for my adventure with the little janitor. "Why, Detective, how could you possibly think that I—? Besides, I was having a fight with my girlfriend at the time. Ah—ex-girlfriend, actually." Because there was absolutely no doubt in my mind that Rita merely wanted to—what was the word we were all using lately? Vent? Yes, Rita wanted me to come over so she could vent on me. I had certain major character flaws that she needed to point out with an accompanying burst of emotion, and my presence was necessary.

Since this was the case, I took an extra minute to clean up. I circled back toward Coconut Grove and parked on the far side of the bridge over the waterway. A good deep channel ran underneath. I rolled a couple of large coral rocks out of the trees at the edge of the waterway, stuffed them into my tote bag, which was loaded with the plastic, gloves, and knife, and flung the thing into the center of the channel.

I stopped once more, at a small, dark park almost to Rita's house, and washed off carefully. I had to be neat and presentable; getting yelled at by a furious woman should be treated as a semiformal occasion.

But imagine my surprise when I rang her doorbell a few minutes later. She did not fling wide the door and begin to hurl furniture and abuse at me. In fact, she opened the door very slowly and carefully, half hiding behind it, as if badly frightened of what might be waiting for her on the other side. And considering that it was me waiting, this showed rare common sense.

"Dexter?" she said, softly, shyly, sounding like she wasn't sure whether she wanted me to answer yes or no. "I . . . didn't think you were coming."

"And yet here I am," I said helpfully.

She didn't answer for a much longer time than seemed right. Finally, she nudged the door slightly more open and said, "Would you . . . come in? Please?"

And if her uncertain, limping tone of voice, unlike any I had ever heard her use before, was a surprise, imagine how astonished I was by her costume. I believe the thing was called a peignoir; or possibly it was a negligee, since it certainly was negligible as far as the amount of fabric used in its construction was concerned. Whatever the correct name, she was certainly wearing it. And as bizarre as the idea was, I believe the costume was aimed at me.

"Please?" she repeated.

It was all a little much. I mean, really, what was I supposed to do here? I was bubbling over with unsatisfied experimentation on the janitor; there were still unhappy murmurings filtering through from the backseat. And a quick check of the situation at large revealed that I was being whipsawed between dear Deb and the dark artist, and now I was expected to do some sort of human thing here, like—well, what, after all? She surely couldn't want— I mean, wasn't she MAD at me? What was going on here? And why was it going on with me?

"I sent the kids next door," Rita said. She bumped the door with her hip.

I went in.

I can think of a great many ways to describe what happened next, but none of them seem adequate. She went to the couch. I followed. She sat down. So did I. She looked uncomfortable and squeezed her left hand with her right. She seemed to be waiting for something, and since I was not quite sure what, I found myself thinking about my unfinished work with Jaworski. If only I'd had a little more time! The things I might have done!

And as I thought of some of those things, I became aware that Rita had quietly started to cry. I stared at her for a moment, trying to suppress the images of a flayed and bloodless janitor. For the life of me I could not understand why she was crying, but since I had practiced long and hard at imitating human beings, I knew that I was supposed to comfort her. I leaned toward her and put an arm across her shoulder. "Rita," I said. "There, there." Not really a line worthy of me, but it was well-thought-of by many experts. And it was effective. Rita lunged forward and leaned her face into my chest. I tightened my arm around her, which brought my hand back into view. Less than an hour ago that same hand had been holding a filet knife over the little janitor. The thought made me dizzy.

And really, I don't know how it happened, but it did. One moment I was patting her and saying, "There, there," and staring at the cords in my hand, feeling the sense memory pulse through the fingers, the surge of power and brightness as the knife explored Jaworski's abdomen. And the next moment—

I believe Rita looked up at me. I am also reasonably certain that I looked back. And yet somehow it was not Rita I saw but a neat stack of cool and bloodless limbs. And it was not Rita's hands I felt on my belt buckle, but the rising unsatisfied chorus from the Dark Passenger. And some little time later—

Well. It's still somewhat unthinkable. I mean, right there on the couch.

How on earth did *that* happen?

By the time I climbed into my little bed I was thoroughly whipped. I don't ordinarily require a great deal of sleep, but I felt as though tonight I might need a nice solid thirty-six hours. The ups and downs of the evening, the strain of so much new experience—it had all been draining. More draining for Jaworski, of course, the nasty wet little thing, but I had used all my adrenaline for the month in this one impetuous evening. I could not even begin to think what any of it meant, from the strange impulse to fly out into the night so madly and rashly, all the way through to the unthinkable things that had happened with Rita. I had left her asleep and apparently much happier. But poor dark deranged Dexter was without a clue once again, and when my head hit the pillow I fell asleep almost instantly.

And there I was out over the city like a boneless bird, flowing and swift and the cold air moved around me and drew me on, pulled me down to where the moonlight rippled on the water and I slash into the tight cold killing room where the little janitor looks up at me and laughs, spread-eagled under the knife and laughing, and the effort of it contorts his face, changes it, and now he is not Jaworski anymore but a woman and the man holding the knife looks up to where I float above the whirling red viscera and as the face comes up I can hear Harry outside the door and I turn just before I can see who it is on the table but—

I woke up. The pain in my head would split a cantaloupe. I felt like I had hardly closed my eyes, but the bedside clock said it was 5:14.

Another dream. Another long-distance call on my phantom party line. No wonder I had steadfastly refused to have dreams for most of my life. So stupid; such pointless, obvious symbols. Totally uncontrollable anxiety soup, hateful, blatant nonsense.

And now I couldn't get back to sleep, thinking of the infantile images. If I had to dream, why couldn't it be more like me, interesting and different?

I sat up and rubbed my throbbing temples. Terrible,

tedious unconsciousness dripped away like a draining
sinus and I sat on the edge of the bed in bleary befuddlement. What was happening to me? And why couldn't it
happen to someone else?

This dream had felt different and I wasn't sure what that
difference was or what it meant. The last time I had been
absolutely certain that another murder was about to happen, and even knew where. But this time—

I sighed and padded into the kitchen for a drink of water.
Barbie's head went *thack thack* as I opened the refrigerator. I
stood and watched, sipping a large glass of cold water. The
bright blue eyes stared back at me, unblinking.

Why had I had a dream? Was it just the strain of last
evening's adventures playing back from my battered subconscious? I had never felt strain before; actually, it had
always been a *release* of strain. Of course, I had never come
so close to disaster before, either. But why dream about it?
Some of the images were too painfully obvious: Jaworski
and Harry and the unseen face of the man with the knife.
Really now. Why bother me with stuff from freshman psy-
chology?

Why bother me with a dream at all? I didn't need it. I
needed rest—and instead, here I was in the kitchen playing
with a Barbie doll. I flipped the head again: *thack thack*. For
that matter, what was Barbie all about? And how was I
going to figure this out in time to rescue Deborah's career?
How could I get around LaGuerta when the poor thing was
so taken with me? And by all that was holy, if anything
actually was, why had Rita needed to do THAT to me?

It seemed suddenly like a twisted soap opera, and it was

far too much. I found some aspirin and leaned against the kitchen counter as I ate three of them. I didn't much care for the taste. I had never liked medicine of any kind, except in a utilitarian way.

Especially since Harry had died.

CHAPTER 16

HARRY DID NOT DIE QUICKLY AND HE DID NOT DIE easily. He took his own terrible long time, the first and last selfish thing he had ever done in his life. Harry died for a year and a half, in little stages, slipping for a few weeks, fighting back to almost full strength again, keeping us all dizzy with trying to guess. Would he go now, this time, or had he beaten it altogether? We never knew, but because it was Harry it seemed foolish for us to give up. Harry would do what was right, no matter how hard, but what did that mean in dying? Was it right to fight and hang on and make the rest of us suffer through an endless death, when death was coming no matter what Harry did? Or was it right to slip away gracefully and without fuss?

At nineteen, I certainly didn't know the answer, although I already knew more about death than most of the other pimple-ridden puddingheads in my sophomore class at the University of Miami.

And one fine autumn afternoon after a chemistry class, as I walked across the campus toward the student union, Deborah appeared beside me. "Deborah," I called to her, sounding very collegiate, I thought, "come have a Coke." Harry had told me to hang out at the union and have Cokes. He'd said it would help me pass for human, and learn how other humans behaved. And of course, he was right. In spite of the damage to my teeth, I was learning a great deal about the unpleasant species.

Deborah, at seventeen, already far too serious, shook her head. "It's Dad," she said. And very shortly we were driving across town to the hospice where they had taken Harry. Hospice was not good news. That meant the doctors were saying that Harry was ready to die, and suggesting that he cooperate.

Harry did not look good when we got there. He looked so green and still against the sheets that I thought we were too late. He was spindly and gaunt from his long fight, looking for all the world as though something inside him was eating its way out. The respirator beside him hissed, a Darth Vader sound from a living grave. Harry was alive, strictly speaking. "Dad," Deborah said, taking his hand. "I brought Dexter."

Harry opened his eyes and his head rolled toward us, almost as if some invisible hand had pushed it from the far side of the pillow. But they were not Harry's eyes. They were murky blue pits, dull and empty, uninhabited. Harry's body might be alive, but he was not home.

"It isn't good," the nurse told us. "We're just trying to make him comfortable now." And she busied herself with a large hypodermic needle from a tray, filling it and holding it up to squirt out the air bubble.

"Wait . . ." It was so faint I thought at first it might be the respirator. I looked around the room and my eyes finally fell on what was left of Harry. Behind the dull emptiness of his eyes a small spark was shining. "Wait . . . ," he said again, nodding toward the nurse.

She either didn't hear him or had decided to ignore him. She stepped to his side and gently lifted his stick arm. She began to swab it with a cotton ball.

"No . . . ," Harry gasped gently, almost inaudibly.

I looked at Deborah. She seemed to be standing at attention in a perfect posture of formal uncertainty. I looked back at Harry. His eyes locked onto mine.

"No . . . ," he said, and there was something very close to horror in his eyes now. "No . . . shot . . ."

I stepped forward and put a restraining hand on the nurse, just before she plunged the needle into Harry's vein. "Wait," I said. She looked up at me, and for the tiniest fraction of a second there was something in her eyes. I almost fell backward in surprise. It was a cold rage, an inhuman, lizard-brain sense of I-Want, a belief that the world was her very own game preserve. Just that one flash, but I was sure. She wanted to ram the needle into my eye for interrupting her. She wanted to shove it into my chest and twist until my ribs popped and my heart burst through into her hands and she could squeeze, twist, rip my life out of me. This was a monster, a hunter, a killer. This was a predator, a soulless and evil thing.

Just like me.

But her granola smile returned very quickly. "What is it, honey?" she said, ever so sweetly, so perfectly Last Nurse.

My tongue felt much too large for my mouth and it seemed like it took me several minutes to answer, but I finally managed to say, "He doesn't want the shot."

She smiled again, a beautiful thing that sat on her face like the blessing of an all-wise god. "Your dad is very sick," she said. "He's in a lot of pain." She held the needle up and a melodramatic shaft of light from the window hit it. The needle sparkled like her very own Holy Grail. "He needs a shot," she said.

"He doesn't want it," I said.

"He's in pain," she said.

Harry said something I could not hear. My eyes were locked on the nurse, and hers on mine, two monsters standing over the same meat. Without looking away from her I leaned down next to him.

"I—WANT . . . pain . . . ," Harry said.

It jerked my gaze down to him. Behind the emerging skeleton, nestled snugly under the crew cut that seemed suddenly too big for his head, Harry had returned and was fighting his way up through the fog. He nodded at me, reached very slowly for my hand and squeezed.

I looked back at Last Nurse. "He wants the pain," I told her, and somewhere in her small frown, the petulant shake of her head, I heard the roar of a savage beast watching its prey scuttle down a hole.

"I'll have to tell the doctor," she said.

"All right," I told her. "We'll wait here."

I watched her sail out into the hallway like some large

and deadly bird. I felt a pressure on my hand. Harry watched me watching Last Nurse.

"You . . . can tell . . . ," Harry said.

"About the nurse?" I asked him. He closed his eyes and nodded lightly, just once. "Yes," I said. "I can tell."

"Like . . . you . . . ," Harry said.

"What?" Deborah demanded. "What are you talking about? Daddy, are you all right? What does that mean, like you?"

"She likes me," I said. "He thinks the nurse may have a crush on me, Deb," I told her, and turned back to Harry.

"Oh, right," Deborah muttered, but I was already concentrating on Harry.

"What has she done?" I asked him.

He tried to shake his head and managed only a slight wobble. He winced. It was clear to me that the pain was coming back, just liked he'd wanted. "Too much," he said. "She . . . gives too much—" he gasped now, and closed his eyes.

I must have been rather stupid that day, because I didn't get what he meant right away. "Too much what?" I said.

Harry opened one pain-blearied eye. "Morphine," he whispered.

I felt like a great shaft of light had hit me. "Overdose," I said. "She kills by overdose. And in a place like this, where it's actually almost her job, nobody would question it— why, that's—"

Harry squeezed my hand again and I stopped babbling. "Don't let her," he said in a hoarse voice with surprising strength. "Don't let her—dope me again."

"Please," Deborah said in a voice that hung on the ragged edge, "what are you guys talking about?" I looked at Harry, but Harry closed his eyes as a sudden stab of pain tore at him.

"He thinks, um . . . ," I started and then trailed off. Deborah had no idea what I was, of course, and Harry had told me quite firmly to keep her in the dark. So how I could tell her about this without revealing anything was something of a problem. "He thinks the nurse is giving him too much morphine," I finally said. "On purpose."

"That's crazy," Deb said. "She's a nurse."

Harry looked at her but didn't say anything. And to be truthful, I couldn't think of anything to say to Deb's incredible naïveté either.

"What should I do?" I asked Harry.

Harry looked at me for a very long time. At first I thought his mind might have wandered away with the pain, but as I looked back at him I saw that Harry was very much present. His jaw was set so hard that I thought the bones might snap through his tender pale skin and his eyes were as clear and sharp as I had ever seen them, as much as when he had first given me his Harry solution to getting me squared away. "Stop her," he said at last.

A very large thrill ran through me. Stop her? Was it possible? Could he mean—*stop* her? Until now Harry had helped me control my Dark Passenger, feeding him stray pets, hunting deer; one glorious time I had gone with him to catch a feral monkey that had been terrorizing a South Miami neighborhood. It had been so close, so almost human—but still not right, of course. And we had gone through all the theoretical steps of stalking, disposing of evidence, and so on. Harry knew that someday It would happen and he wanted me to be ready to do It right. He had always held me back from actually Doing It. But now—stop her? Could he mean it?

"I'll go talk to the doctor," Deborah said. "He'll tell her to adjust your medicine."

I opened my mouth to speak, but Harry squeezed my hand and nodded once, painfully. "Go," he said, and Deborah looked at him for a moment before she turned away and went to find the doctor. When she was gone the room filled with a wild silence. I could think of nothing but what Harry had said: "Stop her." And I couldn't think of any other way to interpret it, except that he was finally turning me loose, giving me permission to do the Real Thing at last. But I didn't dare ask him if that's what he had said for fear he would tell me he meant something else. And so I just stood there for the longest time, staring out the small window into a garden outside, where a splatter of red flowers surrounded a fountain. Time passed. My mouth got dry. "Dexter—" Harry said at last.

I didn't answer. Nothing I could think of seemed adequate. "It's like this," Harry said, slowly and painfully, and my eyes jerked down to his. He gave me a strained half smile when he saw that I was with him at last. "I'll be gone soon," Harry said. "I can't stop you from . . . being who you are."

"Being *what* I am, Dad," I said.

He waved it away with a feeble, brittle hand. "Sooner or later . . . you will—*need*—to do it to a person," he said, and

I felt my blood sing at the thought. "Somebody who . . .
needs it . . ."

"Like the nurse," I said with a thick tongue.

"Yes," he says, closing his eyes for a long moment, and
when he went on his voice had grown hazy with the pain.
"She needs it, Dexter. That's—" He took a ragged breath.
I could hear his tongue clacking as if his mouth was over-
dry. "She's deliberately—overdosing patients . . . killing
them . . . killing them . . . on purpose . . . She's a killer, Dexter . . . A killer . . ."

I cleared my throat. I felt a little clumsy and light-
headed, but after all this was a very important moment in a
young man's life. "Do you want—" I said and stopped as
my voice broke. "Is it all right if I . . . stop her, Dad?"

"Yes," said Harry. "Stop her."

For some reason I felt like I had to be absolutely certain.
"You mean, you know. Like I've been doing? With, you
know, the monkey?"

Harry's eyes were closed and he was clearly floating
away on a rising tide of pain. He took a soft and uneven
breath. "Stop . . . the nurse," he said. "Like . . . the monkey . . . " His head arched back slightly, and he began to
breathe faster but still very roughly.

Well.

There it was.

"Stop the nurse like the monkey." It had a certain wild
ring to it. But in my madly buzzing brain, everything was
music. Harry was turning me loose. I had permission. We
had talked about one day doing this, but he had held me
back. Until now.

Now.

"We talked . . . about this," Harry said, eyes still closed. "You know what to do . . ."

"I talked to the doctor," Deborah said, hurrying into the room. "He'll come down and adjust the meds on the chart."

"Good," I said, feeling something rise up in me, from the base of my spine and out over the top of my head, an electric surge that jolted through me and covered me like a dark hood. "I'll go talk to the nurse."

Deborah looked startled, perhaps at my tone. "Dexter—" she said.

I paused, fighting to control the savage glee I felt towering up inside me. "I don't want any misunderstanding," I said. My voice sounded strange even to me. I pushed past Deborah before she could register my expression.

And in the hallway of that hospice, threading my way between stacks of clean, crisp, white linen, I felt the Dark Passenger become the new driver for the first time. Dexter became understated, almost invisible, the light-colored stripes on a sharp and transparent tiger. I blended in, almost impossible to see, but I was there and I was stalking, circling in the wind to find my prey. In that tremendous flash of freedom, on my way to do the Thing for the first time, sanctioned by almighty Harry, I receded, faded back into the scenery of my own dark self, while the other me crouched and growled. I would do It at last, do what I had been created to do.

And I did.

CHAPTER 17

AND I HAD. SO LONG AGO, YET THE MEMORY STILL pulsed in me. Of course, I still had that first dry drop of blood on its slide. It was my first, and I could call up that memory any time by taking out my little slide and looking at it. I did, every so often. It had been a very special day for Dexter. Last Nurse had been First Playmate, and she had opened up so many wonderful doors for me. I had learned so much, found out so many new things.

But why was I remembering Last Nurse now? Why did this whole series of events seem to be whipping me back through time? I could not afford a fond remembrance of my first pair of long pants. I needed to explode into action, make large decisions, and begin important deeds. Instead of strolling sappily down memory lane, wallowing in sweet memories of my first blood slide.

Which, now that I thought of it, I had not collected from Jaworski. It was the kind of tiny, absurdly unimportant detail that turned strong men of action into fidgeting, whimpering neurotics. I *needed* that slide. Jaworski's death was useless without it. The whole idiotic episode was now worse than a stupid and impulsive foolishness; it was incomplete. I had no slide.

I shook my head, trying spastically to rattle two gray cells into the same synapse. I half wanted to take my boat for an early-morning spin. Perhaps the salt air would clear the stupidity from my skull. Or I could head south to Turkey Point and hope that the radiation might mutate me back into a rational creature. But instead, I made coffee. No slide, indeed. It cheapened the whole experience. Without the slide, I might as well have stayed home. Or almost, at any rate. There had been other rewards. I smiled fondly, recalling the mix of moonlight and muffled screams. Oh, what a madcap little monster I had been. An episode unlike any of my others. It was good to break out of dull routine from time to time. And there was Rita, of course, but I had no idea what to think about that, so I didn't. Instead I thought of the cool breeze flowing across the squirming little man who had liked to hurt children. It had almost been a happy time. But of course, in ten years the memory would fade, and without that slide I could not bring it back. I needed my souvenir. Well, we would see.

While the coffee brewed, I checked for the newspaper, more out of hope than expectation. It was rare for the paper to arrive before six-thirty, and on Sundays it often came after eight. It was another clear example of the disintegration of society that had so worried Harry. Really, now: If you can't get me my newspaper on time, how can you expect me to refrain from killing people?

No paper; no matter. Press coverage of my adventures had never been terribly interesting to me. And Harry had warned me about the idiocy of keeping any kind of scrapbook. He didn't need to; I rarely even glanced at the reviews of my performances. This time was a little different, of course, since I had been so impetuous and was mildly worried that I had not covered my tracks properly. I was just a bit curious to see what might be said about my accidental party. So I sat with my coffee for about forty-five minutes until I heard the paper thump against the door. I brought it in and flipped it open.

Whatever else one can say about journalists—and there is a very great deal, almost an encyclopedia—they are very rarely troubled by memory. The same paper that had so recently trumpeted COPS CORRAL KILLER now screamed ICE MAN'S STORY MELTS! It was a long and lovely piece, very dramatically written, detailing the discovery of a badly abused body at a construction site just off Old Cutler Road. "A Metro Miami police spokesperson"—meaning Detective LaGuerta, I was sure—said that it was much too soon to say anything with certainty, but this was probably a copycat killing. The paper had drawn its own conclusions—another thing they are seldom shy about—and was now wondering aloud if the distinguished gentleman in captivity, Mr. Daryll Earl McHale, was actually, in fact, the killer. Or was the killer still at large, as evidenced by this latest outrage upon public morality? Because, the paper carefully pointed out, how could we believe that two such killers could possibly be on the loose at the same time? It was very neatly reasoned, and it occurred to me that if they had spent as much energy and mental power trying to solve the murders, the whole thing would be over by now.

But it was all very interesting reading, of course. And it certainly made me speculate. Good heavens, was it really possible that this mad animal was still running loose? Was anyone safe?

The telephone rang. I glanced at my wall clock; it was 6:45. It could only be Deborah.

"I'm reading it now," I said into the phone.

"You said bigger," Deborah told me. "Splashier."

"And this isn't?" I asked with great innocence.

"It's not even a hooker," she said. "Some part-time janitor from Ponce Junior High, chopped up at a construction site on Old Cutler. What the hell, Dexter?"

"You did know I'm not perfect, didn't you, Deborah?"

"It doesn't even fit the pattern—where's the cold you said would be there? What happened to the small space?"

"It's Miami, Deb, people will steal anything."

"It's not even a copycat," she said. "It isn't anything like the others. Even LaGuerta got that right. She's already said so in print. Damn it all, Dexter. My butt is way out in the wind here, and this is just some random slasher, or a drug thing."

"It hardly seems fair to blame me for all that."

"Goddamn it, Dex," she said, and hung up.

The early-morning TV shows spent a full ninety seconds on the shocking discovery of the shattered body. Channel 7 had the best adjectives. But nobody knew any more than the paper. They radiated outrage and a grim sense of disaster that even carried over into the weather forecast, but I'm sure a large part of it was caused by the lack of pictures.

Another beautiful Miami day. Mutilated corpses with a chance of afternoon showers. I got dressed and went to work.

I admit I had a minor ulterior motive in heading for the office so early, and I beefed it up by stopping for pastries. I bought two crullers, an apple fritter, and a cinnamon roll the size of my spare tire. I ate the fritter and one cruller as I cheerfully threaded through the lethal traffic. I don't know how I get away with eating so many doughnuts. I don't gain weight or get pimples, and although that may seem unfair, I can't find it in my heart to complain. I came out reasonably well in the genetic crapshoot: high metabolism, good size and strength, all of which helped me in my hobby. And I have been told that I am not awful to look at, which I believe is meant to be a compliment.

I also didn't need a great deal of sleep, which was nice this morning. I had hoped to arrive early enough to beat Vince Masuoka to work, and it seemed that I had. His office was dark when I got there, clutching my white paper bag for camouflage—but my visit had nothing whatever to do with doughnuts. I scanned his work area quickly, looking for the telltale evidence box labeled JAWORSKI and yesterday's date.

I found it and quickly lifted out a few tissue samples. There might be enough. I pulled on a pair of latex gloves and in a moment had pressed the samples to my clean glass slide. I do realize how stupid it was to take yet another risk, but I had to have my slide.

I had just tucked it away in a ziplock baggie when I heard him come in behind me. I quickly put things back in place and whirled to face the door, as Vince came through and saw me.

"My God," I said. "You move so silently. So you *have* had ninja training."

"I have two older brothers," Vince said. "It's the same thing."

I held up the white paper bag and bowed. "Master, I bring a gift."

He looked at the bag curiously. "May Buddha bless you, grasshopper. What is it?"

I tossed him the bag. It hit him in the chest and slid to the floor. "So much for ninja training," I said.

"My finely tuned body needs coffee to function," Vince told me, bending to retrieve the bag. "What's in here? That hurt." He reached into the bag, frowning. "It better not be body parts." He pulled out the huge cinnamon roll and eyed it. "Ay, caramba. My village will not starve this year. We are very grateful, grasshopper." He bowed, holding up the pastry. "A debt repaid is a blessing on us all, my child."

"In that case," I said, "do you have the case file on the one they found last night off Old Cutler?"

Vince took a big bite of cinnamon roll. His lips gleamed with frosting as he slowly chewed. "Mmmpp," he said, and swallowed. "Are we feeling left out?"

"If we means Deborah, yes we are," I said. "I told her I'd take a look at the file for her."

"Wulf," he said, mouth full of pastry, "merf pluddy uh bud is nime."

"Forgive me, master," I said. "Your language is strange to me."

He chewed and swallowed. "I said, at least there's plenty of blood this time. But you're still a wallflower. Bradley got the call for this one."

"Can I see the file?"

He took a bite. "Ee waf awife—"

"Very true, I'm sure. And in English?"

Vince swallowed. "I said, he was still alive when his leg came off."

"Human beings are so resilient, aren't they?"

Vince stuck the whole pastry in his mouth and picked up the file, holding it out to me and taking a large bite of the roll at the same time. I grabbed the folder.

"I've got to go," I said. "Before you try to talk again."

He pulled the roll from his mouth. "Too late," he said.

I walked slowly back to my little cubbyhole, glancing at the contents of the folder. Gervasio César Martez had discovered the body. His statement was on top of the folder. He was a security guard, employed by Sago Security Systems. He had worked for them for fourteen months and had no criminal record. Martez had found the body at approximately 10:17 PM and immediately made a quick search of the area before calling police. He wanted to catch the *pendejo* who had done this thing because no one should do such things and they had done it when he, Gervasio, was on the job. That was like they had done it to him, you know? So he would catch the monster himself. But this had not been possible. There was no sign of the perpetrator, not anywhere, and so he had called the police.

The poor man had taken it personally. I shared his outrage. Such brutality should not be allowed. Of course, I was also very grateful that his sense of honor had given me time to get away. And here I had always thought morality was useless.

I turned the corner into my dark little room and walked right into Detective LaGuerta. "Hah," she said. "You don't see so good." But she didn't move.

"I'm not a morning person," I told her. "My biorhythms are all off until noon."

She looked up at me from an inch away. "They look okay to me," she said.

I slid around her to my desk. "Can I make some small contribution to the full majesty of the law this morning?" I asked her.

She stared at me. "You have a message," she said. "On your machine."

I looked over at my answering machine. Sure enough, the light was blinking. The woman really was a detective.

"It's some girl," LaGuerta said. "She sounds kind of sleepy and happy. You got a girlfriend, Dexter?" There was a strange hint of challenge in her voice.

"You know how it is," I said. "Women today are so forward, and when you are as handsome as I am they absolutely fling themselves at your head." Perhaps an unfortunate choice of words; as I said it I couldn't help thinking of the woman's head flung at me not so long ago.

"Watch out," LaGuerta said. "Sooner or later one of them

will stick." I had no idea what she thought that meant, but it was a very unsettling image.

"I'm sure you're right," I said. "Until then, carpe diem."

"What?"

"It's Latin," I said. "It means, complain in daylight."

"What have you got about this thing last night?" she said suddenly.

I held up the case file. "I was just looking at it," I said.

"It's not the same," she said, frowning. "No matter what those asshole reporters say. McHale is guilty. He confessed. This one is not the same."

"I guess it seems like too much of a coincidence," I said. "Two brutal killers at the same time."

LaGuerta shrugged. "It's Miami, what do they think? Here is where these guys come on vacation. There's lots of bad guys out there. I can't catch them all."

To be truthful, she couldn't catch any of them unless they hurled themselves off a building and into the front seat of her car, but this didn't seem like a good time to bring that up. LaGuerta stepped closer to me and flicked the folder with a dark red fingernail. "I need you to find something here, Dexter. To show it's not the same."

A light dawned. She was getting unpleasant pressure, probably from Captain Matthews, a man who believed what he read in the papers as long as they spelled his name right. And she needed some ammunition to fight back. "Of course it's not the same," I said. "But why come to me?"

She stared at me for a moment through half-closed eyes, a curious effect. I think I had seen the same stare in some of the movies Rita had dragged me to see, but why on earth

Detective LaGuerta had turned the look on me I couldn't say. "I let you in the seventy-two-hour briefing," she said. "Even though Doakes wants you dead, I let you stay."

"Thank you very much."

"Because you have a feeling for these things sometimes. The serial ones. That's what they all say. Dexter has a feeling sometimes."

"Oh, really," I said, "just a lucky guess once or twice."

"And I need somebody in the lab who can find something."

"Then why not ask Vince?"

"He's not so cute," she said. "You find something."

She was still uncomfortably close, so close I could smell her shampoo. "I'll find something," I said.

She nodded at the answering machine. "You gonna call her back? You don't have time for chasing pussy."

She still hadn't backed up, and it took me a moment to realize she was talking about the message on my machine. I gave her my very best political smile. "I think it's chasing me, Detective."

"Hah. You got that right." She gave me a long look, then turned and walked away.

I don't know why, but I watched her go. I really couldn't think of anything else to do. Just before she passed out of sight around the corner, she smoothed her skirt across her hips and turned to look at me. Then she was gone, off into the vague mysteries of Homicidal Politics.

And me? Poor dear dazed Dexter? What else could I do? I sank into my office chair and pushed the play button on my answering machine. "Hi, Dexter. It's me." Of course it was. And as odd as it was, the slow, slightly raspy voice sounded like "me" was Rita. "Mm . . . I was thinking about last night. Call me, mister." As LaGuerta had observed, she sounded kind of tired and happy. Apparently I had a real girlfriend now.

Where would the madness end?

CHAPTER 18

FOR A FEW MOMENTS I JUST SAT AND THOUGHT about life's cruel ironies. After so many years of solitary self-reliance, I was suddenly pursued from all directions by hungry women. Deb, Rita, LaGuerta—they were all apparently unable to exist without me. Yet the one person I wanted to spend some quality time with was being coy, leaving Barbie dolls in my freezer. Was any of this fair?

I put my hand in my pocket and felt the small glass slide, snug and secure in its ziplock. For a moment it made me feel a little better. At least I was doing something. And life's only obligation, after all, was to be interesting, which it certainly was at the moment. "Interesting" did not begin to describe it. I would trade a year off my life to find out more about this elusive will-o'-the-wisp who was teasing me so mercilessly with such elegant work. In fact, I had come far too close to trading more than a year with my little Jaworski interlude.

Yes, things were certainly interesting. And were they

really saying in the department that I had a feeling for serial homicide? That was very troubling. It meant my careful disguise might be close to unraveling. I had been too good too many times. It could become a problem. But what could I do? Be stupid for a while? I wasn't sure I knew how, even after so many years of careful observation.

Ah, well. I opened the case file on Jaworski, the poor man. After an hour of study, I came to a couple of conclusions. First, and most important, I was going to get away with it, in spite of the unforgivable sloppy impulsiveness of the thing. And second—there might be a way for Deb to cash in on this. If she could prove this was the work of our original artist while LaGuerta committed herself to the copycat theory, Deb could suddenly turn from somebody they didn't trust to get their coffee into flavor of the month. Of course, it was not actually the work of the same guy, but that seemed like a very picky objection at this point. And since I knew without any possibility of doubt that there were going to be more bodies found very soon, it wasn't worth worrying about.

And naturally, at the same time, I had to provide the annoying Detective LaGuerta with enough rope to hang herself. Which might also, it occurred to me, come in handy on a more personal level. Pushed into a corner and made to look like an idiot, LaGuerta would naturally try to pin the blame on the nitwit lab tech who had given her the erroneous conclusion—dull dim Dexter. And my reputation would suffer a much-needed relapse into mediocrity. Of course, it would not jeopardize my job, since I was supposed to analyze blood spatter, not provide profiling services. That being the case, it would help to make LaGuerta look like the nitwit she was, and raise Deborah's stock even more.

Lovely when things work out so neatly. I called Deborah.

At half-past one the next day I met Deb at a small restaurant a few blocks north of the airport. It was tucked into a little strip mall, between an auto parts store and a gun shop. It was a place we both knew well, not too far from Miami-Dade Headquarters, and they made the best Cuban sandwiches in the world right there. Perhaps that seems like a small thing, but I assure you there are times when only a *medianoche* will do, and at such times Café Relampago was the only place to get one. The Morgans had been going there since 1974.

And I did feel that some small light touch was in order—if not an actual celebration, then at least an acknowledgment that things were looking up ever so slightly. Perhaps I was merely feeling chipper because I had let off a little steam with my dear friend Jaworski, but in any case I did feel unaccountably good. I even ordered a *batido de mamé*, a uniquely flavored Cuban milk shake that tastes something like a combination of watermelon, peach, and mango.

Deb, of course, was unable to share my irrational mood. She looked like she had been studying the facial expressions of large fish, dour and droopy in the extreme.

"Please, Deborah," I begged her, "if you don't stop, your face will be stuck like that. People will take you for a grouper."

"They're sure not going to take me for a cop," she said. "Because I won't be one anymore."

"Nonsense," I said. "Didn't I promise?"

"Yeah. You also promised that this was going to work. But you didn't say anything about the looks I'd get from Captain Matthews."

"Oh, Deb," I said. "He *looked* at you? I'm so sorry."

"Fuck you, Dexter. You weren't there, and it's not your life going down the tubes."

"I told you it was going to be rough for a while, Debs."

"Well at least you were right about that. According to Matthews, I am this close to being suspended."

"But he did give you permission to use your free time to look into this a little more?"

She snorted. "He said, 'I can't stop you, Morgan. But I am very disappointed. And I wonder what your father would have said.' "

"And did you say, 'My father never would have closed the case with the wrong guy in jail'?"

She looked surprised. "No," she said. "But I was thinking it. How did you know?"

"But you didn't actually *say* it, did you, Deborah?"

"No," she said.

I pushed her glass toward her. "Have some *mamé*, sis. Things are looking up."

She looked at me. "You sure you're not just yanking my chain?"

"Never, Deb. How could I?"

"With the greatest of ease."

"Really, sis. You need to trust me."

She held my eye for a moment and then looked down. She still hadn't touched her shake, which was a shame.

They were very good. "I trust you. But I swear to God I don't know why." She looked up at me, a strange expression flitting back and forth across her face. "And sometimes I really don't think I should, Dexter."

I gave her my very best reassuring big-brother smile. "Within the next two or three days something new will turn up. I promise."

"You can't know that," she said.

"I know I can't, Deb. But I do know. I really do."

"So why do you sound so happy about it?"

I wanted to say it was because the idea made me happy. Because the thought of seeing more of the bloodless wonder made me happier than anything else I could think of. But of course, that was not a sentiment Deb could really share with me, so I kept it to myself. "Naturally, I'm just happy for you."

She snorted. "That's right, I forgot," she said. But at least she took a sip of her shake.

"Listen," I said, "either LaGuerta is right—"

"Which means I'm dead and fucked."

"Or LaGuerta is *wrong*, and you are alive and virginal. With me so far, sis?"

"Mmm," she said, remarkably grumpy considering how patient I was being.

"If you were a betting gal, would you bet on LaGuerta being right? About anything?"

"Maybe about fashion," she said. "She dresses really nice."

The sandwiches came. The waiter dropped them sourly in the middle of the table without a word and whirled away behind the counter. Still, they were very good sandwiches. I don't know what made them better than all the other *medianoches* in town, but they were; bread crisp on the outside and soft on the inside, just the right balance of pork and pickle, cheese melted perfectly—pure bliss. I took a big bite. Deborah played with the straw in her shake.

I swallowed. "Debs, if my deadly logic can't cheer you up, and one of Relampago's sandwiches can't cheer you up, then it's too late. You're already dead."

She looked at me with her grouper face and took a bite of her sandwich. "It's very good," she said without expression. "See me cheer up?"

The poor thing was not convinced, which was a terrible blow to my ego. But after all, I had fed her on a traditional Morgan family delight. And I had brought her wonderful news, even if she didn't recognize it as such. If all this had not actually made her smile—well, really. I couldn't be expected to do everything.

One other small thing I could do, though, was to feed LaGuerta, too—something not quite as palatable as one of Relampago's sandwiches, though delicious in its own way. And so that afternoon I called on the good detective in her office, a lovely little cubby in the corner of a large room containing half a dozen other little cubbies. Hers, of course, was the most elegant, with several very tasteful photographs of herself with celebrities hanging from the fabric of the partitions. I recognized Gloria Estefan, Madonna, and Jorge Mas Canosa. On the desk, on the far side of a jade-green blotter with a leather frame, stood an elegant green onyx pen holder with a quartz clock in the center.

LaGuerta was on the telephone speaking rapid-fire Spanish when I came in. She glanced up at me without seeing me and looked away. But after a moment, her eyes came back to me. This time she looked me over thoroughly, frowned, and said, "Okay-okay. 'Ta luo," which was Cuban for *hasta luego.* She hung up and continued to look at me.

"What have you got for me?" she said finally.

"Glad tidings," I told her.

"If that means good news, I could use some."

I hooked a folding chair with my foot and dragged it into her cubby. "There is no possible doubt," I said, sitting in the folding chair, "that you have the right guy in jail. The murder on Old Cutler was committed by a different hand."

She just looked at me for a moment. I wondered if it took her that long to process the data and respond. "You can back that up?" she asked me at last. "For sure?"

Of course I could back it up for sure, but I wasn't going to, no matter how good confession might be for the soul. Instead, I dropped the folder onto her desk. "The facts speak for themselves," I said. "There's absolutely no question about it." And of course there wasn't any question at all, as only I knew very well. "Look—" I told her, and pulled out a page of carefully selected comparisons I had typed out. "First, this victim is male. All the others were female. This victim was found off Old Cutler. All of McHale's victims were off Tamiami Trail. This victim was found relatively intact, and in the spot where he was killed. McHale's victims were completely chopped up, and they were moved to a different location for disposal."

I went on, and she listened carefully. The list was a good

one. It had taken me several hours to come up with the most obvious, ludicrous, transparently foolish comparisons, and I must say I did a very good job. And LaGuerta did her part wonderfully, too. She bought the whole thing. Of course, she was hearing what she wanted to hear.

"To sum up," I said, "this new murder has the fingerprint of a revenge killing, probably drug related. The guy in jail did the other murders and they are absolutely, positively, 100 percent finished and over forever. Never happen again. Case closed." I dropped the folder on her desk and held out my list.

She took the paper from me and looked at it for a long moment. She frowned. Her eyes moved up and down the page a few times. One corner of her lower lip twitched. Then she placed it carefully on her desk under a heavy jade-green stapler.

"Okay," she said, straightening the stapler so it was perfectly aligned with the edge of her blotter. "Okay. Pretty good. This should help." She looked at me again with her frown of concentration still stitched in place, and then suddenly smiled. "Okay. Thank you, Dexter."

It was such an unexpected and genuine smile that if I only had a soul I'm sure I would have felt quite guilty.

She stood, still smiling, and before I could retreat she had flung her arms around my neck to give me a hug. "I really do appreciate it," she said. "You make me feel—VERY grateful." And she rubbed her body against mine in a way that could only be called suggestive. Surely there could be no question of— I mean, here she was, a defender of public morality, and yet right here in public—and even in the privacy of a bank vault I would have been truly uninterested in being rubbed by her body. Not to mention the fact that I had just handed her a rope with the hope that she would use it to hang herself, which hardly seemed like the sort of thing one would celebrate by— Well really, had the whole world gone mad? What is it with humans? Is this all any of them ever thinks about?

Feeling something very close to panic, I tried to disentangle myself. "Please, Detective—"

"Call me Migdia," she said, clinging and rubbing harder. She reached a hand down to the front of my pants and I jumped. On the plus side, my action dislodged the amorous detective. On the negative side, she spun sideways, hit the desk with her hip, and tripped over her chair, landing sprawled out on the floor.

"I, ah—I really have to get back to work," I stammered. "There's an important, ah—" However, I couldn't think of anything more important than running for my life, so I backed out of the cubicle, leaving her looking after me.

It didn't seem to be a particularly friendly look.

CHAPTER 19

I WOKE UP STANDING AT THE SINK WITH THE WATER running. I had a moment of total panic, a sense of complete disorientation, my heart racing while my crusty eyelids fluttered in an attempt to catch up. The place was wrong. The sink didn't look right. I wasn't even sure who I was—in my dream I had been standing in front of my sink with the water running, but it had not been this sink. I had been scrubbing my hands, working the soap hard, cleansing my skin of every microscopic fleck of horrible red blood, washing it away with water so hot it left my skin pink and new and antiseptic. And the hot of the water bit harder after the cool of the room I had just left behind me; the playroom, the killing room, the room of dry and careful cutting.

I turned off the water and stood for a moment, swaying against the cold sink. It had all been far too real, too little like any kind of dream I knew about. And I remembered so clearly the room. I could see it just by closing my eyes.

I am standing above the woman, watching her flex and bulge against the tape that holds her, seeing the living terror grow in her dull eyes, seeing it blossom into hopelessness, and I feel the great surge of wonder rise up in me and flow down my arm to the knife. And as I lift the knife to begin—

But this is not the beginning. Because under the table there is another one, already dry and neatly wrapped. And in the far corner there is one more, waiting her turn with a hopeless black dread unlike anything I have ever seen before even though it is somehow familiar and necessary, this release of all other possibility so complete it washes me with a clean and pure energy more intoxicating than—

Three.

There are three of them this time.

I opened my eyes. It was me in the mirror. Hello, Dexter. Had a dream, old chap? Interesting, wasn't it? Three of them, hey? But just a dream. Nothing more. I smiled at me, trying out the face muscles, completely unconvinced. And as rapturous as it had been, I was awake now and left with nothing more than a hangover and wet hands.

What should have been a pleasant interlude in my subconscious had me shaking, uncertain. I was filled with dread at the thought that my mind had skipped town and left me behind to pay the rent. I thought of the three carefully trussed playmates and wanted to go back to them and continue. I thought of Harry and knew I couldn't. I was whipsawed between a memory and a dream, and I couldn't tell which was more compelling.

This was just no fun anymore. I wanted my brain back.

I dried my hands and went to bed again, but there was

no sleep left in this night for dear decimated Dexter. I simply lay on my back and watched the dark pools flowing across the ceiling until the telephone rang at a quarter to six.

"You were right," Deb said when I picked up.

"It's a wonderful feeling," I said with a great effort at being my usual bright self. "Right about what?"

"All of it," Deb told me. "I'm at a crime scene on Tamiami Trail. And guess what?"

"I was right?"

"It's him, Dexter. It has to be. And it's a whole hell of a lot splashier, too."

"Splashier how, Deb?" I asked, thinking *three bodies*, hoping she wouldn't say it and thrilled by the certainty that she would.

"There appear to be multiple victims," she said.

A jolt went through me, from my stomach straight up, as if I had swallowed a live battery. But I made a huge effort to rally with something typically clever. "This is wonderful, Deb. You're talking just like a homicide report."

"Yeah, well. I'm starting to feel like I might write one someday. I'm just glad it won't be this one. It's too weird. LaGuerta doesn't know what to think."

"Or even how. What's weird about it, Deb?"

"I gotta go," she said abruptly. "Get out here, Dexter. You have to see this."

By the time I got there the crowd was three deep around the barrier, and most of them were reporters. It is always hard work to push through a crowd of reporters with the scent of blood in their nostrils. You might not think so, since on camera they appear to be brain-damaged wimps with severe eating disorders. But put them at a police barricade and a miraculous thing happens. They become strong, aggressive, willing and able to shove anything and anyone out of the way and trample them underfoot. It's a bit like the stories about aged mothers lifting trucks when their child is trapped underneath. The strength comes from some mysterious place—and somehow, when there is gore on the ground, these anorexic creatures can push their way through anything. Without mussing their hair, too.

Luckily for me, one of the uniforms at the barricade recognized me. "Let him through, folks," he told the reporters. "Let him through."

"Thanks, Julio," I told the cop. "Seems like more reporters every year."

He snorted. "Somebody must be cloning 'em. They all look the same to me."

I stepped under the yellow tape and as I straightened on the far side I had the odd sensation that someone was tampering with the oxygen content of Miami's atmosphere. I stood in the broken dirt of a construction site. They were building what would probably be a three-story office building, the kind inhabited by marginal developers. And as I stepped slowly forward, following the activity around the half-built structure, I knew it was not coincidence that we had all been brought here. Nothing was coincidence with this killer. Everything was deliberate, carefully measured for aesthetic impact, explored for artistic necessity.

We were at a construction site because it was necessary. He was making his statement as I had told Deborah he would. *You got the wrong guy,* he was saying. *You locked up a cretin because you are all cretins. You are too stupid to see it unless I rub your noses in it; so here goes.*

But more than that, more than his message to the police and the public, he was talking to me; taunting me, teasing me by quoting a passage from my own hurried work. He had brought the bodies to a construction site because I had taken Jaworski at a construction site. He was playing catch with me, showing all of us just how good he was and telling one of us—me—that he was watching. *I know what you did, and I can do it, too. Better.*

I suppose that should have worried me a little.

It didn't.

It made me feel almost giddy, like a high-school girl watching as the captain of the football team worked up his nerve to ask for a date. You mean me? Little old me? Oh my stars, really? Pardon me while I flutter my eyelashes.

I took a deep breath and tried to remind myself that I was a good girl and I didn't do those things. But I knew *he* did them, and I truly wanted to go out with him. Please, Harry?

Because far beyond simply doing some interesting things with a new friend, I needed to find this killer. I had to see him, talk to him, prove to myself that he was real and that—

That what?

That he wasn't me?

That I was not the one doing such terrible, interesting things?

Why would I think that? It was beyond stupid; it was

completely unworthy of the attention of my once-proud
brain. Except—now that the idea was actually rattling
around in there, I couldn't get the thought to sit down and
behave. What if it really was me? What if I had somehow
done these things without knowing it? Impossible, of
course, absolutely impossible, but—

I wake up at the sink, washing blood off my hands after
a "dream" in which I carefully and gleefully got blood all
over my hands doing things I ordinarily only dream about
doing. Somehow I know things about the whole string of
murders, things I couldn't possibly know unless—

Unless nothing. Take a tranquilizer, Dexter. Start again.
Breathe, you silly creature; in with the good air, out with the
bad. It was nothing but one more symptom of my recent
feeble-mindedness. I was merely going prematurely senile
from the strain of all my clean living. Granted I had experienced one or two moments of human stupidity in the last
few weeks. So what? It didn't necessarily prove that I was
human. Or that I had been creative in my sleep.

No, of course not. Quite right; it meant nothing of the
kind. So, um—what did it mean?

I had assumed I was simply going crazy, dropping several handfuls of marbles into the recycle bin. Very comforting—but if I was ready to assume that, why not admit that
it was possible I had committed a series of delightful little
pranks without remembering them, except as fragmented
dreams? Was insanity really easier to accept than unconsciousness? After all, it was just a heightened form of sleepwalking. "Sleep murder." Probably very common. Why
not? I already gave away the driver's seat of my conscious-

ness on a regular basis when the Dark Passenger went joyriding. It really wasn't such a great leap to accept that the same thing was happening here, now, in a slightly different form. The Dark Passenger was simply borrowing the car while I slept.

How else to explain it? That I was astrally projecting while I slept and just happened to tune my vibrations to the killer's aura because of our connection in a past life? Sure, that might make sense—if this was southern California. In Miami, it seemed a bit thin. And so if I went into this half building and happened to see three bodies arranged in a way that seemed to be speaking to me, I would have to consider the possibility that I had written the message. Didn't that make more sense than believing I was on some kind of subconscious party line?

I had come to the outside stairwell of the building. I stopped there for a moment and closed my eyes, leaning against the bare concrete block of the wall. It was slightly cooler than the air, and rough. I ground my cheek against it, somewhere between pleasure and pain. No matter how much I wanted to go upstairs and see what there was to see, I wanted just as much not to see it at all.

Talk to me, I whispered to the Dark Passenger. *Tell me what you have done.*

But of course there was no answer, beyond the usual cool, distant chuckle. And that was no actual help. I felt a little sick, slightly dizzy, uncertain, and I did not like this feeling of having feelings. I took three long breaths, straightened up and opened my eyes.

Sergeant Doakes stared at me from three feet away, just

inside the stairwell, one foot on the first step. His face was a dark carved mask of curious hostility, like a rottweiler that wants to rip your arms off but is mildly interested in knowing first what flavor you might be. And there was something in his expression that I had never seen on anybody's face before, except in the mirror. It was a deep and abiding emptiness that had seen through the comic-strip charade of human life and read the bottom line.

"Who are you talkin' to?" he asked me with his bright hungry teeth showing. "You got somebody else in there with you?"

His words and the knowing way he said them cut right through me and turned my insides to jelly. Why choose those words? What did he mean by "in there with me"? Could he possibly know about the Dark Passenger? Impossible! Unless . . .

Doakes knew me for what I was.

Just as I had known Last Nurse.

The Thing Inside calls out across the emptiness when it sees its own kind. Was Sergeant Doakes carrying a Dark Passenger, too? How could it be possible? A homicide sergeant, a Dexter-dark predator? Unthinkable. But how else to explain? I could think of nothing and for much too long I just stared at him. He stared back.

Finally he shook his head, without looking away from me. "One of these days," he said. "You and me."

"I'll take a rain check," I told him with all the good cheer I could muster. "In the meantime, if you'll excuse me . . . ?"

He stood there taking up the entire stairwell and just staring. But finally he nodded slightly and moved to one side. "One of these days," he said again as I pushed past him and onto the stairs.

The shock of this encounter had snapped me instantly out of my sniveling little self-involved funk. Of course I wasn't committing unconscious murders. Aside from the pure ridiculousness of the idea, it would be an unthinkable waste to do these things and not remember. There would be some other explanation, something simple and cold. Surely I was not the only one within the sound of my voice capable of this kind of creativity. After all, I was in Miami, surrounded by dangerous creatures like Sergeant Doakes.

I went quickly up the stairs, feeling the adrenaline rushing through me, almost myself again. There was a healthy spring in my step that was only partly because I was escaping the good sergeant. Even more, I was eager to see this most recent assault on the public welfare—natural curiosity, nothing more. I certainly wasn't going to find any of my own fingerprints.

I climbed the stairs to the second floor. Some of the framing had been knocked into place, but most of the floor was still without walls. As I stepped off the landing and onto the main area of the floor, I saw Angel-no-relation squatting in the center of the floor, unmoving. His elbows were planted on his knees, his hands cupped his face, and he was just staring. I stopped and looked at him, startled. It was one of the most remarkable things I had ever seen, a Miami homicide technician swatted into immobility by what he had found at a crime scene.

And what he had found was even more interesting.

It was a scene out of some dark melodrama, a vaudeville

for vampires. Just as there had been at the site where I had taken Jaworski, there was a stack of shrink-wrapped dry-wall. It had been pushed over against a wall and was now flooded with light from the construction lights and a few more the investigating team had set up.

On top of the drywall, raised up like an altar, was a black portable workbench. It had been neatly centered so the light hit it just right—or rather, so the light illuminated just right the thing that sat on top of the workbench.

It was, of course, a woman's head. Its mouth held the rearview mirror from some car or truck, which stretched the face into an almost comical look of surprise.

Above it and to the left was a second head. The body of a Barbie doll had been placed under its chin so it looked like a huge head with a tiny body.

On the right side was the third head. It had been neatly mounted on a piece of drywall, the ears carefully tacked on with what must be drywall screws. There was no mess of blood puddling around the exhibit. All three heads were bloodless.

A mirror, a Barbie, and drywall.

Three kills.

Bone dry.

Hello, Dexter.

There was absolutely no question about it. The Barbie body was clearly a reference to the one in my freezer. The mirror was from the head left on the causeway, and the drywall referred to Jaworski. Either someone was so far inside my head they might as well be me, or they actually were me.

I took a slow and very ragged breath. I'm quite sure my emotions were not the same as his, but I wanted to squat down in the middle of the floor beside Angel-no-relation. I needed a moment to remember how to think, and the floor seemed a great place to start. Instead, I found myself moving slowly toward the altar, pulled forward as if I was on well-oiled rails. I could not make myself stop or slow down or do anything but move closer. I could only look, marvel, and concentrate on getting the breath to come in and go out in the right place. And all around me I slowly became aware that I was not the only one who couldn't quite believe what he was seeing.

In the course of my job—to say nothing of my hobby—I had been on the scene of hundreds of murders, many of them so gruesome and savage that they shocked even me. And at each and every one of those murders the Miami-Dade team had set up and gone on with their job in a relaxed and professional manner. At each and every one of them someone had been slurping coffee, someone had sent out for *pasteles* or doughnuts, someone was joking or gossiping as she sponged up the gore. At each and every crime scene I had seen a group of people who were so completely unimpressed with the carnage that they might as well have been bowling with the church league.

Until now.

This time the large, bare concrete room was unnaturally quiet. The officers and technicians stood in silent groups of two and three, as if afraid to be alone, and simply looked at

what had been displayed at the far end of the room. If anybody accidentally made a small sound, everyone jumped
and glared at the noisemaker. The whole scene was so positively comically strange that I certainly would have
laughed out loud if I hadn't been just as busy staring as all
the other geeks.

Had I done this?

It was beautiful—in a terrible sort of way, of course. But
still, the arrangement was perfect, compelling, beautifully
bloodless. It showed great wit and a wonderful sense of
composition. Somebody had gone to a lot of trouble to
make this into a real work of art. Somebody with style, tal-
ent, and a morbid sense of playfulness. In my whole life I
had only known of one such somebody.

Could that somebody possibly be darkly dreaming Dexter?

CHAPTER 20

I STOOD AS CLOSE AS I COULD GET TO THE TABLEAU without actually touching it, just looking. The little altar had not been dusted for prints yet; nothing had been done to it at all, although I assumed pictures had been taken. And oh how I wanted a copy of one of those pictures to take home. Poster sized, and in full, bloodless color. If I *had* done this, I was a much better artist than I had ever suspected. Even from this close the heads seemed to float in space, suspended above the mortal earth in a timeless, bloodless parody of paradise, literally cut off from their bodies—

Their bodies: I glanced around. There was no sign of them, no telltale stack of carefully wrapped packages. There was only the pyramid of heads.

I stared some more. After a few moments Vince Masuoka swam slowly over, his mouth open, his face pale. "Dexter," he said, and shook his head.

"Hello, Vince," I said. He shook his head again. "Where are the bodies?"

He just stared at the heads for a long moment. Then he looked at me with a face full of lost innocence. "Somewhere else," he said.

There was a clatter on the stairs and the spell was broken. I moved away from the tableau as LaGuerta came in with a few carefully selected reporters—Nick Something and Rick Sangre from local TV, and Eric the Viking, a strange and respected columnist from the newspaper. For a moment the room was very busy. Nick and Eric took one look and ran back down the stairs with their hands covering their mouths. Rick Sangre frowned deeply, looked at the lights, and then turned to LaGuerta.

"Is there a power outlet? I gotta get my camera guy," he said.

LaGuerta shook her head. "Wait for those other guys," she said.

"I need pictures," Rick Sangre insisted.

Sergeant Doakes appeared behind Sangre. The reporter looked around and saw him. "No pictures," Doakes said. Sangre opened his mouth, looked at Doakes for a moment, and then closed his mouth again. Once again the sterling qualities of the good sergeant had saved the day. He went back and stood protectively by the displayed body parts, as if it was a science-fair project and he was its guardian.

There was a strained coughing sound at the door, and Nick Something and Eric the Viking returned, shuffling slowly up the stairs and back onto the floor like old men. Eric wouldn't look at the far end of the room. Nick tried not to look, but his head kept drifting around toward the awful sight, and then he would snap it back to face LaGuerta again.

LaGuerta began to speak. I moved close enough to hear. "I asked you three to come see this thing before we allow any official press coverage," she said.

"But we can cover it unofficially?" Rick Sangre interrupted.

LaGuerta ignored him. "We don't want any wild speculation in the press about what has happened here," she said. "As you can see, this is a vicious and bizarre crime—" she paused for a moment and then said very carefully, "Unlike Anything We Have Ever Seen Before." You could actually hear her capitalize the letters.

Nick Something said, "Huh," and looked thoughtful. Eric the Viking got it immediately. "Whoa, wait a minute," he said. "You're saying this is a brand-new killer? A whole different set of murders?"

LaGuerta looked at him with great significance. "Of course it's too soon to say anything for sure," she said, sounding sure, "but let's look at this thing logically, okay? First," she held up a finger, "we got a guy who confessed the other stuff. He's in jail, and we didn't let him out to do this. Second, this doesn't look like anything I ever saw, does it? 'Cause there's three and they're stacked up all pretty, okay?" Bless her heart, she had noticed.

"Why can't I get my camera guy?" Rick Sangre asked.

"Wasn't there a mirror found at one of the other murders?" Eric the Viking said weakly, trying very hard not to look.

"Have you identified the, uh—" Nick Something said. His head started to turn toward the display and he caught himself, snapped back around to LaGuerta. "Are the victims prostitutes, Detective?"

"Listen," LaGuerta said. She sounded a little annoyed, and a small trace of Cuban accent showed in her voice for just a second. "Let me *esplain* something. I don't care if they're prostitutes. I don't care if they got a mirror. I don't care about any of that." She took a breath and went on, much calmer. "We got the other killer locked up in the jail. We've got a confession. This is a whole new thing, okay? That's the important thing. You can see it—this is different."

"Then why are you assigned to it?" asked Eric the Viking, very reasonably, I thought.

LaGuerta showed shark teeth. "I solved the other one," she said.

"But you're sure this is a brand-new killer, Detective?" Rick Sangre asked.

"There's no question. I can't tell you any details, but I got lab work to back me up." I was sure she meant me. I felt a small thrill of pride.

"But this is kind of close, isn't it? Same area, same general technique—" Eric the Viking started. LaGuerta cut him off.

"Totally different," she said. "Totally different."

"So you're completely satisfied that McHale committed all those other murders and this one is different," Nick Something said.

"One hundred percent," LaGuerta said. "Besides, I never said McHale did the others."

For a second, the reporters all forgot the horror of not having pictures. "What?" Nick Something finally said.

LaGuerta blushed, but insisted, "I never said McHale did it. McHale said he did it, okay? So what am I supposed to do? Tell him go away, I don't believe you?"

Eric the Viking and Nick Something exchanged a meaningful glance. I would have, too, if only there had been someone for me to look at. So instead I peeked at the central head on the altar. It didn't actually wink at me, but I'm sure it was just as amazed as I was.

"That's nuts," Eric muttered, but he was overrun by Rick Sangre.

"Are you willing to let us interview McHale?" Sangre demanded. "With a camera present?"

We were saved from LaGuerta's answer by the arrival of Captain Matthews. He clattered up the stairs and stopped dead as he saw our little art exhibit. "Jesus Christ," he said. Then his gaze swung to the group of reporters around LaGuerta. "What the hell are you guys doing up here?" he asked.

LaGuerta looked around the room, but nobody volunteered anything. "I let them in," she said finally. "Unofficially. Off the record."

"You didn't say off the record," Rick Sangre blurted out. "You just said unofficially."

LaGuerta glared at him. "Unofficially *means* off the record."

"Get out," Matthews barked. "Officially and on the record. Out."

Eric the Viking cleared his throat. "Captain, do you agree with Detective LaGuerta that this is a brand-new string of murders, a different killer?"

"Out," Matthews repeated. "I'll answer questions downstairs."

"I need footage," Rick Sangre said. "It will only take a minute."

Matthews nodded toward the exit. "Sergeant Doakes?"

Doakes materialized and took Rick Sangre's elbow. "Gentlemen," he said in his soft and scary voice. The three reporters looked at him. I saw Nick Something swallow hard. Then they all three turned without a sound and trooped out.

Matthews watched them go. When they were safely out of earshot he turned on LaGuerta. "Detective," he said in a voice so venomous he must have learned it from Doakes, "if you ever pull this kind of shit again you'll be lucky to get a job doing parking lot security at Wal-Mart."

LaGuerta turned pale green and then bright red. "Captain, I just wanted—" she said. But Matthews had already turned away. He straightened his tie, combed his hair back with one hand, and chased down the stairs after the reporters.

I turned to look at the altar again. It hadn't changed, but they were starting to dust for prints now. Then they would take it apart to analyze the pieces. Soon it would all be just a beautiful memory.

I trundled off down the stairs to find Deborah.

Outside, Rick Sangre already had a camera rolling. Captain Matthews stood in the wash of lights with microphones thrusting at his chin, giving his official statement. ". . . always the policy of this department to leave the investigating officer autonomy on a case, until such time as it becomes evident that a series of major errors in judgment call the officer's competence into question. That time has not yet arrived, but I am monitoring the situation closely. With so much at stake for the community—"

I spotted Deborah and moved past them. She stood at the barrier of yellow tape, dressed in her blue patrol uniform. "Nice suit," I told her.

"I like it," she said. "You saw?"

"I saw," I told her. "I also saw Captain Matthews discussing the case with Detective LaGuerta."

Deborah sucked in her breath. "What did they say?"

I patted her arm. "I think I once heard Dad use a very colorful expression that would cover it. He was 'reaming her a new asshole.' Do you know that one?"

She looked startled, then pleased. "That's great. Now I really need your help, Dex."

"As opposed to what I've been doing, of course?"

"I don't know what you think you've been doing, but it isn't enough."

"So unfair, Deb. And so very unkind. After all, you are actually at a crime site, and wearing your uniform, too. Would you prefer the sex suit?"

She shuddered. "That's not the point. You've been holding back something about this all along and I want it now."

For a moment I had nothing to say, always an uncomfortable feeling. I'd had no idea she was this perceptive. "Why, Deborah—"

"Listen, you think I don't know how this political stuff works, and maybe I'm not as smart about it as you are, but I know they're all going to be busy covering their own asses for a while. Which means nobody is going to be doing any real police work."

"Which means you see a chance to do some of your own? Bravo, Debs."

"And it also means I need your help like never before." She put a hand out and squeezed mine. "Please, Dexy?"

I don't know what shocked me more—her insight, her hand-squeezing, or her use of the nickname "Dexy." I hadn't heard her say that since I was ten years old. Whether she intended it or not, when she called me Dexy she put us both firmly back in Harry Land, a place where family mattered and obligations were as real as headless hookers. What could I say?

"Of course, Deborah," I said. Dexy indeed. It was almost enough to make me feel emotion.

"Good," she said, and she was all business again, a wonderfully quick change that I had to admire. "What's the one thing that really sticks out right now?" she asked with a nod toward the second floor.

"The body parts," I said. "As far as you know, is anybody looking for them?"

Deborah gave me one of her new Worldly Cop looks, the sour one. "As far as I know, there are more officers assigned to keeping the TV cameras out than to doing any actual work on this thing."

"Good," I said. "If we can find the body parts, we might get a small jump on things."

"Okay. Where do we look?"

It was a fair question, which naturally put me at a disadvantage. I had no idea where to look. Would the limbs be left in the killing room? I didn't think so—it seemed messy to me, and if he wanted to use that same room again, it would be impossible with that kind of nasty clutter lying around.

All right, then I would assume that the rest of the meat had gone somewhere else. But where?

Or perhaps, it slowly dawned on me, the real question should be: Why? The display of the heads was for a reason. What would be the reason for putting the rest of the bodies somewhere else? Simple concealment? No—nothing was simple with this man, and concealment was evidently not a virtue he prized too highly. Especially right now, when he was showing off a bit. That being the case, where would he leave a stack of leftovers?

"Well?" Deborah demanded. "How about it? Where should we look?"

I shook my head. "I don't know," I said slowly. "Wherever he left the stuff, it's part of his statement. And we're not really sure what his statement is yet, are we?"

"Goddamn it, Dexter—"

"I know he wants to rub our noses in it. He needs to say that we did something incredibly dumb, and even if we hadn't he's still smarter than we are."

"So far he's right," she said, putting on her grouper face.

"So . . . wherever he dumped the stuff, it has to continue

that statement. That we're stupid— No, I'm wrong. That
we DID something stupid."

"Right. Very important difference."

"Please, Deb, you'll hurt your face like that. It is important, because he's going to comment on the ACT, and not on
the ACTORS."

"Uh-huh. That's really good, Dex. So we should probably head for the nearest dinner theater and look around for
an actor with blood up to his elbows, right?"

I shook my head. "No blood, Deb. None at all. That's one
of the most important things."

"How can you be so sure?"

"Because there's been no blood at any of the scenes.
That's deliberate, and it's vital to what he's doing. And this
time, he'll repeat the important parts, but comment on
what he's already done, because we've missed it, don't you
see?"

"Sure, I see. Makes perfect sense. So why don't we go
check Office Depot Center? He's probably got the bodies
stacked up in the net again."

I opened my mouth to make some wonderfully clever
reply. The hockey rink was all wrong, completely and obviously wrong. It had been an experiment, something different, but I knew he wouldn't repeat it. I started to explain
this to Deb, that the only reason he would ever repeat the
rink would be— I stopped dead, my mouth hanging open.
Of course, I thought. *Naturally*.

"Now who's making a fish face, huh? What is it, Dex?"

For a moment I didn't say anything. I was far too busy
trying to catch my whirling thoughts. *The only reason he*

would repeat the hockey rink was to show us we had the wrong guy locked up.

"Oh, Deb," I said at last. "Of course. You're right, the arena. You are right for all the wrong reasons, but still—"

"Beats the hell out of being wrong," she said, and headed for her car.

CHAPTER 21

"**Y**OU DO UNDERSTAND IT'S A LONG SHOT?" I SAID. "Probably we won't find anything at all."

"I know that," Deb said.

"And we don't actually have any jurisdiction here. We're in Broward. And the Broward guys don't like us, so—"

"For Christ's sake, Dexter," she snapped. "You're chattering like a schoolgirl."

Perhaps that was true, although it was very unkind of her to say so. And Deborah, on the other hand, appeared to be a bundle of steely, tightly wrapped nerves. As we turned off the Sawgrass Expressway and drove into the parking lot of the Office Depot Center she bit down harder. I could almost hear her jaw creak. "Dirty Harriet," I said to myself, but apparently Deb was eavesdropping.

"Fuck off," she said.

I looked from Deborah's granite profile to the arena. For one brief moment, with the early-morning sunlight hitting it just right, it looked like the building was surrounded by a fleet of flying saucers. Of course it was only the outdoor lighting fixtures that sprouted around the arena like over-sized steel toadstools. Someone must have told the architect they were distinctive. "Youthful and vigorous," too, most likely. And I'm sure they were, in the right light. I did hope they would find the right light sometime soon.

We drove one time around the arena, looking for signs of life. On the second circuit, a battered Toyota pulled up beside one of the doors. The passenger door was held closed with a loop of rope that ran out the window and around the doorpost. Opening the driver's door as she parked, Deborah was already stepping out of the car while it was still rolling.

"Excuse me, sir?" she said to the man getting out of the Toyota. He was fifty, a squat guy in ratty green pants and a blue nylon jacket. He glanced at Deb in her uniform and was instantly nervous.

"Wha'?" he said. "I din't do nothin'."

"Do you work here, sir?"

"Shoor. 'Course, why you think I'm here, eight o'clock in the morning?"

"What's your name, please sir?"

He fumbled for his wallet. "Steban Rodriguez. I got a ID."

Deborah waved that off. "That's not necessary," she said. "What are you doing here at this hour, sir?"

He shrugged and pushed his wallet back into the pocket. "I s'posed to be here earlier most days, but the team is on the road—Vancouver, Ottawa, and L.A. So I get here a little later."

"Is anyone else here right now, Steban?"

"Naw, jus' me. They all sleep late."

"What about at night? Is there a guard?"

He waved an arm around. "The security goes around the parking lot at night, but not too much. I the first one here mos' days."

"The first one to go inside, you mean?"

"Yeah, tha's right, what I say?"

I climbed out of the car and leaned across the roof. "Are you the guy who drives the Zamboni for the morning skate?" I asked him. Deb glanced at me, annoyed. Steban peered at me, taking in my natty Hawaiian shirt and gabardine slacks. "Wha' kinda cop you are, ha?"

"I'm a nerd cop," I said. "I just work in the lab."

"Ooohhh, shoor," he said, nodding his head as if that made sense.

"Do you run the Zamboni, Steban?" I repeated.

"Yeah, you know. They don' lemme drive her in the games, you know. Tha's for the guys with suits. They like to put a kid, you know. Some celebrity maybe. Ride around and wave, that shit. But I get to do it for the morning skate, you know. When the team is in town. I run the Zamboni just the morning, real early. But they on the road now so I come later."

"We'd like to take a look inside the arena," Deb said, clearly impatient with me for speaking out of turn. Steban turned back to her, a crafty gleam lighting up half of one eye.

"Shoor," he said. "You got a warrant?"

Deborah blushed. It made a wonderful contrast to the

blue of her uniform, but it was possibly not the most effective choice for reinforcing her authority. And because I knew her well, I knew she would realize she had blushed and get mad. Since we did not have a warrant and did not, in fact, have any business here whatsoever that could remotely be considered officially sanctioned, I did not think that getting mad was our best tactical maneuver.

"Steban," I said before Deb could say anything regrettable.

"Hah?"

"How long have you worked here?"

He shrugged. "Since the place open. I work at the old arena two year before that."

"So you were working here last week when they found the dead body on the ice?"

Steban looked away. Under his tan, his face turned green. He swallowed hard. "I never want to see something like that again, man," he said. "Never."

I nodded with genuine synthetic sympathy. "I really don't blame you," I said. "And that's why we're here, Steban."

He frowned. "Wha' you mean?"

I glanced at Deb to make sure she wasn't drawing a weapon or anything. She glared at me with tight-lipped disapproval and tapped her foot, but she didn't say anything.

"Steban," I said, moving a little closer to the man and making my voice as confidential and manly as I could, "we think there's a chance that when you open those doors this morning, you might find the same kind of thing waiting for you."

"Shit!" he exploded. "I don' want nothin' to do with that."

"Of course you don't."

"*Me cago en diez* with that shit," he said.

"Exactly," I agreed. "So why not let us take a peek first? Just to be sure."

He gaped at me for a moment, then at Deborah, who was still scowling—a very striking look for her, nicely set off by her uniform.

"I could get in trouble," he said. "Lose my job."

I smiled with authentic-looking sympathy. "Or you could go inside and find a stack of chopped-up arms and legs all by yourself. A lot more of them this time."

"Shit," he said again. "I get in trouble, lose my job, huh? Why I should do that, huh?"

"How about civic duty?"

"Come on, man," he said. "Don't fuck with me. What do you care about if I lose my job?"

He did not actually hold out his hand, which I thought was very genteel, but it was clear that he hoped for a small present to insulate him against the possible loss of his job. Very reasonable, considering that this was Miami. But all I had was $5, and I really needed to get a cruller and a cup of coffee. So I just nodded with manly understanding.

"You're right," I said. "We hoped you wouldn't have to see all the body parts—did I say there were quite a few this time? But I certainly don't want you to lose your job. Sorry to bother you, Steban. Have a nice day!" I smiled at Deborah. "Let's go, Officer. We should get back to the other scene and search for the fingers."

Deborah was still scowling, but at least she had the native wit to play along. She opened her car door as I cheerfully waved to Steban and climbed in.

"Wait!" Steban called. I glanced at him with an expression of polite interest. "I swear to God, I don' wanna find that shit ever again," he said. He looked at me for a moment, perhaps hoping I would loosen up and hand him a fistful of Krugerands, but as I said, that cruller was weighing heavily on my mind and I did not relent. Steban licked his lips, then turned away quickly and jammed a key into the lock of the large double door. "Go 'head. I wait out here."

"If you're sure—" I said.

"Come on, man, what you want from me? Go 'head!"

I stood up and smiled at Deborah. "He's sure," I said. She just shook her head at me, a strange combination of little-sister exasperation and cop sour humor. She walked around the car and led the way in through the door and I followed.

Inside, the arena was cool and dark, which shouldn't have surprised me. It was, after all, a hockey rink early in the morning. No doubt Steban knew where the light switch was, but he had not offered to tell us. Deb unsnapped the large flashlight from her belt and swung the beam around the ice. I held my breath as the light picked out one goalie's net, then the other. She swept back around the perimeter one time, slowly, pausing once or twice, then back to me.

"Nothing," she said. "Jack shit."

"You sound disappointed."

She snorted at me and headed back out. I stayed in the

middle of the rink, feeling the cool radiate up off the ice, and thinking my happy thoughts. Or, more precisely, not quite *my* happy thoughts.

Because as Deb turned to go out I heard a small voice from somewhere over my shoulder; a cool and dry chuckle, a familiar feather touch just under the threshold of hearing. And as dear Deborah departed, I stood motionless there on the ice, closed my eyes and listened to what my ancient friend had to say. It was not much—just a sub-whisper, a hint of unvocal, but I listened. I heard him chuckle and mutter soft and terrible things in one ear, while the other ear let me know that Deborah had told Steban to come in and turn on the lights. Which moments later he did, as the small off-voice whisper rose in a sudden crescendo of rattling jolly humor and good-natured horror.

What is it? I asked politely. My only answer was a surge of hungry amusement. I had no idea what it meant. But I was not greatly surprised when the screaming started.

Steban was really terrible at screaming. It was a hoarse, strangled grunting that sounded more like he was being violently sick than anything else. The man brought no sense of music to the job.

I opened my eyes. It was impossible to concentrate under these circumstances, and anyway there was nothing more to hear. The whispering had stopped when the screaming began. After all, the screams said it all, didn't they? And so I opened my eyes just in time to see Steban catapult out of the little closet at the far end of the arena and vault onto the rink. He went clattering across the ice, slipping and sliding and moaning hoarsely in Spanish and finally hurling headlong into the boards. He scrabbled up and skittered toward the door, grunting with horror. A small splotch of blood smeared the ice where he had fallen.

Deborah came quickly through the door, her gun drawn, and Steban clawed past her, stumbling out into the light of day. "What is it?" Deborah said, holding her weapon ready.

I tilted my head, hearing one last echo of the final dry chuckle, and now, with the grunting horror still ringing in my ears, I understood.

"I believe Steban has found something," I said.

CHAPTER 22

POLICE POLITICS, AS I HAD TRIED SO HARD TO impress on Deborah, was a slippery and many-tentacled thing. And when you brought together two law enforcement organizations that really didn't care for each other, mutual operations tended to go very slowly, very much by the book, and with a good deal of foot-dragging, excuse-making, and veiled insults and threats. All great fun to watch, of course, but it did draw out the proceedings just a trifle more than necessary. Consequently it was several hours after Steban's dreadful yodeling exhibition before the jurisdictional squabbling was straightened out and our team actually began to examine the happy little surprise our new friend Steban had discovered when he opened the closet door.

During that time Deborah stood off to one side for the most part, working very hard at controlling her impatience but not terribly hard at hiding it. Captain Matthews arrived with Detective LaGuerta in tow. They shook hands with their Broward County counterparts, Captain Moon and Detective McClellan. There was a lot of barely polite sparring, which boiled down to this: Matthews was reasonably certain that the discovery of six arms and six legs in Broward was part of his department's investigation of three heads lacking the same pieces in Miami-Dade. He stated, in terms that were far too friendly and simple, that it seemed a bit farfetched to think that he would find three heads without bodies, and then three totally different bodies without heads would turn up here.

Moon and McClellan, with equal logic, pointed out that people found heads in Miami all the time, but in Broward it was a little more unusual, and so maybe they took it a bit more seriously, and anyway there was no way to know for sure they were connected until some preliminary work had been done, which clearly ought to be done by them, since it was in their jurisdiction. Of course they would cheerfully pass on the results.

And of course that was unacceptable to Matthews. He explained carefully that the Broward people didn't know what to look for and might miss something or destroy a piece of key evidence. Not, of course, through incompetence or stupidity; Matthews was quite sure the Broward people were perfectly competent, considering.

This was naturally not taken in a cheerful spirit of cooperation by Moon, who observed with a little bit of feeling that this seemed to imply that his department was full of second-rate morons. By this point Captain Matthews was mad enough to reply much too politely, oh, no, not second-rate at all. I'm sure it would have ended in a fistfight if the gentleman from the Florida Department of Law Enforcement had not arrived to referee.

The FDLE is a sort of state-level FBI. They have jurisdiction anywhere in the state at any time, and unlike the feds they are respected by most of the local cops. The officer in question was a man of average height and build with a shaved head and a close-cropped beard. He didn't really seem out of the ordinary to me, but when he stepped between the two much larger police captains they instantly shut up and took a step back. In short order he had things settled down and organized and we got quickly back to being the neat and well-ordered scene of a multiple homicide.

The man from FDLE had ruled that it was Miami-Dade's investigation unless and until tissue samples proved the body parts here and the heads down there were unrelated. In practical and immediate terms, this meant that Captain Matthews got to have his picture taken first by the mob of reporters already clustering outside.

Angel-no-relation arrived and went to work. I was not at all sure what to make of it, and I don't mean the jurisdictional squabbling. No, I was far more concerned with the event itself, which had left me with a great deal to think about—not merely the fact of the killings and the redistribution of the meat, which was piquant enough. But I had of course managed to sneak a peak into Steban's little closet of horrors earlier, before the troops arrived—can you blame me, really? I had only wanted to sample the carnage and try to understand why my dear unknown business associate had chosen to stack the leftovers there; truly, just a quick look-see.

So immediately after Steban had skidded out the door squealing and grunting like a pig choking on a grapefruit, I had skipped eagerly back to the closet to see what had set him off.

The parts were not wrapped carefully this time. Instead, they were laid out on the floor in four groups. And as I looked closer I realized a wonderful thing.

One leg had been laid straight along the left-hand side of the closet. It was a pale, bloodless blue-white, and around the ankle there was even a small gold chain with a heart-shaped trinket. Very cute, really, unspoiled by awful bloodstains; truly elegant work. Two dark arms, equally well cut, had been bent at the elbow and placed alongside the leg, with the elbow pointing away. Right next to this the remaining limbs, all bent at the joint, had been arranged in two large circles.

It took me a moment. I blinked, and suddenly it swam into focus and I had to frown very hard to keep myself from giggling out loud like the schoolgirl Deb had accused me of being.

Because he had arranged the arms and legs in letters, and the letters spelled out a single small word: BOO.

The three torsos were carefully arranged below the BOO in a quarter-circle, making a cute little Halloween smile.

What a scamp.

But even as I admired the playful spirit this prank exposed, I wondered why he had chosen to put the display here, in a closet, instead of out on the ice where it could gain the recognition of a wider audience. It was a very spacious closet, granted, but still close quarters, just enough room for the display. So why?

And as I wondered, the outer door of the arena swung open with a clatter—the first of the arriving rescue team, no doubt. And the door crashing wide sent, a moment later, a draft of cool air over the ice and onto my back—

The cold air went over my spine and was answered by a flow of warmth moving upward along the same pathway. It ran light-fingered up into the unlit bottom of my consciousness and something changed somewhere deep in the moonless night of my lizard brain and I felt the Dark Passenger agree violently with something that I did not even hear or understand except that it had to do somehow with the primal urgency of cool air and the walls closing in and an attacking sense of—

Rightness. No question about it. Something here was just plain right and made my obscure hitchhiker pleased and excited and satisfied in a way I did not begin to understand. And floating in above all that was the strange notion that this was very familiar. None of it made any sense to me, but there it was. And before I could explore these strange revelations any further I was being urged by a squat young man in a blue uniform to step away and keep my hands in plain sight. No doubt he was the first of the arriving troops, and he was holding his weapon on me in a very convincing way. Since he had only one dark eyebrow running all the way across his face and no apparent forehead, I decided it would be a very good idea to go along with his wishes. He looked to be just the sort of dull-witted brute who might shoot an innocent person—or even me. I stepped away from the closet.

Unfortunately, my retreat revealed the little diorama in the closet, and the young man was suddenly very busy finding someplace to put his breakfast. He made it to a large trash can about ten feet away before commencing his ugly blargging sounds. I stood quite still and waited for him to finish. Nasty habit, hurling half-digested food around like that. So unsanitary. And this was a guardian of public safety, too.

More uniforms trotted in, and soon my simian friend had several buddies sharing the trash can with him. The noise was extremely unpleasant, to say nothing of the smell now wafting my way. But I waited politely for them to finish, since one of the fascinating things about a handgun is that it can be fired almost as well by someone who is throwing up. But one of the uniforms eventually straightened up, wiped his face on his sleeve, and began to question me. I was soon sorted out and pushed over to one side with instructions not to go anywhere or touch anything.

Captain Matthews and Detective LaGuerta had arrived soon after, and when they finally took over the scene I relaxed a bit. But now that I could actually go somewhere and touch something, I simply sat and thought. And the things I thought about were surprisingly troublesome.

Why had the display in the closet seemed familiar?

Unless I was going to return to my idiocy of earlier in the day and persuade myself that I had done this, I was at a loss as to why it should seem so delightfully unsurprising. Of course I hadn't done it. I was already ashamed of the stupidity of that notion. Boo, indeed. It was not even worth taking the time to scoff at the idea. Ridiculous.

So, um—why did it seem familiar?

I sighed and experienced one more new feeling, befuddlement. I simply had no notion of what was going on, except that somehow I was a part of it. This did not seem a terribly helpful revelation, since it matched exactly all my other closely reasoned analytical conclusions so far. If I ruled out the absurd idea that I had done this without knowing it—and I did—then each subsequent explanation became even more unlikely. And so Dexter's summary of the case reads as follows: he is involved somehow, but doesn't even know what that means. I could feel the little wheels in my once-proud brain leaping off their tracks and clattering to the floor. Clang-clang. Whee. Dexter derailed.

Luckily, I was saved from complete collapse by the appearance of dear Deborah. "Come on," she said brusquely, "we're going upstairs."

"May I ask why?"

"We're going to talk to the office staff," she said. "See if they know anything."

"They must know something if they have an office," I offered.

She looked at me for a moment, then turned away. "Come on," she said.

It may have been the commanding tone in her voice, but I went. We walked to the far side of the arena from where I had been sitting and into the lobby. A Broward cop stood beside the elevator there, and just outside the long row of glass doors I could see several more of them standing at a barrier. Deb marched up to the cop at the elevator and said, "I'm Morgan." He nodded and pushed the up button. He looked at me with a lack of expression that said a great deal. "I'm Morgan, too," I told him. He just looked at me, then turned his head away to stare out the glass doors.

There was a muted chime and the elevator arrived. Deborah stalked in and slammed her hand against the button hard enough to make the cop look up at her and the door slid shut.

"Why so glum, sis?" I asked her. "Isn't this what you wanted to do?"

"It's make-work, and everybody knows it," she snarled.

"But it's detective-type make-work," I pointed out.

"That bitch LaGuerta stuck her oar in," she hissed. "As soon as I'm done spinning my wheels here, I have to go back out on hooker duty."

"Oh, dear. In your little sex suit?"

"In my little sex suit," she said, and before I could really formulate any magical words of consolation we arrived at the office level and the elevator doors slid open. Deb stalked out and I followed. We soon found the staff lounge, where the office workers had been herded to wait until the full majesty of the law had the time to get around to them. Another Broward cop stood at the door of the lounge, presumably to make certain that none of the staff made a break for the Canadian border. Deborah nodded to the cop at the door and went into the lounge. I trailed behind her without much enthusiasm and let my mind wander over my problem. A moment later I was startled out of my reverie when

Deborah jerked her head at me and led a surly, greasy-faced young man with long and awful hair toward the door. I followed again.

She was naturally separating him from the others for questioning, very good police procedure, but to be perfectly honest it did not light a fire in my heart. I knew without knowing why that none of these people had anything meaningful to contribute. Judging from this first specimen, it was probably safe to apply that generalization to his life as well as to this murder. This was just dull routine makework that had been doled out to Deb because the captain thought she had done something good, but she was still a pest. So he had sent her away with a piece of real detective drudgery to keep her busy and out of sight. And I had been dragged with her because Deb wanted me along. Possibly she wanted to see if my fantastic ESP powers could help determine what these office sheep had eaten for breakfast. One look at this young gentleman's complexion and I was fairly sure he had eaten cold pizza, potato chips, and a liter of Pepsi. It had ruined his complexion and given him an air of vacuous hostility.

Still, I followed along as Mr. Grumpy directed Deborah to a conference room at the back of the building. There was a long oak table with ten black high-backed chairs in the center of the room, and a desk in the corner with a computer and some audio-visual equipment. As Deb and her pimply young friend sat and began trading frowns, I wandered over to the desk. A small bookshelf sat under the window beside the desk. I looked out the window. Almost directly below me I could see the growing crowd of reporters and squad cars that now surrounded the door where we had gone in with Steban.

I looked at the bookshelf, thinking I would clear a small space and lean there, tastefully away from the conversation. There was a stack of manila folders and perched on top of it was a small gray object. It was squarish and looked to be plastic. A black wire ran from the thing over to the back of the computer. I picked it up to move it.

"Hey!" the surly geek said. "Don't mess with the webcam!"

I looked at Deb. She looked at me and I swear I saw her nostrils flair like a racehorse at the starting gate. "The what?" she said quietly.

"I had it focused down on the entrance," he said. "Now I gotta refocus it. Man, why do you have to mess with my stuff?"

"He said webcam," I said to Deborah.

"A camera," she said to me.

"Yes."

She turned to young Prince Charming. "Is it on?"

He gaped at her, still concentrating on maintaining his righteous frown. "What?"

"The camera," Deborah said. "Does it work?"

He snorted, and then wiped his nose with a finger. "What do you think, I would get all worked up if it didn't? Two hundred bucks. It totally works."

I looked out the window where the camera had been pointing as he droned on in his surly grumble. "I got a Web site and everything. Kathouse.com. People can watch the team when they get here and when they leave."

Deborah drifted over and stood beside me, looking out the window. "It was pointed at the door," I said.

"Duh," our happy pal said. "How else are people on my Web site gonna see the team?"

Deborah turned and looked at him. After about five seconds he blushed and dropped his eyes to the table. "Was the camera turned on last night?" she said.

He didn't look up, just mumbled, "Sure. I mean, I guess so."

Deborah turned to me. Her computer knowledge was confined to knowing enough to fill out standardized traffic reports. She knew I was a little more savvy.

"How do you have it set up?" I asked the top of the young man's head. "Do the images automatically archive?"

This time he looked up. I had used archive as a verb, so I must be okay. "Yeah," he said. "It refreshes every fifteen seconds and just dumps to the hard drive. I usually erase in the morning."

Deborah actually clutched my arm hard enough to break the skin. "Did you erase this morning?" she asked him.

He glanced away again. "No," he said. "You guys came stomping in and yelling and stuff. I didn't even get to check my e-mail."

Deborah looked at me. "Bingo," I said.

"Come here," she said to our unhappy camper.

"Huh?" he said.

"Come here," she repeated, and he stood up slowly, mouth hanging open, and rubbed his knuckles.

"What," he said.

"Could you please come over here, sir?" Deborah ordered with truly veteran-cop technique, and he stuttered into motion and came over. "Can we see the pictures from last night, please?"

He gaped at the computer, then at her. "Why?" he said. Ah, the mysteries of human intelligence.

"Because," Deborah said, very slowly and carefully. "I think you might have taken a picture of the killer."

He stared at her and blinked, then blushed. "No way," he said.

"Way," I told him.

He stared at me, and then at Deb, his jaw hanging open. "Awesome," he breathed. "No shit? I mean— No, really? I mean—" He blushed even harder.

"Can we look at the pictures?" Deb said. He stood still for a second, then plunged into the chair at the desk and touched the mouse. Immediately the screen came to life, and he began typing and mouse-clicking furiously. "What time should I start?"

"What time did everybody leave?" Deborah asked him.

He shrugged. "We were empty last night. Everybody gone by, what—eight o'clock?"

"Start at midnight," I said, and he nodded.

" 'Kay," he said. He worked quietly for a moment, then, "Come on," he mumbled. "It's only like a six hundred megaherz," he said. "They won't update. They keep saying it's fine, but sooooo freaking slow, and it won't— Okay," he said, breaking off suddenly.

A dark image appeared on the monitor: the empty parking lot below us. "Midnight," he said, and stared at the screen. After fifteen seconds, the picture changed to the same picture.

"Do we have to watch five hours of this?" Deborah asked.

"Scroll through," I said. "Look for headlights or something moving."

"Riiiiiight," he said. He did some rapid point-and-click, and the pictures began to flip past at one per second. They didn't change much at first; the same dark parking lot, one bright light out at the edge of the picture. After about fifty frames had clicked past, an image jumped into view. "A truck!" Deborah said.

Our pet nerd shook his head. "Security," he said, and in the next frame the security car was visible.

He kept scrolling, and the pictures rolled by, eternal and unchanging. Every thirty or forty frames we would see the security truck pass, and then nothing. After several minutes of this, the pattern stopped, and there was a long stretch of nothing. "Busted," my greasy new friend said.

Deborah gave him a hard look. "The camera is broken?"

He looked up at her, blushed again, and looked away. "The security dudes," he explained. "They totally suck. Every night at, like, three? They park over at the other side and go to sleep." He nodded at the unchanging pictures scrolling past. "See? Hello! Mr. Security Dude? Hard at work?" He made a wet sound deep in his nose that I had to assume was meant to be laughter. "Not very!" He repeated the snorting sound and started the pictures scrolling again.

And then suddenly— "Wait!" I called out.

On-screen, a van popped into view at the door below us. There was another pop as the image changed, and a man stood beside the truck. "Can you make it go closer?" Deborah asked.

"Zoom in," I said before he could do more than frown a little. He moved the cursor, highlighted the dark figure on the screen, and clicked the mouse. The picture jumped to a closer look.

"You're not gonna get much more resolution," he said. "The pixels—"

"Shut up," said Deborah. She was staring at the screen hard enough to melt it, and as I stared too I could see why.

It was dark, and the man was still too far away to be certain, but from the few details I could make out, there was something oddly familiar about him; the way he stood frozen in the image on the computer, his weight balanced on both feet, and the overall impression of the profile. Somehow, as vague as it was, it added up to something. And as a very loud wave of sibilant chuckling erupted from deep in the backseat of my brain, it fell on me with the impact of a concert grand piano that, actually, he looked an awful lot like—

"Dexter . . . ?" Deborah said, in a sort of hushed and strangled croak.

Yes indeed.

Just like Dexter.

CHAPTER 23

I AM PRETTY SURE THAT DEBORAH TOOK YOUNG MR. Bad Hair Day back to the lounge, because when I looked up again, she was standing in front of me, alone. In spite of her blue uniform she did not look at all like a cop right now. She looked worried, like she couldn't decide whether to yell or to cry, like a mommy whose special little boy had let her down in a big way.

"Well?" she demanded, and I had to agree that she had a point.

"Not terribly," I said. "You?"

She kicked a chair. It fell over. "Goddamn it, Dexter, don't give me that clever shit! Tell me something. Tell me that wasn't you!" I didn't say anything. "Well then, tell me it *is* you! Just tell me SOMETHING! Anything at all!"

I shook my head. "I—" There was really nothing to say, so I just shook my head again. "I'm pretty sure it isn't me," I said. "I mean, I don't think so." Even to me that sounded like I had both feet firmly planted in the land of lame answers.

"What does that mean, 'pretty sure'?" Deb demanded. "Does that mean you're not sure? That it might be you in that picture?"

"Well," I said, a truly brilliant riposte, considering. "Maybe. I don't know."

"And does 'I don't know' mean you don't know whether you're going to tell me, or does it mean that you really don't know if that's you in the picture?"

"I'm pretty sure it isn't me, Deborah," I repeated. "But I really don't know for sure. It looks like me, doesn't it?"

"Shit," she said, and kicked the chair where it lay. It slammed into the table. "How can you not know, goddamn it?!"

"It *is* a little tough to explain."

"Try!"

I opened my mouth, but for once in my life nothing came out. As if everything else wasn't bad enough, I seemed to be all out of clever, too. "I just—I've been having these . . . dreams, but—Deb, I really don't know," I said, and I may have actually mumbled it.

"Shit shit SHIT!" said Deborah. Kick kick kick.

And it was very hard to disagree with her analysis of the situation.

All my stupid, self-mutilating musings swam back at me with a bright and mocking edge. *Of course it wasn't me—how could it be me? Wouldn't I know it if it was me?* Apparently not, dear boy. Apparently you didn't actually know anything at all. Because our deep dark dim little brains tell us all kinds of things that swim in and out of reality, but pictures do not lie.

Deb unleashed a new volley of savage attacks on the chair, and then straightened up. Her face was flushed very red and her eyes looked more like Harry's eyes than they ever had before. "All right," she said. "It's like this," and she blinked and paused for a moment as it occurred to both of us that she had just said a Harry thing.

And for a second Harry was there in the room between me and Deborah, the two of us so very different, and yet still both Harry's kids, the two strange fists of his unique legacy. Some of the steel went out of Deb's back and she looked human, a thing I hadn't seen for a while. She stared at me for a long moment, and then turned away. "You're my brother, Dex," she said. I was very sure that was not what she had originally intended to say.

"No one will blame you," I told her.

"Goddamn you, you're my *brother*!" she snarled, and the ferocity of it took me completely by surprise. "I don't know what went on with you and Dad. The stuff you two never talked about. But I know what he would have done."

"Turned me in," I said, and Deborah nodded. Something glittered in the corner of her eye. "You're all the family I have, Dex."

"Not such a great bargain for you, is it?"

She turned to me, and I could see tears in both eyes now. For a long moment she just looked at me. I watched the tear run from her left eye and roll down her cheek. She wiped it, straightened up, and took a deep breath, turning away to the window once again.

"That's right," she said. "He would've turned you in. Which is what I am going to do." She looked away from me, out the window, far out to the horizon.

"I have to finish these interviews," she said. "I'm leaving you in charge of determining if this evidence is relevant. Take it to your computer at home and figure out whatever you have to figure out. And when I am done here, before I go back out on duty, I am coming to get it, to hear what you have to say." She glanced at her watch. "Eight o'clock. And if I have to take you in then, I will." She looked back at me for a very long moment. "Goddamn it, Dexter," she said softly, and she left the room.

I moved over to the window and had a look for myself. Below me the circus of cops and reporters and gawking geeks was swirling, unchanged. Far away, beyond the parking lot, I could see the expressway, filled with cars and trucks blasting along at the Miami speed limit of ninety-five miles per hour. And beyond that in the dim distance was the high-rise skyline of Miami.

And here in the foreground stood dim dazed Dexter, staring out the window at a city that did not speak and would not have told him anything even if it did.

Goddamn it, Dexter.

I don't know how long I stared out the window, but it eventually occurred to me that there were no answers out there. There might be some, though, on Captain Pimple's computer. I turned to the desk. The machine had a CD-RW drive. In the top drawer I found a box of recordable CDs. I put one into the drive, copied the entire file of pictures, and took the CD out. I held it, glanced at it; it didn't have much to say, and I probably imagined the faint chuckling I thought I heard from the dark voice in the backseat. But just to be safe, I wiped the file from the hard drive.

On my way out, the Broward cops on duty didn't stop me, or even speak, but it did seem to me that they looked at me with a very hard and suspicious indifference.

I wondered if this was what it felt like to have a conscience. I supposed I would never really know—unlike poor Deborah, being torn apart by far too many loyalties that could not possibly live together in the same brain. I admired her solution, leaving me in charge of determining if the evidence was relevant. Very neat. It had a very Harry feel to it, like leaving a loaded gun on the table in front of a guilty friend and walking away, knowing that guilt would pull the trigger and save the city the cost of a trial. In Harry's world, a man's conscience couldn't live with that kind of shame.

But as Harry had known very well, his world was long dead—and I did not have any conscience, shame, or guilt. All I had was a CD with a few pictures on it. And of course, those pictures made even less sense than a conscience.

There had to be some explanation that did not involve Dexter driving a truck around Miami in his sleep. Of course, most of the drivers on the road seemed to manage it, but they were at least partially awake when they started out, weren't they? And here I was, all bright-eyed and cheerfully alert and not at all the kind of guy who would ever prowl the city and kill unconsciously; no, I was the kind of guy who wanted to be awake for every moment of it. And to get right down to the bottom line, there was the night on the causeway. It was physically impossible that I could have thrown the head at my own car, wasn't it?

Unless I had made myself believe that I could be in two places at once, which made a great deal of sense—considering that the only alternative I could come up with was believing that I only *thought* I had been sitting there in my car watching someone else throw the head, when in fact I had actually thrown the head at my own car and then—

No. Ridiculous. I could not ask the last few shreds of my brain to believe in this kind of fairy tale. There would be some very simple, logical explanation, and I would find it, and even though I sounded like a man trying to convince himself that there was nothing under the bed, I said it out loud.

"There is a simple, logical explanation," I said to myself. And because you never know who else is listening, I added, "And there is nothing under the bed."

But once again, the only reply was a very meaningful silence from the Dark Passenger.

In spite of the usual cheerful bloodlust of the other drivers, I found no answers on the drive home. Or to be perfectly truthful, I found no answers that made sense. There were plenty of stupid answers. But they all revolved around the same central premise, which was that all was not well inside the skull of our favorite monster, and I found this very hard to accept. Perhaps it was only that I did not feel any crazier than I had ever felt. I did not notice any missing gray tissue, I did not seem to be thinking any slower or more strangely, and so far I'd had no conversations with invisible buddies that I was aware of.

Except in my sleep, of course—and did that really count? Weren't we all crazy in our sleep? What was sleep, after all, but the process by which we dumped our insanity into a dark subconscious pit and came out on the other side ready to eat cereal instead of the neighbor's children?

And aside from the dreams I'd had, everything made sense: someone else had thrown the head at me on the causeway, left a Barbie in my apartment, and arranged the bodies in intriguing ways. Someone else, not me. Someone other than dear dark Dexter. And that someone else was finally captured, right here, in the pictures on this CD. And I would look at the pictures and prove once and for all that—

That it looked very much like the killer might be me?

Good, Dexter. Very good. I told you there was a logical explanation. Someone else who was actually me. Of course. That made wonderful sense, didn't it?

I got home and peeked into my apartment carefully. There did not appear to be anyone waiting for me. There was no reason why there should have been, of course. But knowing that this archfiend who was terrorizing the metropolis knew where I lived was a little unsettling. He had proven he was the kind of monster who might do any-thing—he could even come in and leave more doll parts at any time. Especially if he was me.

Which of course he was not. Certainly not. The pictures would show some small something to prove that the resemblance was only coincidental—and the fact that I was so strangely attuned to the murders was also coincidental, no doubt. Yes, this was clearly a series of perfectly logical monstrous coincidences. Perhaps I should call the Guinness Book people. I wondered what the world record was for not being sure whether you committed a string of murders?

I put on a Philip Glass CD and sat in my chair. The music stirred the emptiness inside me and after a few minutes something like my usual calm and icy logic returned. I went to my computer and turned it on. I put the CD into the drive and looked at the pictures. I zoomed in and out and did everything I knew how to do in an attempt to clean up the images. I tried things I had only heard about and things that I made up on the spot, and nothing worked. At the end I was no further along than I had been when I started. It was just not possible to get enough resolution to make the face of the man in the picture come clear. Still I stared at the pictures. I moved them around to different angles. I printed them out and held them up to the light. I did everything a normal person would do, and while I was pleased with my imitation, I did not discover anything except that the man in the picture looked like me.

I just could not get a clear impression of anything, even his clothing. He wore a shirt that could have been white, or tan, or yellow, or even light blue. The parking lot light that shone on him was one of the bright Argon anticrime lights and it cast a pinkish-orange glow; between that and the lack of resolution in the picture it was impossible to tell any more. His pants were long, loosely cut, light-colored. Altogether a standard outfit that anyone might have worn—

including me. I had clothing just like it several times over, enough to outfit an entire platoon of Dexter lookalikes.

I did manage to zoom in on the side of the truck enough to make out the letter "A" and, below it, a "B," followed by an "R" and either a "C" or an "O." But the truck was angled away from the camera and that was all I could see.

None of the other pictures offered me any hints. I watched the sequence again: the man vanished, reappeared, and then the van was gone. No good angles, no fortuitous accidental glimpses of his license plate—and no reason to say with any authority that either it was or was not deftly dreaming Dexter.

When I finally looked up from the computer night had come and it was dark outside. And I did what a normal person almost certainly would have done several hours ago: I quit. There was nothing else I could do except wait for Deborah. I would have to let my poor tormented sister haul me away to jail. After all, one way or another I was guilty. I really should be locked up. Perhaps I could even share a cell with McHale. He could teach me the rat dance.

And with that thought I did a truly wonderful thing.

I fell asleep.

CHAPTER 24

I HAD NO DREAMS, NO SENSE OF TRAVELING OUTSIDE my body; I saw no parade of ghostly images or headless, bloodless bodies. No visions of sugarplums danced in my head. There was nothing there, not even me, nothing but a dark and timeless sleep. And yet when the telephone woke me up I knew that the call was about Deborah, and I knew that she was not coming. My hand was already sweating as I grabbed up the receiver. "Yes," I said.

"This is Captain Matthews," the voice said. "I need to speak to Detective Morgan, please."

"She isn't here," I said, a small part of me sinking from the thought and what it meant.

"Hmmp. Aahh, well, that's not— When did she leave?"

I glanced at the clock instinctively; it was a quarter after nine and I fell deeper into the sweats. "She was never here," I told the captain.

"But she's signed out to your place. She's on duty—she's supposed to be there."

"She never got here."

"Well goddamn it," he said. "She said you have some evidence we need."

"I do," I said. And I hung up the telephone.

I did have some evidence, I was terribly sure of that. I just didn't quite know what it was. But I had to figure it out, and I did not think I had a great deal of time. Or to be more accurate, I did not think Deb had a great deal of time.

And again, I was not aware of how I knew this. I did not consciously say to myself, "He has Deborah." No alarming pictures of her impending fate popped into my brain. And I did not have to experience any blinding insights or think, "Gee, Deb should have been here by now; this is unlike her." I simply knew, as I had known when I woke up, that Deb had come for me, and she had not made it. And I knew what that meant.

He had her.

He had taken her entirely for my benefit, this I knew. He had been circling closer and closer to me—coming into my apartment, writing small messages with his victims, teasing me with hints and glimpses of what he was doing. And now he was as close as he could get without being in the same room. He had taken Deb and he was waiting with her. Waiting for me.

But where? And how long would he wait before he became impatient and started to play without me?

And without me, I knew very well who his playmate would be—Deborah. She had turned up at my place dressed for work in her hooker outfit, absolutely gift-wrapped for him. He must have thought it was Christmas.

He had her and she would be his special friend tonight. I did not want to think of her like that, taped and stretched tight and watching slow awful pieces of herself disappear forever. But that was how it would be. Under other circumstances, it might make a wonderful evening's entertainment—but not with Deborah. I was pretty sure I didn't want that, didn't want him to do anything permanent and wonderful, not tonight. Later, perhaps, with someone else. When we knew each other a little better. But not now. Not with Deborah.

And with that thought of course everything seemed better. It was just so nice to have that settled. I preferred my sister alive, rather than in small bloodless sections. Lovely, almost human of me. Now that was settled: What next? I could call Rita, perhaps take in a movie, or a walk in the park. Or, let's see—maybe, I don't know . . . save Deborah? Yes, that sounded like fun. But—

How?

I had a few clues, of course. I knew the way he thought—after all, I had been thinking that way myself. And he wanted me to find him. He had been sending that message loud and clear. If I could put all the distracting stupidity out of my head—all the dreams and New Age fairy-chasing and everything else—then I was certain that I could arrive at the logical and correct location. He would not have taken Deb unless he thought he had given me everything a clever monster would need to know in order to find him.

All right then, clever Dexter—find him. Track down the Deb-napper. Let your relentless logic slash across the back trail like an icy wolf pack. Kick the giant brain into high gear; let the wind race across the rocketing synapses of your powerful mind as it speeds to its beautiful, inevitable conclusion. Go, Dexter, go!

Dexter?

Hello? Is anybody in there?

Apparently not. I heard no wind from rocketing synapses. I was as empty as if I had never been. There was no swirl of debilitating emotions, of course, since I didn't have any emotions to swirl. But the result was just as daunting. I was as numb and drained as if I really could feel something. Deborah was gone. She was in terrible danger of becoming a fascinating work of performance art. And her only hope of maintaining any kind of existence beyond a series of still pictures tacked up on a police lab board was her battered, brain-dead brother. Poor dog-dumb Dexter, sitting in a chair with his brain running in circles, chasing its tail, howling at the moon.

I took a deep breath. Of all the times I had ever needed to be me, this was one of the foremost. I concentrated very hard and steadied me, and as a small amount of Dexter returned to fill the echo in my brain cavity, I realized just how human and stupid I had become. There was really no great mystery here. In fact, it was patently obvious. My friend had done everything but send a formal invitation reading, "The honor of your presence is requested at the vivisection of your sister. Black heart optional." But even this small blob of logic was wiped out of my throbbing skull by a new thought that wormed its way in, oozing rotten logic.

I had been asleep when Deb disappeared.

Could that mean that once again I had done it without knowing it? What if I had already taken Deb apart some-where, stacked the pieces in some small, cold storage room and—

Storage room? Where had that come from?

The closed-in feeling . . . the rightness of the closet at the hockey rink . . . the cool air blowing across my spine . . . Why did that matter? Why did I keep coming back to that? Because no matter what else happened, I did; I returned to those same illogical sense memories, and there was no rea-son for them that I could see. What did it mean? And why did I actually give a single hummingbird's fart what it meant? Because whether it meant something or not, it was all I had to go on. I had to find a place that matched that sense of cool and pressing rightness. There was simply no other way to go: find the box. And there I would find Deb, too, and find either myself or my not-self. Wasn't that sim-ple?

No. It wasn't simple at all, just simpleminded. It made absolutely no sense to pay any attention to the ghostly secret messages floating up at me from my dreams. Dreams had no existence in reality, left no Freddy Krueger–crossover claw marks on our wake-up world. I couldn't very well dash out of the house and drive aimlessly around in a psychic funk. I was a cool and logical being. And so it was in a cool and logical manner that I locked my apartment door and strolled to the car. I still had no idea where I was going, but the need to get there quickly had grabbed the reins and whipped me down to the building's parking area, where I kept my car. But twenty feet away from my trusty vehicle I slammed to a stop as though I had run into an invisible wall.

The dome light was on.

I had certainly not left it on—it had been daylight when I parked, and I could see that the doors were closed tightly. A casual thief would have left the door ajar to avoid the noise from closing it.

I approached slowly, not at all sure what I expected to see or whether I really wanted to see it. From five feet away I could see something in the passenger seat. I circled the car carefully and peered down at it, my nerves tingling, and peeked in. And there it was.

Barbie again. I was getting quite a collection.

This one was dressed in a little sailor hat and a shirt with a bare midriff, and tight pink hot pants. In one hand she clutched a small suitcase that said CUNARD on the side.

I opened the door and picked up the doll. I pulled the little suitcase from Barbie's hand and popped it open. Some small something fell out and rolled onto the floorboard. I picked it up. It looked an awful lot like Deborah's class ring. On the inside of the band was etched D.M., Deborah's initials.

I collapsed onto the seat, clutching Barbie in my sweaty hands. I turned her over. I bent her legs. I waved her arms. And what did you do last night, Dexter? Oh, I played with my dolls while a friend chopped up my sister.

I did not waste any time wondering how Cruise Line Hooker Barbie had gotten into my car. This was clearly a message—or a clue? But clues really ought to hint at something, and this one seemed to lead in the wrong direction.

Clearly he had Debbie—but Cunard? How did that fit in with tight cold killing space? I could see no connection. But there was really only one place in Miami where it did fit.

I drove up Douglas and turned right through Coconut Grove. I had to slow down to thread my way through the parade of happy imbeciles dancing between the shops and cafés. They all seemed to have far too much time and money and very few clues beyond that, and it took me much longer than it should have to get through them, but it was hard to be too upset since I didn't actually know where I was going. Onward to somewhere; along Bayfront Drive, over to Brickle, and into downtown. I saw no huge neon signs bedecked with flashing arrows and encouraging words to direct me: "This way to the dissection!" But I drove on, approaching American Airlines Arena and, just beyond, MacArthur Causeway. In the quick glimpse I got on the near side of the arena, I could see the superstructure of a cruise ship in Government Cut, not a Cunard Lines ship, or course, but I peered anxiously for some sign. It seemed obvious that I was not actually being directed onto a cruise ship; too crowded, too many snooping officials. But somewhere nearby, somewhere related—which of course had to mean what? No further clues. I looked hard enough at the cruise ship to melt the poop deck, but Deborah did not spring from the hold and dance down the gangway.

I looked some more. Beside the ship, cargo cranes reared up into the night sky like abandoned props from *Star Wars*. A little farther and the stacks of cargo boxes were just barely visible in the dark below the cranes, great untidy heaps of them, scattered across the ground as if a gigantic

and very bored child had flung out his toy box full of building blocks. Some of the storage boxes were refrigerated.
And then beyond these boxes—

Back up just for a moment, dear boy.

Who was that whispering to me, muttering what soft
words to all-alone darkly driving Dexter? Who sat behind
me now; whose dry chuckling filled the backseat? And
why? What message was rattling into my brainless, echo-
empty head?

Storage boxes.

Some of them refrigerated.

But why the storage boxes? What possible reason could I
have to be interested in a pile of cold, tightly enclosed
spaces?

Oh, yes. Well. Since you put it that way.

Could this be the place, the future home of the Dexter's
Birthplace Museum? With authentic, lifelike exhibits, including a rare live performance by Dexter's only sister?

I yanked my steering wheel hard, cutting off a BMW
with a very loud horn. I extended my middle finger, for
once driving like the Miami native I was, and accelerated
over the causeway.

The cruise ship was off to the left. The area with all the
boxes was on the right, surrounded by a chain-link fence
topped with razor wire. I drove around one time on the
access road, wrestling a rising tide of certainty and a
swelling chorus of what sounded like college fight songs
from the Dark Passenger. The road dead-ended at a guard
booth well before I got to the containers. There was a gate
with several uniformed gentlemen lounging about, and no

way through without answering some fairly embarrassing questions. Yes, officer, I wondered if I could come in and look around? You see, I thought it might be a good place for a friend of mine to slice up my sister.

I cut through a line of orange cones in the middle of the road thirty feet from the gate and turned around, back the way I had come. The cruise ship loomed on the right now. I turned left just before I came to the bridge back to the mainland and drove into a large area with a terminal on one end and a chain-link fence on the other. The fence was gaily decorated with signs that threatened dire punishment to anyone who strayed into the area, signed by U.S. Customs.

The fence led back to the main road along a large parking lot, empty at this time of night. I cruised its perimeter slowly, staring at the containers on the far side. These would be from foreign ports, needing to go through customs, access tightly controlled. It would be much too difficult for anyone to get in and out of this area, especially if they were carrying questionable loads of body parts and the like. I would either need to find a different area or admit that chasing vague feelings dredged up from a series of taunting dreams and a scantily clad doll was a waste of time. And the sooner I admitted that, the better my chance of finding Deb. She was not here. There was no reason she should be.

At last, a logical thought. I felt better already, and certainly would have been smug about it—if I had not seen a familiar panel truck parked right up against the inside of the fence, parked to display the lettering on the side that said ALLONZO BROTHERS. My private crowd in the basement of my brain sang too loudly for me to hear myself smirk, so I pulled over and parked. The clever-boy part of me was knocking on the front door of my brain and calling out, "Hurry! Hurry! Go-go-go!" But around back the lizard slithered up to the window and flicked its cautious tongue, and so I sat for a long moment before I finally climbed out of the car.

I walked to the fence and stood like a bit-part actor in a World War II prison camp movie, my fingers locked in the mesh of the fence, peering hungrily at what lay beyond, only a few impossible yards away. I was sure that there must be a very simple way for a marvelously intelligent creature like me to get in, but it was some indication of the state I was in that I could not seem to fasten one thought onto another. I had to get in, but I could not. And so I stood there clinging to the fence and looking in, knowing full well that everything that mattered was right there, only a few yards away, and I was completely unable to fling my giant brain at the problem and catch a solution as it bounced back. The mind picks some very bad times to take a walk, doesn't it?

My backseat alarm clock went off. I had to move away, and right now. I was standing suspiciously in a well-guarded area, and it was night; any moment one of the guards was certain to take an interest in the handsome young man peering intelligently through the fence. I would have to move on and find some way in as I rolled along in my car. I stepped back from the fence, giving it one last, loving look. Right there where my feet had touched the fence, a break was barely visible. The fence links had been snipped just enough to allow entry for one human being, or even a good copy like me. The flap was pinned in place by the weight of the parked truck so it would not swing out and give itself away. It must have been done recently, this evening, since the truck had arrived.

My final invitation.

I backed away slowly, feeling an automatic hello-there kind of absentminded smile climb up on my face as a disguise. Hello there, officer, just out for a walk. Lovely evening for a dismemberment, isn't it? I cheerfully scuffed over to my car, looking around at nothing but the moon over the water, whistling a happy tune as I climbed in and drove away. No one seemed to be paying any attention whatsoever—except, of course, for the Hallelujah chorus in my mind. I nudged my car into a parking place over by the cruise ship office, perhaps one hundred yards from my little handmade gate into Paradise. A few other cars were scattered nearby. No one would pay any mind to mine.

But as I parked another car slid into the spot next to me, a light blue Chevy with a woman behind the wheel. I sat still for a moment. So did she. I opened my door and got out.

So did Detective LaGuerta.

CHAPTER 25

I HAVE ALWAYS BEEN VERY GOOD AT AWKWARD SO-
cial situations, but I must admit that this one had me
stumped. I just didn't know what to say, and for a
moment I stared at LaGuerta and she looked back at me
with her eyes unblinking and her fangs slightly exposed,
like a predatory feline trying to decide whether to play with
you or eat you. I could think of no remark that did not
begin with a stammer, and she seemed interested only in
watching me. So we simply stood there for a long moment.
At last she broke the ice with a light quip.

"What's in there?" she asked, nodding toward the fence,
some one hundred yards away.

"Why, Detective!" I gushed, hoping that she wouldn't
notice what she had said, I suppose. "What are you doing
here?"

"I followed you. What's in there?"

"In there?" I said. I know, a really dumb remark, but honestly, I had just about run out of the smart ones and I can't

be expected to come up with something good under such circumstances.

She cocked her head to one side and poked her tongue out, letting it run along her bottom lip; slowly to the left, right, left, and back into her mouth again. Then she nodded. "You must think I'm stupid," she said. And of course that thought had crossed my mind fleetingly once or twice, but it didn't seem politic to say so. "But you got to remember," she went on, "I'm a full detective, and this is Miami. How do you think I got that, huh?"

"Your looks?" I asked, giving her a dashing smile. It never hurts to compliment a woman.

She showed me her lovely set of teeth, even brighter in the high crime lights that lit up the parking area. "That's good," she said, and she moved her lips into a strange half smile that hollowed her cheeks and made her look old. "That's the kind of shit I used to fall for when I thought you liked me."

"I do like you, Detective," I told her, perhaps a little too eagerly. She didn't seem to hear me.

"But then you push me on the floor like I'm some kind of pig, and I wonder what's wrong with me? I got bad breath? And it hits me. It's not me. It's you. There's something wrong about you."

Of course she was right, but it still hurt to hear her say so. "I don't— What do you mean?"

She shook her head again. "Sergeant Doakes wants to kill you and he doesn't even know why. I should've listened to him. Something is wrong about you. And you're connected to this hooker stuff some way."

"Connected— What do you mean?"

This time there was an edge of savage glee to the smile she showed me and the trace of accent snuck back into her voice. "You can save the cute acting for your lawyer. And maybe a judge. 'Cause I think I got you now." She looked at me for a long hard moment and her dark eyes glittered. She looked as inhuman as I am and it made a small shiver run across the back of my neck. Had I truly underestimated her? Was she really this good?

"And so you followed me?"

More teeth. "That's right, yeah," she said. "Why are you looking around at the fence? What's in there?"

I am sure that under ordinary circumstances I would have thought of this before, but I plead duress. It truly didn't occur to me until that very moment. But when it did, it was like a small and painful light flashing on. "When did you pick me up? At my house? At what time?"

"Why do you keep changing the subject? Something's in there, huh?"

"Detective, please—this could be very important. When and where did you start to follow me?"

She studied me for a minute, and I began to realize that I had, in fact, underestimated her. There was a great deal more to this woman than political instinct. She really did seem to have something extra. I was still not convinced that any of it was intelligence, but she did have patience, and sometimes that was more important than smarts in her line of work. She was willing to simply wait and watch me and keep repeating her question until she got an answer. And then she would probably ask the same question a few more times, wait and watch some more, to see what I would do. Ordinarily I could outwit her, but I could not possibly outwait her, not tonight. So I put on my best humble face and repeated myself. "Please, Detective . . ."

She stuck her tongue out again, and then finally put it away. "Okay," she said. "When your sister was gone for a few hours and no word where, I started to think maybe she's up to something. And I know she can't do anything herself, so where would she go?" She arched an eyebrow at me, then continued in a triumphant tone. "To your place, that's where! To talk with you!" She bobbed her head, pleased with her deductive logic. "And so I think about you for a while. How you're always showing up and looking, even when you don't have to. How you figure out those serial killers sometimes, except this one? And then how you fuck me over with that stupid list, make me look stupid, push me on the fucking floor—" Her face looked harder, a little older again for a moment. Then she smiled and went on. "I said something out loud, in my office, and Sergeant Doakes says, 'I told you about him but you don't listen.' And all of a sudden it's your big handsome face all over the place and it shouldn't be." She shrugged. "So I went to your place, too."

"When? At what time, did you notice?"

"Naw," she said. "But I'm only there like twenty minutes and then you come out and play with your faggot Barbie doll and then drive over here."

"Twenty minutes—" So she hadn't been there in time to

see who or what had taken Deborah. And quite probably she was telling the truth and had simply followed me to see—to see what?

"But why follow me at all?"

She shrugged. "You're connected to this thing. Maybe you didn't do it, I don't know. But I'm gonna find out. And some of what I find is gonna stick to you. What's in there, in those boxes? You gonna tell me, or we just going to stand here all night?"

In her own way, she had put her finger right on it. We could not stand here all night. We could not, I was sure, stand here much longer at all before terrible things happened to Deborah. If they hadn't already happened. We had to go, right now, go find him and stop him. But how did I do that with LaGuerta along for the ride? I felt like a comet with a tail I didn't want.

I took a deep breath. Rita had once taken me to a New Age Health Awareness Workshop which had stressed the importance of deep cleansing breaths. I took one. I did not feel any cleaner after my breath, but at least it made my brain whirl into brief action, and I realized I would have to do something I had rarely done before—tell the truth. LaGuerta was still staring at me, waiting for an answer.

"I think the killer is in there," I told LaGuerta. "And I think he has Officer Morgan."

She watched me for a moment without moving. "Okay," she said at last. "And so you come stand at the fence and look in? 'Cause you love your sister so much you want to watch?"

"Because I wanted to get in. I was looking for a way in through the fence."

"Because you forget that you work for the police?"

Well there it was, of course. She had actually jumped right to the real problem spot, and all by herself, too. I had no good answer for that. This whole business of telling the truth just never seems to work without some kind of awkward unpleasantness. "I just—I wanted to be sure, before I made a big fuss."

She nodded. "Uh-huh. That's really good," she said. "But I tell you what I think. Either you did something bad, or you know about it. And you're either hiding it, or you wanna find it by yourself."

"By myself? But why would I want that?"

She shook her head to show how stupid that was. "So you get all the credit. You and that sister of yours. Think I didn't figure that out? I told you I'm not stupid."

"I'm not your slasher, Detective," I said, throwing myself on her mercy and now completely confident that she had even less than I did. "But I think he's in there, in one of the storage boxes."

She licked her lips. "Why do you think that?"

I hesitated, but she kept her unblinking lizard stare on me. As uncomfortable as it made me, I had to tell her one more piece of truth. I nodded at the Allonzo Brothers van parked just inside the fence. "That's his truck."

"Ha," she said, and at last she blinked. Her focus left me for a moment and seemed to wander away into some deep place. Her hair? Her makeup? Her career? I couldn't tell.

But there were a lot of awkward questions a good detective might have asked here: How did I know that was his truck? How had I found it here? Why was I so sure he hadn't simply dumped the truck and gone somewhere else? But in the final analysis LaGuerta was not a good detective; she simply nodded, licked her lips again, and said, "How are we gonna find him in there in all that?"

Clearly, I really had underestimated her. She had gone from "you" to "we" with no visible transition. "Don't you want to call for backup?" I asked her. "This is a very dangerous man." I admit I was only needling her. But she took it very seriously.

"If I don't catch this guy by myself, in two weeks I'm a meter maid," she said. "I got my weapon. Nobody's gonna get away from me. I'll call for backup when I have him." She studied me without blinking. "And if he's not in there, I'll give them you."

It seemed like a good idea to let that go. "Can you get us through the gate?"

She laughed. " 'Course I can. I got my badge, get us through anywhere. And then what?"

This was the tricky part. If she went for this, I might well be home free. "Then we split up and search until we find him."

She studied me. Again I saw in her face the thing I had seen when she first got out of her car—the look of a predator weighing her prey, wondering when and where to strike, and how many claws to use. It was horrible—I actually found myself warming to the woman. "Okay," she said at last, and tilted her head toward her car. "Get in."

I got in. She drove us back out onto the road and over to the gate. Even at this hour there was some traffic. Most of it seemed to be people from Ohio looking for their cruise ship, but a few of them wound up at the gate, where the guards sent them back the way they came. Detective LaGuerta cut ahead of them all, bulling her big Chevy to the front of the line. Their Midwest driving skills were no match for a Miami Cuban woman with good medical insurance driving a car she didn't care about. There was a blare of horns and some muffled shouting and we were at the guard booth.

The guard leaned out, a thin, muscular black man. "Lady, you can't—"

She held up her badge. "Police. Open the gate." She said it with such hard-edged authority that I almost jumped out of the car to open the gate myself.

But the guard froze, took a breath through his mouth, and glanced nervously back into the booth. "What you want with—"

"Open the fucking gate, Rental," she told him, jiggling her badge, and he finally unfroze.

"Lemme see the badge," he said. LaGuerta held it up limply, making him take the extra step over to peer at it. He frowned at it and found nothing to object to. "Uh-huh," he said. "Can you tell me what you want in there?"

"I can tell you that if you don't open the gate in two seconds I'm gonna put you in the trunk of my car and take you downtown to a holding cell full of gay bikers and then I'm gonna forget where I put you."

The guard stood up. "Just trying to help," he said, and called over his shoulder, "Tavio, open the gate!"

The gate went up and LaGuerta gunned her car through. "Sonnova bitch got something going he doesn't want me to know about," she said. There was amusement in her voice to go with the rising edge of excitement. "But I don't care about smuggling tonight." She looked at me. "Where we going?"

"I don't know," I said. "I guess we should start over where he left his truck."

She nodded, accelerating down the path between stacks of storage boxes. "If he's got a body to carry, he probably parked pretty close to wherever he was going." As we got closer to the fence she slowed down, nosing the car quietly to within fifty feet of the truck and then stopping. "Let's take a look at the fence," she said, slamming the transmission into park and sliding out of the car as it rocked to a stop.

I followed. LaGuerta stepped in something she didn't like and lifted her foot to look at her shoe. "Goddamint," she said. I moved past her, feeling my pulse hammering loud and fast, and went to the truck. I walked around it, trying the doors. They were locked, and although there were two small back windows, these were painted over from the inside. I stood on the bumper and tried to peek in anyway, but there were no holes in the paint job. There was nothing more to be seen on this side, but I squatted anyway and looked on the ground. I felt rather than heard LaGuerta slither up behind me.

"What you got?" she asked, and I stood.

"Nothing," I said. "The back windows are painted over on the inside."

"Can you see in the front?"

I went around to the front of the truck. It was bare of any hint as well. Inside the windshield, a pair of the sunscreens so popular in Florida had been unfolded across the dashboard, blocking out any possible view into the cab. I climbed on the front bumper and up onto the hood, crawled along it from right to left, but there were no gaps in the sunscreen. "Nothing," I said and climbed down.

"Okay," LaGuerta said, looking at me with lidded eyes and just the smallest tip of her tongue protruding. "Which way you wanna go?"

This way, someone whispered deep inside my brain. *Over here.* I glanced to the right, where the chuckling mental fingers had pointed and then back to LaGuerta, who was staring at me with her unblinking hungry tiger stare. "I'll go left and circle around," I said. "Meet you halfway."

"Okay," LaGuerta said with a feral smile. "But I go left."

I tried to look surprised and unhappy, and I suppose I managed a reasonable facsimile, because she watched me and then nodded. "Okay," she repeated, and turned down the first row of stacked shipping containers.

Then I was alone with my shy interior friend. And now what? Now that I had tricked LaGuerta into leaving me the right-hand path, what did I do with it? After all, I had no reason to think it was any better than the left-hand, or for that matter, better than standing by the fence and juggling coconuts. There was only my sibilant internal clamor to direct me, and was that really enough? When you are an icy tower of pure reason as I have always been, you naturally look for logical hints to direct your course of action. Just as

naturally, you ignore the nonobjective irrational screeching
of loud musical voices from the bottom floor of your brain
that try to send you reeling along the path, no matter how
urgent they have become in the rippling light of the moon.

And as to the rest, the particulars of where I should go
now—I looked around, down the long irregular rows of
containers. Off to the side where LaGuerta had gone spike-
heeling along, there were several rows of brightly colored
truck trailers. And in front of me, stretching off to the right,
were the shipping containers.

Suddenly, I was very uncertain. I didn't like the feeling. I
closed my eyes. The moment I did, the whispering became
a cloud of sound and without knowing why I found myself
moving toward a clutter of shipping containers down near
the water. I had no conscious notion that these particular
containers were any different or better or that this direction
was more proper or rewarding. My feet simply jerked into
motion and I followed them. It was as if they were tracing
some path only the toes could see, or as if some compelling
pattern was being sung by the whisper-wail of my internal
chorus, and my feet translated and dragged me along.

As they moved the sound grew inside me, a muted hilar-
ious roar, pulling me faster than my feet, yanking me clum-
sily down the crooked path between boxes with powerful
invisible jerks. And yet at the same time a new voice, small
and reasonable, was pushing me backward, telling me I did
not want to be here of all places, yammering at me to run,
go home, get away from this place, and it made no more
sense than any of the other voices. I was pulled forward
and pushed back at the same time so powerfully that I

could not make my legs work properly and I stumbled and fell flat-faced onto the hard rocky ground. I rose to my knees, mouth dry and heart pounding, and paused to finger a rip in my beautiful Dacron bowling shirt. I pushed my fingertip through the hole and wiggled it at myself. Hello, Dexter, where are you going? Hello, Mr. Finger. I don't know, but I'm almost there. I hear my friends calling.

And so I climbed to suddenly unsteady feet and listened. I heard it clearly now, even with my eyes open, and felt it so strongly I could not even walk. I stood for a moment, leaning against one of the containers. A very sobering thought, as if I needed one. Something nameless was born in this place, something that lived in the darkest hidey-hole of the thing that was Dexter, and for the first time that I could remember I was scared. I did not want to be here where horrible things lurked. Yet I had to be here to find Deborah. I was being ripped in half by an invisible tug-of-war. I felt like Sigmund Freud's poster child, and I wanted to go home and go to bed.

But the moon roared in the dark sky above me, the water howled along Government Cut, and the mild night breeze shrieked over me like a convention of banshees, forcing my feet forward. And the singing swelled within me like some kind of gigantic mechanical choir, urging me on, reminding me of how to move my feet, pushing me lock-kneed down the rows of boxes. My heart hammered and yammered, my short gasps of breath were much too loud, and for the first time I could remember I felt weak, woozy, and stupid—like a human being, like a very small and helpless human being.

I staggered along the strangely familiar path on borrowed feet until I could stagger no more and once again I put an arm out to lean against a box, a box with an air-conditioning compressor attached, pounding away at the back and mixing with the shriek of the night, all thumping in my head so loudly now that I could hardly see. And as I leaned against the box the door swung open.

The inside of the box was lit by a pair of battery-powered hurricane lamps. Against the back wall there was a temporary operating table made of packing crates.

And held unmoving in place on the table was my dear sister Deborah.

CHAPTER 26

FOR A FEW SECONDS IT DIDN'T REALLY SEEM NEC-
essary to breathe. I just looked. Long, slick strands of
duct tape wrapped around my sister's arms and legs.
She wore gold lamé hot pants and a skimpy silk blouse tied
above her navel. Her hair was pulled back tight, her eyes
were unnaturally wide, and she breathed rapidly through
her nose, since her mouth, too, was held closed by a strip of
duct tape that went across her lips and down to the table to
hold her head still.

I tried to think of something to say, but realized my
mouth was too dry to say it and so I just looked. Deborah
looked back. There were many things in her eyes, but the
plainest was fear, and that held me there in the doorway. I
had never seen that look on her before and I was not sure
what to think about it. I took half a step toward Deborah
and she flinched against the duct tape. Afraid? Of course—
but afraid of me? I was here to rescue her, most likely. Why
should she be afraid of me? Unless—

Had I done this?

During my little "nap" earlier this evening what if Deborah had arrived at my apartment, as scheduled, and found my Dark Passenger behind the wheel of the Dexter-mobile? And unknown to me I had brought her here and taped her so tantalizingly to the table without consciously realizing it—which made absolutely no sense, naturally. Had I raced home and left myself the Barbie doll, then gone upstairs and flopped on the bed and woke up as "me" again, like I was running some kind of homicidal relay race? Impossible: but . . .

How else had I known to come here?

I shook my head; there was no way I could have picked this one cold box out of all the places in Miami, unless I already knew where it was. And I did. The only way that could be possible was if I had been here before. And if not tonight with Deb, then when and with whom?

"I was almost sure this was the right spot," a voice said, a voice so very like my own that for a moment I thought I had said it, and I wondered what I meant by that.

The hair went up on the back of my neck and I took another half step toward Deborah—and he came forward out of the shadow. The soft light of the lanterns lit him up and our eyes met; for a moment the room spun back and forth and I did not quite know where I was. My sight shifted between me at the door and him at the small makeshift worktable, and I saw me seeing him, then I saw him seeing me. In a blinding flash I saw me on the floor, sitting still and unmoving, and I did not know what that vision meant. Very unsettling—and then I was myself again, although I was somewhat uncertain what that meant.

"Almost sure," he said again, a soft and happy voice like Mr. Rogers's troubled child. "But now here you are, so this must be the right place. Don't you think?"

There is no pretty way for me to say this, but the truth is, I stared at him with my mouth hanging open. I am quite sure I was almost drooling. I just stared. It was him. There was no question about it. Here was the man in the pictures we had found on the webcam, the man both Deb and I had thought might very well be me.

This close I could see that he was not, in fact, me; not quite, and I felt a small wave of gratitude at that realization. Hurray—I was someone else. I was not completely crazy yet. Seriously antisocial, of course, and somewhat sporadically homicidal, nothing wrong with that. But not crazy. There was somebody else, and he was not me. Three cheers for Dexter's brain.

But he was very much like me. Perhaps an inch or two taller, thicker through the shoulders and chest as though he had been doing a great deal of heavy weight lifting. That, combined with the paleness of his face, made me think that he might have been in prison recently. Behind the pallor, though, his face was very similar to mine; the same nose and cheekbones, the same look in the eyes that said the lights were on but nobody was home. Even his hair had the same awkward half wave to it. He did not really look like me, but very similar.

"Yes," he said. "It is a little bit of a shock the first time, isn't it?"

"Just a little," I said. "Who are you? And why is all this so—" I left it unfinished, because I did not know what all this was.

He made a face, a very Dexter-disappointed face. "Oh, dear. And I was so sure you had figured it out."

I shook my head. "I don't even know how I got here," I said.

He smiled softly. "Somebody else driving tonight?" As the hair stood up on the back of my neck he chuckled just a little, a mechanical sound that was not worth mentioning—except that the lizard voice from the underside of my brain matched it note for note. "And it isn't even a full moon, is it?"

"But not actually an empty moon," I said. Hardly great wit, but some kind of attempt, which under the circumstances seemed significant. And I realized that I was half drunk with the realization that here at last was someone who *knew*. He was not making idle remarks that coincidentally stabbed into my own personal bull's-eye. It was his bull's-eye, too. He knew. For the first time I could look across the gigantic gulf between my eyes and someone else's and say without any kind of worry, *He is like me.*

Whatever it was that I was, he was one, too.

"But seriously," I said. "Who are you?"

His face stretched into a Dexter-the-Cheshire-Cat smile, but because it was so much like my own I could see there was no real happiness behind it. "What do you remember from before?" he said. And the echo of that question bounced off the container's walls and nearly shattered my brain.

CHAPTER 27

WHAT DO YOU REMEMBER FROM BEFORE? HARRY had asked me.

Nothing, Dad.

Except—

Images tugged at my underbrain. Mental pictures—dreams? memories?—very clear visions, whatever they were. And they were here—this room? No; impossible. This box could not have been here very long, and I had certainly never been in it before. But the tightness of the space, the cool air flowing from the thumping compressor, the dim light—everything called out to me in a symphony of homecoming. Of course it had not been this same box—but the pictures were so clear, so similar, so completely almost-right, except for—

I blinked; an image fluttered behind my eyes. I closed them.

And the inside of a different box jumped back out at me. There were no cartons in this other box. And there were—things over there. Over by . . . Mommy? I could see her face there, and she was somehow hiding and peeking up over the—things—just her face showing, her unwinking unblinking unmoving face. And I wanted to laugh at first, because Mommy had hidden so well. I could not see the rest of her, just her face. She must have made a hole in the floor. She must be hiding in the hole and peeking up— but why didn't she answer me now that I saw her? Why didn't she even wink? And even when I called her really loud she didn't answer, didn't move, didn't do anything but look at me. And without Mommy, I was alone.

But no—not quite alone. I turned my head and the memory turned with me. I was not alone. Someone was with me. Very con- fusing at first, because it was me—but it was someone else—but it looked like me—but we both looked like me—

But what were we doing here in this box? And why wasn't Mommy moving? She should help us. We were sitting here in a deep puddle, of, of—Mommy should move, get us out of this, this—

"Blood . . . ?" I whispered.

"You remembered," he said behind me. "I'm so happy."

I opened my eyes. My head was pounding hideously. I could almost see the other room superimposed on this one. And in this other room tiny Dexter sat right *there.* I could put my feet on the spot. And the other me sat beside me, but he was not me, of course; he was some other someone, a someone I knew as well as myself, a someone named—

"Biney . . . ?" I said hesitantly. The sound was the same, but the name did not seem quite right.

He nodded happily. "That's what you called me. At the

time you had trouble saying Brian. You said Biney." He patted my hand. "That's all right. It's nice to have a nickname." He paused, his face smiling but his eyes locked onto my face. "Little brother."

I sat down. He sat next to me.

"What—" was all I could manage to say.

"Brother," he repeated. "Irish twins. You were born only one year after me. Our mother was somewhat careless." His face twisted into a hideous, very happy smile. "In more ways than one," he said.

I tried to swallow. It didn't work. He—Brian—my brother—went on.

"I'm just guessing with some of this," he said. "But I had a little time on my hands, and when I was encouraged to learn a useful trade, I did. I got very good at finding things with the computer. I found the old police files. Mommy dearest hung out with a very naughty crowd. In the import business, just like me. Of course, their product was a little more sensitive." He reached behind him into a carton and pulled out a handful of hats with a springing panther on them. "My things are made in Taiwan. Theirs came from Colombia. My best guess is that Mumsy and her friends tried a little independent project with some product that strictly speaking did not actually belong to her, and her business associates were unhappy with her spirit of independence and decided to discourage her."

He put the hats carefully back in the carton and I felt him looking at me, but I could not even turn my head. After a moment he looked away.

"They found us here," he said. "Right here." His hand went to the floor and touched the exact spot where the small other not-me had been sitting in that long-ago other box. "Two and a half days later. Stuck to the floor in dried blood, an inch deep." His voice here was grating, horrible; he said that awful word, *blood*, just the way I would have said it, with contemptuous and utter loathing. "According to the police reports, there were several men here, too. Probably three or four. One or more of them may well have been our father. Of course, the chain saw made identification very difficult. But they are fairly sure there was only one woman. Our dear old mother. You were three years old. I was four."

"But," I said. Nothing else came out.

"Quite true," Brian told me. "And you were very hard to find, too. They are so fussy with adoption records in this state. But I did find you, little brother. I did, didn't I?" Once again he patted my hand, a strange gesture I had never seen from anyone in my life. Of course, I had never before seen a flesh-and-blood sibling, either. Perhaps hand-patting was something I should practice with my brother, or with Deborah—and I realized with a small flutter of concern that I had forgotten all about Deborah.

I looked over at her, some six feet away, all neatly taped into place.

"She's fine," my brother said. "I didn't want to begin without you."

It may seem a very strange thing for my first coherent question, but I asked him, "How did you know I would want to?" Which perhaps made it sound as though I truly did want to—and of course I didn't really want to explore Deborah. Certainly not. And yet—here was my big brother, wanting to play, surely a rare enough opportunity. More than our ties of mutual parent, far more, was the fact that he was like me. "You couldn't really know," I said, sounding far more uncertain than I would have thought possible.

"I didn't know," he said. "But I thought there was a very good chance. The same thing happened to both of us." His smile broadened and he lifted a forefinger into the air. "The Traumatic Event—you know that term? Have you done any reading on monsters like us?"

"Yes," I said. "And Harry—my foster father—but he would never say exactly what had happened."

Brian waved a hand around at the interior of the little box. "This happened, little brother. The chain saw, the flying body parts, the . . . *blood*—" With that same fearful emphasis again. "Two and a half days of sitting in the stuff. A wonder we survived at all, isn't it? Almost enough to make you believe in God." His eyes glittered and, for some reason or other, Deborah squirmed and made a muffled noise. He ignored her. "They thought you were young enough to recover. I was just a bit over the age limit. But we both suffered a classic Traumatic Event. All the literature agrees. It made me what I am—and I had a thought that it might do the same for you."

"It did," I said, "exactly the same."

"Isn't that nice," he said. "Family ties."

I looked at him. My brother. That alien word. If I had said it aloud I am sure I would have stuttered. It was utterly impossible to believe—and even more absurd to deny it. He looked like me. We liked the same things. He even had my wretched taste in jokes.

"I just—" I shook my head.

"Yes," he said. "It takes a minute to get used to the idea that there are two of us, doesn't it?"

"Perhaps slightly longer," I said. "I don't know if I—"

"Oh, dear, are we being squeamish? After what happened? Two and a half days of sitting here, bubba. Two little boys, sitting for two and a half days in *blood*," he said, and I felt sick, dizzy, heart floundering, head hammering.

"No," I gagged, and I felt his hand on my shoulder.

"It doesn't matter," he said. "What matters is what happens now."

"What—happens," I said.

"Yes. What happens. Now." He made a small, strange, snuffling, gurgling noise that was surely intended to sound like laughter, but perhaps he had not learned to fake it as well as I had. "I think I should say something like: My whole life has been leading up to this!" He repeated the snuffling sound. "Of course, neither one of us could manage that with real feeling. After all, we can't actually feel anything, can we? We've both spent our lives playing a part. Moving through this world reciting lines and pretending we belong in a world made for human beings, and never really human ourselves. And always, forever, reaching for a way to *feel* something! Reaching, little brother, for a moment just like this! Real, genuine, unfaked feeling! It takes your breath away, doesn't it?"

And it did. My head was whirling and I did not dare to

close my eyes again for fear of what might be waiting there for me. And, far worse, my brother was right beside me, watching me, demanding that I be myself, be just like him. And to be myself, to be his brother, to be who I was, I had to, had to—what? My eyes turned, all by themselves, toward Deborah.

"Yes," he said, and all the cold happy fury of the Dark Passenger was in his voice now. "I knew you'd figure it out. This time we do it together," he said.

I shook my head, but not very convincingly. "I can't," I said.

"You have to," he said, and we were both right. The feather touch on my shoulder again, almost matching the push from Harry that he could never understand and yet seemed every bit as powerful as my brother's hand, as it lifted me to my feet and pushed me forward; one step, two—Deborah's unblinking eyes were locked onto mine, but with that other presence behind me I couldn't tell her that I was certainly not going to—

"Together," he said. "One more time. Out with the old. In with the new. Onward, upward, inward—!" Another half step—Deborah's eyes were yelling at me, but—

He was beside me now, standing with me, and something gleamed in his hand, two somethings. "One for all, both for one— Did you ever read *The Three Musketeers*?" He flipped one knife into the air; it arced up and into his left hand and he held it out toward me. The weak dim light grew on the flat of the blades he held up and burned into me, matched only by the gleam in Brian's eyes. "Come on,

Dexter. Little brother. Take the knife." His teeth shone like the knives. "Showtime."

Deborah in her tightly wrapped tape made a thrashing sound. I looked up at her. There was frantic impatience in her eyes, and a growing madness, too. Come on, Dexter! Was I really thinking of doing this to her? Cut her loose and let's go home. Okay, Dexter? Dexter? Hello, Dexter? It is you, isn't it?

And I didn't know.

"Dexter," Brian said. "Of course I don't mean to influence your decision. But ever since I learned I had a brother just like me, this is all I could think about. And you feel the same, I can see it in your face."

"Yes," I said, still not taking my eyes off Deb's very anxious face, "but does it have to be her?"

"Why not her? What is she to you?"

What indeed. My eyes were locked onto Deborah's. She was not actually my sister, not really, not a real relation of any kind, not at all. Of course I was very fond of her, but—

But what? Why did I hesitate? Of course the thing was impossible. I knew it was unthinkable, even as I thought it. Not just because it was Deb, although it was, of course. But such a strange thought came into my poor dismal battered head and I could not bat it away: *What would Harry say?*

And so I stood uncertain, because no matter how much I wanted to begin I knew what Harry would say. He had already said it. It was unchangeable Harry truth: *Chop up the bad guys, Dexter. Don't chop up your sister.* But Harry had never foreseen anything like this—how could he? He had never imagined when he wrote the Code of Harry that I would be faced with a choice like this; to side with Deborah—not my real sister—or to join my authentic 100 percent real live brother in a game that I so very much wanted to play. And Harry could not have conceived that when he set me on my path. Harry had never known that I had a brother who would—

But wait a moment. Hold the phone, please. Harry did know—Harry had been there when it happened, hadn't he? And he had kept it to himself, never told me I had a brother. All those lonely empty years when I thought I was the only me there was—and he knew I was not, knew and had not told me. The most important single fact about me—I was not alone—and he had kept it from me. What did I really owe Harry now, after this fantastic betrayal?

And more to the immediate point, what did I owe this squirming lump of animal flesh quivering beneath me, this creature masquerading as my sibling? What could I possibly owe her in comparison to my bond with Brian, my own flesh, my brother, a living replication of my selfsame precious DNA?

A drop of sweat rolled across Deborah's forehead and into her eye. She blinked at it frantically, making ugly squinting faces in an effort to keep watching me and clear the sweat out of her eye at the same time. She really looked somewhat pathetic, helplessly taped and struggling like a dumb animal; a dumb, human animal. Not at all like me, like my brother; not at all clever clean no-mess bloodless razor-sharp Moondancer snicker-snee Dexter and his very own brother.

"Well?" he said, and I heard impatience, judgment, the beginning of disappointment.

I closed my eyes. The room dove around me, got darker, and I could not move. There was Mommy watching me, unblinking. I opened my eyes. My brother stood so close behind me I could feel his breath on my neck. My sister looked up at me, her eyes as wide and unblinking as Mommy's. And the look she gave me held me, as Mommy's had held me. I closed my eyes; Mommy. I opened my eyes; Deborah.

I took the knife.

There was a small noise and a rush of warm wind came into the cool air of the box. I spun around.

LaGuerta stood in the doorway, a nasty little automatic pistol in her hand.

"I knew you'd try this," she said. "I should shoot you both. Maybe all three," she said, glancing at Deborah, then back at me. "Hah," she said, looking at the blade in my hand. "Sergeant Doakes should see this. He was right about you." And she pointed the gun toward me, just for half a second.

It was long enough. Brian moved fast, faster than I would have thought possible. Still, LaGuerta got off one shot and Brian stumbled slightly as he slid the blade into LaGuerta's midsection. For a moment they stood like that, and then both of them were on the floor, unmoving.

A small pool of blood began to spread across the floor, the mingled blood of them both, Brian and LaGuerta. It was not deep, it did not spread far, but I shrank away from it, the horrible stuff, with something very near to panic. I only took two backward steps and then I bumped into something that made muffled sounds to match my own panic.

Deborah. I ripped the duct tape off her mouth.

"Jesus Christ that hurt," she said. "For God's sake let me out of this shit and quit acting like a fucking lunatic."

I looked down at Deborah. The tape had left a ring of blood around the outside of her lips, awful red blood that drove me back behind my eyes and into the yesterday box with Mommy. And she lay there—just like Mommy. Just like last time with the cool air of the box lifting the hair on my neck and the dark shadows chattering around us. Just exactly like last time in the way she lay there all taped and staring and waiting like some kind of—

"Goddamn it," she said. "Come on, Dex. Snap out of it."

And yet this time I had a knife, and she was still helpless, and I could change everything now, I could—

"Dexter?" said Mommy.

I mean, Deborah. Of course that's what I meant. Not Mommy at all who had left us here in this same place just like this, left us in this place where it began and now might finally finish, with a burning absolutely must-do-it already on its large dark horse and galloping along under the wonderful moon and the one thousand intimate voices whispering, *Do it—do it now—do it and everything can change—the way it should be—back with—*

"Mommy?" someone said.

"Dexter, come on," said Mommy. I mean Deborah. But

the knife was moving. "Dexter, for Christ's sake, cut the shit! It's me! Debbie!"

I shook my head and of course it was Deborah, but I could not stop the knife. "I know, Deb. I'm really very sorry." The knife crept higher. I could only watch it, couldn't stop it now for anything. One small spiderweb touch of Harry still whipped at me, demanding that I pay attention and get squared away, but it was so small and weak, and the need was big, strong, stronger than it had ever been before, because this was everything, the beginning and the end, and it lifted me up and out of myself and sent me washing away down the tunnel between the boy in the blood and the last chance to make it right. This would change everything, would pay back Mommy, would show her what she had done. Because Mommy should have saved us, and this time had to be different. Even Deb had to see that.

"Put the knife down, Dexter." Her voice was a little calmer now, but those other voices were so much louder that I could barely hear her. I tried to put the knife down, really I did, but I only managed to lower it a few inches.

"I'm sorry, Deb, I just can't," I said, fighting to speak at all with the rising howl around me of the storm that had built for twenty-five years—and now with my brother and me brought together like thunderheads on a dark and moony night—

"Dexter!" said wicked Mommy, who wanted to leave us here alone in the awful cold blood, and the voice of my brother inside hissed out with mine, "Bitch!" and the knife went all the way back up—

A noise came from the floor. LaGuerta? I couldn't tell,

and it didn't matter. I had to finish, had to do this, had to let this happen now.

"Dexter," Debbie said. "I'm your sister. You don't want to do this to me. What would Daddy say?" And that hurt, I'll admit it, but— "Put down the knife, Dexter."

Another sound behind me, and a small gurgle. The knife in my hand went up.

"Dexter, look out!" Deborah said and I turned.

Detective LaGuerta was on one knee, gasping, straining to raise her suddenly very heavy weapon. Up came the barrel, slowly, slowly—pointed at my foot, my knee—

But did it matter? Because this was going to happen now no matter what and even though I could see LaGuerta's finger tighten on the trigger the knife in my hand did not even slow down.

"She's going to shoot you, Dex!" Deb called, sounding somewhat frantic now. And the gun was pointed at my navel, LaGuerta's face was screwing itself into a frown of tremendous concentration and effort and she really was going to shoot me. I half turned toward LaGuerta but my knife was still fighting its way down toward—

"Dexter!" said Mommy/Deborah on the table, but the Dark Passenger called louder and moved forward, grabbing my hand and guiding the knife down—

"Dex—!"

You're a good kid, Dex," whispered Harry from behind in his feather-hard ghost voice, just enough to twitch the knife so very little up again.

"I can't help it," I whispered back, so very much growing into the handle of the quivering blade.

"Choose what . . . or WHO . . . you kill," he said with the hard and endless blue of his eyes now watching me from Deborah's same eyes, watching now loud enough to push the knife a full half inch away. *"There are plenty of people who deserve it,"* said Harry so softly above the rising angry yammer of the stampede inside.

The tip of the knife winked and froze in place. The Dark Passenger could not send it down. Harry could not pull it away. And there we were.

Behind me I heard a rasping sound, a heavy thump, and then a moan so very full of emptiness that it crawled across my shoulders like a silk scarf on spider legs. I turned.

LaGuerta lay with her gun hand stretched out, pinned to the floor by Brian's knife, her lower lip trapped between her teeth and her eyes alive with pain. Brian crouched beside her, watching the fear scamper across her face. He was breathing hard through a dark smile.

"Shall we clean up, brother?" he said.

"I . . . can't," I said.

My brother lurched to his feet and stood in front of me, weaving slightly from side to side. "Can't?" he said. "I don't think I know that word." He pried the knife from my fingers and I could not stop him and I could not help him.

His eyes were on Deborah now, but his voice whipped across me and blasted at the phantom Harry fingers on my shoulder. "Must, little brother. Absolutely *must*. No other way." He gasped and bent double for a moment, slowly straightening, slowly raising the knife. "Do I have to remind you of the importance of family?"

"No," I said, with both my families, living and dead,

crowded around me clamoring for me to do and not do. And with one last whisper from the Harry-blue eyes of my memory, my head began to shake all by itself and I said it again, "No," and this time I meant it, "No. I can't. Not Deborah."

My brother looked at me. "Too bad," he said. "I'm so disappointed."

And the knife came down.

EPILOGUE

I KNOW IT IS A NEARLY HUMAN WEAKNESS, AND IT may be no more than ordinary sentimentality, but I have always loved funerals. For one thing they are so clean, so neat, so completely given over to careful ceremonies. And this was really a very good one. It had rows of blue-uniformed policemen and -women, looking solemn and neat and—well, ceremonial. There was the ritual salute with the guns, the careful folding of the flag, all the trimmings—a proper and wonderful show for the deceased. She had been, after all, one of our own, a woman who had served with the few, the proud. Or is that the marines? No matter, she had been a Miami cop, and Miami cops know how to throw a funeral for one of their own. They have had so much practice.

"Oh, Deborah," I sighed, very softly, and of course I knew she couldn't hear me, but it really did seem like the right thing to do, and I wanted to do this right.

I almost wished I could summon up a tear or two to wipe

away. She and I had been very close. And it had been a messy and unpleasant death, no way for a cop to go, hacked to death by a homicidal maniac. Rescue had come too late; it was all over long before anyone could get to her. And yet, by her example of selfless courage, she had helped to show how a cop should live and die. I'm quoting, of course, but that's the gist of it. Really very good stuff, quite moving if one has anything inside that can be moved. Which I don't, but I know it when I hear it and this was the real thing. And very much caught up in the silent bravery of the officers in their clean blues and the weeping of the civilians, I could not help myself. I sighed heavily. "Oh, Deborah," I sighed, a little louder this time, almost feeling it. "Dear, dear Deborah."

"Quiet, you moron!" she whispered, and poked me hard with her elbow. She looked lovely in her new outfit—a sergeant at last, the least they could do for her after all her hard work identifying and nearly catching the Tamiami Slasher. With the APB out on him, no doubt they would find my poor brother sooner or later—if he didn't find them first, of course. Since I had just been reminded so forcefully that family is important, I did hope he could stay free. And Deborah would come around, now that she had accepted her promotion. She really wanted to forgive me, and she was already more than half convinced of the Wisdom of Harry. We were family, too, and that had shown in the end, hadn't it? It was not such a great leap to accept me as I was after all, was it? Things being what they are. What they have, in fact, always been.

I sighed again. "Quit it!" she hissed, and nodded at the

far end of the line of stiff Miami cops. I glanced where she indicated; Sergeant Doakes glared at me. He had not taken his eyes off me, not once the whole time, even when he had dropped his handful of earth on Detective LaGuerta's coffin. He was so very sure that things were not what they seemed. I knew with a total certainty that he would come for me now, track me like the hound he was, snort at my footsteps and sniff my back trail and hunt me down, bring me to bay for what I had done and what I would quite naturally do again.

I squeezed my sister's hand and with my other hand I fingered the cool hard edge of the glass slide in my pocket, one small drop of dried blood that would not go into the grave with LaGuerta but live forever on my shelf. It gave me comfort, and I did not mind Sergeant Doakes, or whatever he thought or did. How could I mind? He could no more control who he was and what he did than anyone else could. He would come for me. Truly, what else could he do?

What can any of us do? Helpless as we all are, in the grip of our own little voices, what indeed can we do?

I really wished I could shed a tear. It was all so beautiful. As beautiful as the next full moon would be, when I would call on Sergeant Doakes. And things would go on as they were, as they had always been, beneath that lovely bright moon.

The wonderful, fat, musical red moon.

ABOUT THE AUTHOR

JEFF LINDSAY lives in South Florida with his wife and three daughters. He is currently finishing a second novel featuring Dexter.